THE SAINT VALENTINE'S DAY
MURDERS

RUTH DUDLEY EDWARDS

The Saint Valentine's Day Murders

St. Martin's Press
New York

Library of Congress Cataloging in Publication Data

Edwards, Ruth Dudley.
    The Saint Valentine's Day murders.

    I. Title.
PR6055.D98S2   1985   823'.914   85-1703
ISBN 0-312-69732-5

First published in Great Britain by Quartet Books Ltd.

First U.S. Edition

10 9 8 7 6 5 4 3 2 1

To Jack and Marie Mattock

THE SAINT VALENTINE'S DAY MURDERS

Prologue

February

'The Department is offering you the opportunity of a lifetime.'

Amiss looked doubtfully at the expressionless face of his career manager. 'But I had been hoping for a secondment to a real industry.' And then, seeing from the stiffening across the desk that he had been tactless: 'Of course, I'm not implying that British Conservation isn't a proper commercial outfit. It's just that it's such a recent spin-off from the Department of Conservation that it can't be operating like an ordinary firm.'

'The British Conservation Corporation may have been set up with government funding,' said his interlocutor coldly, 'but its profit targets are such that it is required to be dynamic and competitive. You are not, I trust, suggesting that the presence within it of a number of ex-civil servants is likely to prove a hindrance to efficiency?'

Amiss felt his courage desert him. He wasn't going to get anywhere with a wanker like this. 'No, no. Of course not. It sounds very interesting.'

'Good. That's settled. You will take up a managerial job with the corporation at the beginning of May for a period of one year. Their Personnel Department will be in touch with you beforehand to give you details of the post allocated to you. In the meantime, they insist that you take a number of courses to fit you for this challenging work. It has been agreed that you will spend two months undergoing training in management, business studies and computing.'

Amiss reflected that it didn't say much for Authority's view of the intricacy of these sciences that he was supposed to mug them up just like that, but he kept his mouth shut and tried to look eager.

'In addition. Immediately before taking up your duties with

the BCC you will attend a full week's induction course on its organization and responsibilities.'

Amiss was feeling a bit dazed, but he hadn't forgotten the key question. 'I will have Principal rank in the BCC, won't I?'

'Er . . . not quite.'

'But that was the whole idea. You said weeks ago that my promotion would be confirmed if I were seconded.'

The face opposite stared at him bleakly. 'The whole idea – as you put it – is to give you an opportunity to develop skills outside the service which will in the future be of use within the service. You already know that with the present government cut-backs your chances of finding a Principal post within the Department during the next eighteen months are negligible. In the BCC you will have a rank roughly on a par with – but rather better paid than – a Senior Executive Officer. I think the BCC has been extremely generous in agreeing to accept one of your comparative inexperience at such a responsible level. You should not run away with the idea that your good fortune in having worked for the Permanent Secretary entitles you to special consideration.'

Their eyes met. Amiss's dropped first. 'Oh, all right,' he muttered weakly. 'I'm sure I'll find the year very rewarding.'

1

It was a chastened Amiss who set off for BCC headquarters on his first day of work. He was filled with doubts about his ability to perform adequately in an organization apparently so dedicated, so thrusting and so demanding of its staff. His confidence, already somewhat eroded by the bewildering succession of intensive courses, had fallen towards zero during his week of induction. The corporation was clearly no place for a gifted amateur. He had been singled out from among his fellow newcomers for many a diatribe about the importance of professionalism, single-mindedness and expertise. No man, it appeared, could hope to succeed in the BCC without years of practical experience advising industry on conservation. The Department of Conservation, the instructor had pointed out with an ill-concealed sneer, had to be there to deal with politicians, but its activities were only peripheral. It was the BCC – muscular and sinewy – that was single-handedly fighting the battle against waste in industry. Its research scientists were second to none; its advisory service was working flat-out to convert the factories of Great Britain to energy saving and reprocessing. In the five years since the corporation had been formed from a nucleus of Departmental scientists and administrators, it had been transformed into a profitable enterprise. Men of commerce had been recruited; cost effectiveness was the watchword; growth was unstoppable. There were now over 1,000 employees – whizz kids to a man. 'The BCC,' said the instructor without the glimmer of a smile, 'is where it is all at.'

There still remained within Amiss's battered psyche some small corner of scepticism. After all, there was no getting away from the fact that the instructor was a prat of the first order, and probably also a hyperbolic prat. His apprehensions about the new job were disproportionate. What was it the behavioural scientist had said during that seminar on Stress Situations? – that natural fears about a new job should be counteracted by listing to oneself one's areas of competence. Well, if he was rather lacking in technical skills and experience, at least he was a finely trained flanneler on matters about which he knew nothing.

What was the new job, anyway? It was hardly a sign of superhuman efficiency that the Personnel Department hadn't told him anything about it until the previous Friday. Appeals for information over the preceding weeks had been met with procrastinating mutters. Even now, all he knew was that he was to present himself at 9 a.m. to a Mr D. Shipton at the headquarters building in south London, when all would be revealed. Dammit, even the civil service usually gave people more advance notice than that.

He struck out bravely from the tube station, looking about him alertly in the intervals between consulting the map. What an odd place to site the headquarters of a major company, he thought. Grime was the district's main feature. There were miserable rows of depressed housing, interleaved with un-painted chip shops, dingy cafes, fly-by-night surplus stores, grocery shops with a range suited to the needs of octogenarians of a conservative disposition, greengrocers that had never heard of any fruit or *légume* more exotic than a banana. It was only fitting that his long walk through the main streets should be taken in the grey light, chilling breeze and insidious rain that heralded the beginning of an English May.

His sense of relief on arriving at the street that boasted the BCC was swiftly overtaken by a wave of desolation. Ahead of him lay a vast and largely undeveloped wasteland. Not a tree graced the barren acres, in the centre of which had been erected an apologetic-looking high block dominated by slabs of plate glass tastefully set off by yellowish-grey concrete. Even by the standards of contemporary British architecture, this building was a notable bummer. The architect had clearly been a man of unusual modesty, terrified lest he allow any signs of individual-ity in the design which might make it possible to identify him.

The rain was intensifying, so Amiss ran towards the entrance for cover. The inside wasn't quite so bad. Someone had made a bit of an effort with a paint pot and a few plants. Perhaps it wasn't the fault of the BCC that they had been cursed with this

God-forsaken hole: it had probably been foisted on them by a malevolent decision from what was humorously known as the Department of the Environment. The receptionist, too, was agreeable enough, even if it took her a moment or two to remember the whereabouts of Mr D. Shipton and despatch Amiss to the fifth floor.

Shipton's office had a strangely familiar aura. It could have been the room of any middle ranking civil servant – the same off-white walls, bulk-purchase teak furniture and regulation coat stand. Shipton himself was at the far end of the room, lying rather than sitting in his leather chair, a mass of supine fat clothed in shiny navy blue. As Amiss introduced himself, Shipton's right arm waved him lethargically towards the armchair. He looked like a man about to expire from exhaustion. Amiss wondered if he was recovering from jet-lag or all-night negotiations. That tired old frame might have been sacrificing its health and strength in the pursuit of a higher profit margin.

'Tell me about yourself,' said Shipton uninterestedly. Amiss obligingly ran through an account of his civil service career, and then, seeing no flicker of reaction on the flabby face in front of him, tore into a summary of what he had studied on his recent training marathon. He looked hopefully at Shipton. Nothing. Shipton moved suddenly, but it was only to make an ill-disguised attempt to smother a yawn. Amiss didn't give up, but embarked on a peroration about his enthusiasm for this new challenge and his determination to work his balls off in the service of the corporation. This time he got Shipton's attention: an expression of mild bewilderment spread across the crumpled features. 'Fine,' said Shipton. 'Fine, fine.'

Silence fell. In some desperation, Amiss broke it with a question about his new job. Shipton stirred slightly and looked vacantly across the desk. 'Oh, haven't they told you? You're PD2.'

Amiss racked his memory of BCC organization charts and drew a blank. 'I'm sorry, Mr Shipton. I'm afraid I'm not quite *au fait* with things yet. What is PD2?'

'You are,' said Shipton, and then – visibly struggling to be helpful – 'Purchasing Department, Branch 2. That's you. You'll be running it.'

Amiss suppressed a feeling of disappointment. This didn't

sound like the centre of decision-making, but then again it might well be where at least some of it was all at. After all, this department must have a budget of millions if it was to meet the widespread requirements of a highly sophisticated company. He adjusted to the tempo of the dialogue and began to daydream about buying trips across Europe. And surely much of the really advanced technology would have to be bought from Japan and the States?

'That sounds very interesting.'

'Does it?' asked Shipton. 'Oh, good. Well, I'll tell you what. I haven't got time to brief you myself. Not with all this . . .' and he flapped his hand towards an in-tray that contained two envelopes. 'I'll get Horace. He's PD1. He'll tell you everything you need to know.'

He pressed a button on his intercom, called 'Horace' and relapsed into his stupor. There was the sound of hurrying feet and an alert form catapulted into the room.

'Ah, Horace. This is . . . What did you say your name was?'

'Robert Amiss.'

'Ah, yes. He's PD2, Horace. Take him away and show him the ropes.'

As Horace took him away, Shipton spoke again. 'Oh . . . Robert. Don't forget. My door is always open.'

Amiss noticed without surprise that Horace closed it firmly behind them.

2

By midday, a numbed Amiss had come to the conclusion that his session with Horace Underhill would go on for ever if he didn't do something drastic to shut him up. There was no doubt about Horace's dedication, though it seemed to be to the part rather than to the whole. By now Amiss had learned that no business could succeed without centralized purchasing; that the BCC top brass didn't seem to understand this; that, far from being supportive of PD, they were cravenly yielding to irresponsible demands from all over the organization for autonomy in purchasing; that PD had so far lost computers, vehicles, laboratory equipment and catering equipment; that enemies were even now trying to take away calculators; that none of this would have happened had he, Horace, been PD instead of Donald Shipton; that Shipton was a spent force; that Horace was confidently expecting him to take early retirement any day now; that when that day dawned and Horace took over, PD would come into its own again and recover all its old powers.

Amiss had to admit that at least Horace knew what he wanted. But he was already nursing a growing conviction that he wasn't going to get it. He didn't look like a man before whom Authority would capitulate. His face was lined with anxiety; his dandruff was out of control; his knobbly form would have defeated the best tailor, whom Horace had anyway not sought out; and despite his aggressively jet-black hair he didn't look a day under fifty-five. Still, at least he was pleasant enough and concerned to get Amiss on his side. His initial suspicion had evaporated as soon as he discovered that the new PD2 would definitely be returning to the civil service at the end of a year.

'What happened to my predecessor?' asked Amiss idly.

'He died two weeks ago.'

'Good heavens! How awful.'

'Yes. All very sad – though hardly unexpected. The poor fellow had emphysema for years. We knew it would carry him off in the end. In fact, to be perfectly honest, it was a bit of a relief that he didn't die in the office. That kind of thing is always a bit unsettling and distracts people from their work.'

Amiss couldn't think of an answer to that. His own experience of corpses on official premises had better be kept quiet.

'Anyway,' said Horace with a jolly beam, 'we've been very lucky to get a replacement so soon. Personnel seem to have no idea of the importance of prompt filling of vacancies here. I've been run off my feet trying to keep an eye on both branches simultaneously.'

'But presumably the workload has been somewhat reduced since so much of the purchasing was decentralized?'

Horace's face contorted. 'Certainly not. You wouldn't believe how much there is to do now that I've instituted these new allocation procedures. I can tell you we've plenty to keep

7

us occupied. When we get back centralized purchasing of everything we'll have to quadruple the staff.'

He went off into a long account of recent administrative reforms, from which Amiss gathered little except that paperwork seemed magically to have increased in inverse proportion to the actual purchasing responsibilities. He stopped him short. 'That's fascinating, Horace. But as you can imagine, it's a bit hard to understand all at once. Could you tell me something about my precise areas of responsibility and the people who'll be working for me?'

Horace was happy to oblige. Amiss listened with a mounting sense of unreality. He was to be in charge of buying furniture and stationery, and his main job, in Horace's view, was to make it impossible for Authority to take away from him his role as calculator-purchasing supremo. Horace's branch didn't seem to purchase anything at all, but they had manifold duties of figure gathering and paper regurgitation. 'And, of course, staff management is a very important part of our work,' concluded Horace, fishing a piece of paper out of a file. 'Here you are. It's all set out here. This is one of my innovations, having a staff plan for each branch kept up-to-date. I've even written in the names of your staff and explained the grades.'

Amiss studied it attentively.

PD2 – SPE
(Robert Amiss)

PD2.1 PE (Henry Crump)	PD2.2 PE (Tony Farson)	PD2.3 PE (Bill Thomas)
PD2.1.1 APE (Tiny Short)	PD2.2.1 APE (Graham Illingworth)	PD2.3.1 APE (Charlie Collins)

SPE – Senior Purchasing Executive
PE – Purchasing Executive
APE – Assistant Purchasing Executive

Amiss denied himself speculation about an organization that could call junior staff APEs, and tried to sound intelligent. 'So

8

there are just the two branches, and both of us work to Donald.'

'That's right. Not that Donald's any use. Why, would you believe –'

Amiss interrupted hastily. 'Why all the numbers?'

Horace looked hurt. 'That's one of my innovations too. It provides for continuity in the event of staff changes. It would be invaluable if we were properly staffed, of course, and each PE had several APEs. And of course APEs should really be backed up by clerical support. Then one might have, for instance, a clerical officer on Henry Crump's team who could instantly be pinpointed by the designation PD2.1.1.1. You see the advantages?'

'Oh, certainly.' Amiss felt he shouldn't give too much encouragement to Horace. He'd be sewing numbers on the blokes' suits next. 'What are my staff like?'

'Well, perhaps not as dynamic as one would wish,' Horace said sadly. 'Though I'm sure that now you've arrived they'll have more of a sense of purpose. They're all experienced and reliable men, of course. I'd keep my eye on Charlie Collins, though. He doesn't seem to take his work as seriously as he should. I'm afraid he's a bit flippant.'

Suppressing a flash of fellow-feeling for Charlie, Amiss nodded knowingly. 'I'd better get out there and talk to them now,' he said. 'It's nearly lunchtime. Perhaps we could all have an informal drink?'

Horace was flabbergasted. 'We don't encourage our staff to drink.'

The reproof drove Amiss into stumbling fatuousness. 'Oh, just a symbolic quick one, you know. Breaks the ice and all that.'

'Well, of course I don't want to tell you how to do your job. But when you've been around as long as I have you'll discover that too much informality breeds contempt for management.'

Amiss felt a pang of homesickness for his cheerfully irreverent staff back in the DOC, but answered obediently. 'Yes. I quite understand. I'll watch that.'

'Just one thing before you go. It's about your office.'

'I didn't think I had one. When we walked through the general office I saw an empty desk that I assumed was mine.'

Horace corrected him gravely. 'That was for a special reason.

George couldn't work in an enclosed space because his cigarette smoke could have been bad for his chest. You'll be having a proper office like this to yourself.' He gesticulated vigorously around the cramped and claustrophobic cubicle which Amiss had already dubbed 'the command module'.

'Oh, really. I'd rather sit with my staff. It's what I'm used to.'

'It's not a question of what you'd like, if you don't mind me saying so. It's a question of what is correct for an SPE. The union wouldn't be very pleased if you allowed management to deny you the privileges it has won for you. In any case, the carpenters are coming in to construct it tomorrow.'

Amiss gave up. There was no point in alienating Horace – or the bloody union for that matter. He stood up. 'Well, that's fine, then. Thanks for everything, Horace. You've been very helpful.'

Horace was a hard man to shake off. 'I'll come with you and introduce you to your chaps. Might as well do the thing properly.'

He led Amiss out and they skirted the long row of filing cabinets that cut the branches off from easy contact with each other. Horace cleared his throat. 'This is your new SPE, Robert Amiss.'

Amiss's ingratiating smile died abruptly as he glanced over the small group and encountered a concerted glare of hostility.

3

Purchasing Department,
British Conservation Corporation
14 May

Dear Rachel,

You won't be the only person to be surprised by an unexpected letter from me. After almost five days in my new job on secondment to the above I've decided to occupy my office hours by writing incessantly to old neglected friends. To be seen reading for pleasure is considered bad for discipline.

I would describe this place as a mad-house, except that it's nothing so exciting – more like a geriatric home. Between

9 a.m. and 5 p.m. I'm walled up in a ten foot by four foot plywood cubby-hole where I pretend to spend eight hours on work that wouldn't occupy a half-wit for three. My staff of six sit outside discussing old and new grievances (I'm one of the latter), exchanging badinage, reading newspapers on the pretext that they need to keep in touch with technical developments, and covertly pursuing their hobbies. They and I are supposed to concentrate full-time on purchasing furniture, stationery and calculators for the BCC.

All our furniture is bought from the same source the civil service uses, so all we have to do is rubber-stamp requests and fill out order forms. Stationery needs more attention. If so minded, one can spend many happy hours engaging in exchanges of memoranda with irresponsible colleagues who have ordered a stapler we consider surplus to their needs.

Calculators are our hot potato. As far as I can gather from the files, we've been making a cock-up here for some time. Our last achievement was to buy – two years ago – two hundred expensive models because we were impressed by promises of longevity. It is now alleged by our critics that these are obsolete and that smaller, more sophisticated calculators can be bought at Woolworths at a tenth of the price. A war has been raging for some considerable time. We are fighting a last-ditch action to persuade Authority that it shouldn't decentralize calculator purchasing as it has in recent years – and clearly with good reason – decentralized damn near everything from computers to teapots. The only weapon we've got is to blame the whole mess on my predecessor, who was not at his sparkling best when the decision was taken. If I am to gain any popularity here, it will be by winning at least a stay of execution, and at best a confirmation that I am to be left with my rightful responsibilities in this matter.

As yet I haven't the faintest grasp of why an apparently efficient outfit like this should tolerate the existence of a department in which fifteen men do the work of three. And what a shower they are! My boss, Donald Shipton, sleeps his life away down the corridor. My opposite number, Horace Underhill, devotes all his efforts to complicating our work to a level where even an Indian bureaucrat would cry halt. I know next to nothing about my staff except that St Francis of Assisi would find it hard to love them. They have made it abundantly

11

clear that they take a dim view of being lumbered with an alien
– worse, a young alien. They've resisted all my attempts to be
friendly. Over the one drink I persuaded them to have with me
all I got were snide remarks about graduates who thought they
knew it all, the superiority of those who had been to the
university of life, and animadversions on the inefficiency of civil
servants. Which last is a bit thick when you consider that they
are all people who transferred from the DOC when the BCC
was set up – presumably because the salaries here are slightly
higher – and must have been among the worst duds in the whole
of the Home Civil Service. (From all this I exempt Charlie
Collins, the only human being in the group, but more of him
later.)

Henry Crump is particularly ghastly. He's in his early fifties,
all spreading belly and bum. His main hobby is making a
nuisance of himself to the two women in the room. (In addition
to Horace's other burdens, he controls the Clerical Assistant,
Cathy, a long-suffering middle-aged Irishwoman who bears on
her face signs of the 800 years of sorrow and oppression of her
race, and Janice, a dishy eighteen-year-old West Indian typist.)
Henry, though like most of PD a sexist xenophobe, never
misses an opportunity to squeeze up against either of them in
narrow spaces. When he isn't doing that he's finding opportunities to lean over Janice and peer down her front. He's got a sort
of underhand leer, if you know what I mean, that makes one
cringe and blush for him. He is also, I gather from occasional
pronouncements drifting through my wall, in favour of capital
and corporal punishment, repatriation, the outlawing of strikes
and getting the trains to run on time. He manages cleverly to be
anti-Semitic and fascist while referring to Chancellor Kohl and
the rest of his nation as Nazis who should have been eliminated
in 1945.

Graham Illingworth is about ten years younger and combines
dullness, obstinacy and pessimism to a unique degree. All
requests, whether from me or elsewhere, are initially answered
by 'Doubt it very much', 'No chance' or 'I see trouble'. When
I've tried to get him to talk about his interests (because I'm still
trying, and I do sit and talk to them sometimes), I can
occasionally get him to say something about DIY or the merits
of taking the A1 rather than the M1, but it's mostly monosylla-
bic. He's mousey-looking and without a single distinguishing

feature physically, and I fear that some day I'll meet him outside the office and won't recognize him.

Tiny, God help us, is called that because he has the surname Short. Also, as you will instantly have guessed, he is in fact large and exuberant. He must weigh sixteen stone in the buff and he keeps himself fit with Saturday rugger. I might possibly like him if he didn't confine his conversation in my hearing to anti-queer jokes of a crudity that throws even me, on the undoubted assumption that I'm queer myself. Moreover, I suspect him of being responsible for upending a plant pot into one of the drawers of my filing cabinets yesterday. I had an hour of happy fun clearing the mess up. In my anxiety to avoid trouble so early in my time here, I said nothing about it.

Bill Thomas is sweaty, bespectacled, forty-five-ish and almost entirely bald. As far as I can gather he has no interests outside his house and garden. He certainly spends enough time looking at seed catalogues under the desk. So far I've discovered that he won't go abroad because he didn't like it when there on National Service, that he doesn't like books or music and that he won't have a TV set because it's rubbish. (He's the only bachelor among them, by the way. It figures.) The lack of a TV set cuts him off from much of the general conversation among his peers.

Tony Farson is small, weedy and late forties. He spends a great deal of his time peering over the financial pages and is, I suspect, as mean as hell. The only time I've seen him animated was when I shocked him to the core by admitting that I was renting rather than buying a flat.

Then there's Charlie. I can't imagine what he's doing here. He's not much older than me, nice-looking, quick-witted and quick-moving. He's not exactly friendly towards me, but he does throw me a civil and occasionally funny word from time to time.

What all of them have in common is a total lack of interest in the work they do and a deep resentment about poor promotion prospects. They ransack *Personnel News* looking for jobs of a higher grade for which they can apply, but Horace has admitted that for the last three years, no one from PD has ever been transferred, let alone promoted. Their journeys to work are horrendous. Every one of them commutes from outside London and then has a long tube journey and a twenty-minute walk at the end of that. They loathe London and get the hell out each evening as fast as their employers and British Rail will allow. Their travelling habits are as regular as their bowel movements (about which I am well informed, as they seem to save up evacuation for office hours).

They're all discontented with their personal lives as well (except possibly bachelor Bill). None of them has a good word to say about marriage, though those with children seem to like them. The younger ones are financially crippled by mortgages and travel costs. In my kindlier moments – when they aren't particularly thick or unpleasant – I feel sorry for them, but they wouldn't thank me for that. They abhor me even more than they would otherwise, because I live in London, have no dependants to fritter my money, and, worse again, I earn more than they do.

I forgot to tell you about their chief diversion – persecuting Cathy with Irish jokes which she pretends not to hear.

I feel better now. Sorry to have whined so much, but it has been a considerable shock to my self-esteem to find that someone saw fit to send me to this hell-hole. Did you ever see Sartre's *Huis Clos*? If you did, you'll get the general idea.

I'm going to make efforts to get a transfer, but my chances are slim, especially since I've got to do it without antagonizing Horace. On the plus side, I've got more spare time than I've had for years and I intend to enjoy it. I might even come over to Paris some weekend if you renew last year's invitation with sufficient enthusiasm.

And now, on to news of common acquaintances . . .

4

PD2
BCC
11 June

Dear Rachel,

You're very decent to go on writing so regularly. Yes. The weekend after next will be fine. I'll be on the plane that arrives at Charles de Gaulle at 7:45 your time. It's kind of you to offer to introduce me to some of the embassy people, but if it's all the same to you I'd prefer not to be sociable. Could we just eat and drink a lot and catch up on the last two years? You haven't really told me much about your job and I've mostly just been maundering on in my letters about the horrors of my exile. Absence has certainly made my heart grow fonder of the good old DOC – although I'd like to strangle that shit who sent me here.

I can't resist giving you some more of the same. You shouldn't have given me the opening by asking about my attempts to get out of here. The simple answer is no dice. Personnel tell me stiffly that they would consider it only if I got Shipton to recommend it. Apart from the fact that he'd resist the physical effort of signing his name, he's too satisfied with me to think of letting me go. I realize from something Horace said recently that the last PD2 was given to wheezing up the corridor and trying to pass decisions up to Shipton. Stupidly, I haven't bothered him at all: the trickiest issue I've been faced with so far has been whether to let the paper recycling lab have an unscheduled batch of pencils. I said yes and Graham the DIY fanatic is still sulking.

Speaking of Graham, the other day I found in a file a memo which sums up magnificently his approach to his job. It reads thus:

P/Lab: Mr E.B. White
With reference to your request for a paper-punch (PP14976) I must point out that you have failed to fill in on your CP/3A the box in which you are required to give your reasons for needing this item. Without this the requisition cannot be considered.

I should point out additionally that we have been experiencing considerable delays from the PP14976 suppliers and I think it is very unlikely that even if we approve your request there will be a delivery situation before October at the earliest.

G. Illingworth APE
PD2.2.1

Mr E.B. White is clearly a patient man. He returned a CP/3A with the crucial box filled in with the words 'For punching holes in pieces of paper.' Graham duly did the necessary with his rubber stamp. I contributed my mite by sending a rocket to the suppliers which had the effect of securing a delivery within the week. Graham's pissed off about that too.

News from Henry (mostly through the partition) is that he thinks that any woman who says no means yes. However, he also thinks that rapists should be castrated. He has informed his colleagues that all black men have enormous dongs. I won't commit to paper what he thinks all black women have.

Bill has had a record crop of lettuces. He's now bent over the summer seed catalogue.

Horace is in his element. He's standing in for Shipton, who's on holiday, and is trying to get approval for some mad scheme for a PD brainstorming weekend at the BCC's Hertfordshire training centre. I am fearful that Shipton won't have the energy to countermand the plans when gets back. Brainstorming! Sweet Jesus! How can I get out of it?

Janice, splendid girl, finally flipped last week when Henry's hand connected with her bum and screamed at him to fuck himself as no one else would. She has now been transferred. Her replacement is a superannuated lady who bears a strong resemblance to Eleanor Roosevelt and sports knee-length pink woollen knickers. Henry's prospects are bleak.

Oh, I forgot. Horace is threatening to invite me home to dinner so that I can meet his wife and see the slides of their last Spanish holiday.

Yesterday someone put drawing pins on my chair. My cry of pain was answered from without by a raucous laugh from Tiny.

On the plus side, I have come the heavy with Personnel over Charlie's future prospects and the omens are propitious. He really is bright. I wouldn't mind getting to know him better, but I can't of course. It would finish him off with his associates.

I must stop now as I have an important meeting to prepare for. Horace and I are to state our calculator retention case before a higher court. Even the civil service never expected me to prostitute truth in such a cause – but I can't quite see it as a resignation issue.

Love,
Robert

5

The sound of bird-shot in the near distance jerked Amiss out of his drunken doze. Diving panic-stricken for cover, he caught his foot on the leg of his chair and his head struck the sharp edge of his desk. As he sprawled, the chair fell painfully across his twisted right leg. Full-blooded, throaty laughter sounded through the wall and his senses returned, bringing with them clashing emotions of anger and embarrassment.

What he wanted to do now was to hurtle out into the general office and throttle the fool who had launched what must have been an entire carton of paperclips at his plywood wall. What he had to do was recover his composure and think of an appropriate wise-crack to deliver when he sauntered out in a few minutes, apparently unruffled. It was his own fault anyway. He shouldn't have drunk so much at Charlie's goodbye party.

Wincing, he disentangled himself from the chair, set it upright and examined the damage in the mirror. His face was flushed and a discoloured swelling was beginning to appear high up on his left temple. The relief of finding that his hair was long enough to cover the evidence of his fall made the pain easier to bear, though the throbbing of his right leg demanded great will-power if he was to avoid exhibiting a limp. It was worth it, though. If the chair hadn't fallen on his leg it would have made a resounding crash and the bastards would have been chortling for the rest of the afternoon.

It had to be Tiny, of course. Only he had the strength to create a din of this magnitude with the missiles to hand. Amiss wondered for the hundredth time why Tiny seemed determined to annoy a reasonably well-disposed boss, who was in a position to counteract the effect of the vicious reports that Henry put in on him. But then he probably didn't realize that Henry was selling him down the river, or that Amiss was struggling hopelessly to persuade Shipton that Tiny deserved a break. Fat chance. It had taken six months of constant effort to wangle Charlie a temporary promotion to another department and that had really only been possible because Bill's reports on him had been so innocuous. Thinking back to what he had endured from Tiny over the six months, Amiss was impressed by his own generosity of spirit. Of course, he couldn't be certain that Tiny had been behind all the practical jokes, but he couldn't think of any other likely perpetrator. God! They were so wearisome and unfunny. Plastering his office with soft-porn pin-ups was one thing; lining his briefcase with green jelly was another. And those damn bogus alarm calls in the middle of the night were especially hard to bear. Maybe he should have come down on Tiny like a ton of bricks when the jokes started, rather than ignoring them. But then he'd probably have denied responsibility.

Amiss shook his head and strolled out of his command module. Paperclips littered the floor. 'Oh, come on, Bill,' he said reprovingly, 'now that you've thrown them you should pick them up.' Bill was opening his mouth to protest when the laughter from the others indicated to him that this was a witticism, since no one could ever imagine him departing from orthodox behaviour – especially since he had confined himself to orange squash at lunchtime. Amiss congratulated himself. Bill would now feel it incumbent on him to persuade Tiny to clear up. Or, more likely, timid poor sod that he was, he'd do it himself.

He glanced round the group. 'Can you come in for a minute, Charlie?' Charlie followed him in.

'Have you time for a quick one tonight? Just to say a personal goodbye.'

Charlie looked dubious for a moment. Then he said, 'Oh, hell. Why not for once? I'll just phone the wife and tell her I'll be a bit late. She can't complain considering you got me the promotion.'

'Will you phone from here? I'd rather the others didn't know. They'd accuse me of favouritism and you of crawling!'

'They do already,' grinned Charlie, dialling a number. Amiss found his muttered excuses to his wife almost more dispiriting than the total lack of warmth in his voice. No wonder they all regarded marriage as a concentration camp. He'd never known any of them vary his evening routine by five minutes.

As they walked across the tarmac, Charlie stopped and looked up at the BCC offices. 'I only wish I had the guts to set the whole bloody building on fire.'

'Why don't you find a job somewhere else?'

'Are you being funny? I've no qualifications and I'd get a lousy reference – temporary promotion or no temporary promotion. I've got job security here, and that counts for a lot when you've got a wife, two kids and a mortgage to support.'

'Sorry. I see the problem. But things should be looking up a bit now.'

'Oh, yeah. The job I'm going to looks all right. It's just that I can't forgive the swine for leaving me so long in that PD hell-hole. Sorry. I know you're stuck there, but at least you've got a short sentence.'

They walked on.

'The Star all right?' asked Amiss.

'It's no more disgusting than anywhere else around here.'

Entering the bar, they found a free stained and pitted plastic table. Amiss bought the beer from the grudging barman, averting his eyes from the sweaty hairy chest revealed by the almost buttonless shirt. As he sat down beside Charlie he looked at him despairingly. 'I didn't suggest a drink just to say goodbye. I've been hoping you'd be able to explain things to me. You see, after six months here I still don't understand what's going on in the BCC. Everyone must know PD is a disaster area. I know the union blocked Personnel's attempts to abolish it, but surely the top brass could have pushed it through if they'd wanted to?'

Charlie began to snigger. 'You mean you haven't realized they don't want to? Hasn't anyone told you?'

'Who the hell is going to tell me anything?'

'True, true, I suppose I only know because I've still got a few friends scattered about. It's funny, really. You see, because the unions got a no-redundancy deal, the BCC can't get rid of duds so they send them off to serve out their lives in PD. They can't do any harm there because all their work's crap. It's a sump.'

Amiss digested this in silence and spotted a flaw. 'But you weren't a dud?'

'No. But my last boss thought I was cheeky and needed taking down a peg. I think it was supposed to be a short, sharp shock. Maybe he didn't realize that everyone in PD with any authority is making bloody sure that if he can't get out, no one can.'

'Well, what about me, then? What did I do to deserve this?'

Charlie's snigger was even louder this time. He composed himself and took a swig from his glass. 'A pal of mine told me that the BCC didn't really want secondees. They agreed because they were being leant on by your Department, but they stuck you in a crap job on purpose. They figure you'll be the first and last guinea-pig.'

Amiss felt a wave of fury sweep over him and then caught Charlie's eye. They both burst out laughing.

'I suppose you've got to admire their ingenuity.'

'Sure. No flies on those fuckers.'

'Wait a minute. If they only want duds in PD, why are we getting a graduate entrant to replace you?'

'There'll be a reason. It's a girl, for a start. Personnel aren't too keen on them. She's probably got something else wrong with her as well.'

'So everyone else in PD is doomed to spend the rest of his life there?'

'Yeah. Well, why not? Look at them. What a shower of shits! I don't know how I haven't gone mad, what with Henry drooling over his girlie-mags and Tony counting his money. I used to spend hours trying to decide if Graham was more boring than Bill or the other way around. Tiny's a bit better, but you get sick of all those practical jokes.'

'I thought most of them were directed at me.'

'Christ, no. You don't know what's going on, living in that stupid box of yours. He never stops: funny labels on people's coats, hoax messages, out-of-order notices on the lift, hiding briefcases. I used to get back at him sometimes, but it only made things worse, so I just put up with it. Anyway, he livens the place up a bit, and that's got to be good. And he'd probably go mad if he didn't have some safety valve.'

Amiss sighed. 'You're probably right. I might as well go on letting him get away with it.'

Charlie looked at his watch. 'Sorry. I'll have to be off.'

'Yes, of course. Just one more thing while I'm finishing my pint. What do the others think of me now? Is it as bad as when I came? I sometimes think I'm not getting through to them at all.'

'You're wasting your time trying. I'm the only one that

changed my mind about you. And in the beginning that was because you were my only hope. The rest still can't stand you because you've had all the breaks with education and career and all that. You've got a snotty accent. You earn more than any of us and you've got freedom to spend it the way you like. The last straw has been you coming into the office a few times with a bag of duty-free goodies from Paris airport. Monday mornings, too, with all the lads plunged in gloom. Guaranteed to choke them.'

'Oh, God. I never thought of that. It's only because I go there for the odd weekend to visit a girlfriend and I come straight to the office from the airport.'

'Oh, that's it, is it? Henry thinks you're having it off with every whore in Paris. Takes it as a personal insult that you're living out his fantasies.'

Amiss picked up his briefcase. 'I'll put the bottles in this next time. Beyond that, I give up. I think I'll take a leaf out of Shipton's book and sleep away the rest of my time in BCC. Good luck, Charlie. I'm glad you've got out anyway. Makes me feel this whole year isn't a complete write-off.'

'I won't forget what you've done. But you shouldn't be saying goodbye, Robert. We'll be meeting up in a couple of weeks at the PD training weekend. Horace insisted I must come as well in case I had any bright ideas.'

'What did you want to remind me of that for? I've been trying not to think about it. *Au revoir*, then. I'm catching a bus. I've found one that takes me most of the way home.'

'Lucky sod. Good night.'

Amiss watched Charlie's hurrying form disappear around the corner and felt suddenly very forlorn.

6

13 November

Amiss had been looking forward to this Saturday night during the whole of the fraught five days that had preceded it. As he walked towards the Miltons' house, he was trying to recall a worse week during the whole of his time in that frightful office.

For a start, on Monday the staff had been in a state of gloomy resentment occasioned by the sight of Charlie's empty chair. One of their number had got away and they rotted in Colditz. The following day had brought the news that calculator purchasing was to be decentralized immediately. On Wednesday, *Personnel News* announced the names of those employees at equivalent rank to PEs and APEs who had been called for promotion board interviewing. Only Charlie's name was on the lists. Amiss had called his staff in one by one to try to comfort them and offer some cheery word of hope. He had expected them to be upset, but hadn't anticipated how far removed they were from the civil service ethos of licking wounds in private. Tiny had raged; Henry had griped; Graham had actually wept. Only Tony and Bill had said little other than that life was unfair and someone had a down on them. Amiss had an uncomfortable suspicion that they all – to a greater or lesser extent – blamed him for this new rebuff, despite the fact that not one of them had been even considered for promotion in years.

Thursday, to cap it all, had seen the arrival of the egregious Melissa Taylor. Amiss shuddered. This was not the time to think about her. Better to focus on Jim and Ann Milton, whom he hadn't seen since before he left the Department. He wondered if Jim had yet become a Chief Superintendent. Ann, presumably, was still coining it as a management consultant. Agreeable people, he thought, as he negotiated their garden gate and looked at the unpretentious Edwardian house that lay a little back from the street. They would help renew his faith in the possibility of making a happy marriage. Even his feelings for Rachel were insufficient to withstand the horrors that overcame him every time he thought about what that state was doing to the people he worked with.

Milton opened the door and greeted Amiss with a slightly forced heartiness that was unsettling. When Ann followed him into the hall looking flustered and strained and made an unnecessary fuss about taking his coat and overnight case, Amiss's unease deepened. Fighting? They all began to relax as they chatted over pre-dinner drinks, and, to Amiss's relief, by the time they had finished soup and were on their second bottle of wine, they were both looking more as he remembered them. Over dinner he went to great lengths to make his account of PD as entertaining as possible and was gratified by the hilarity with which his best stories were greeted. He had been saving for the end his *pièce de resistance*.

'And now we've got our graduate trainee – Melissa Taylor.'

'Don't keep us in suspense,' said Ann. 'What's wrong with her?'

Amiss was savouring the moment. 'Nice wine, this.'

'Come on!'

'Melissa is a dedicated member of the sisterhood.'

'You don't mean she's a lesbian?'

'She hasn't actually said so yet, but there isn't much doubt. She is certainly preoccupied to an inordinate degree with the struggle against male oppression. Not only is she an enthusiastic supporter of the separatists, but her spare time is spent in raising funds to aid the establishment of a women's colony in Devon, on the sacred turf of which no man will ever set foot.'

'But what in the name of heaven is she doing working in the BCC?' asked Milton.

'Oh, she was quite frank about that with me. She couldn't find an ideologically OK job so she eventually compromised her principles and kept quiet to the BCC recruiters about her private beliefs. They were impressed by her first-class Economics degree and thrilled to learn that she had been accepted by a university in London to do a part-time MSc. Of course, as she explained it to me, once she had been offered the job formally, she couldn't compromise any further, so she gave the relevant chap in Personnel a lecture on sexism. He retaliated by posting her to PD. She doesn't care. She has no desire to spend more than a couple of years in a male-dominated capitalist organization, but the salary is useful at present. She's scrapping the MSc, of course.'

'How are the others taking it?' Milton wanted to know. 'Particularly Henry?'

'Henry is so mesmerized by her bra-less tits that he hasn't taken in the full horror yet. The others are in a bit of a state. Tiny's the only one who's fighting back. He's trying to rally the others to back him in a litany of anti-feminist jokes, but they're too scared of her, poor wretches. She's cleverer than they are, overpowering in debate and she uses words and concepts that befog them completely. And she's a nasty cow with it. She's deliberately setting out to undermine them, sneer at the way they conduct their lives and threaten their manhood by dark statements about the irrelevance of men now that sperm banks are really getting going.'

'How do you get on with her?'

'Well, of course I think she's appalling, but I know her kind and she doesn't bother me overmuch. I'm adopting the Tiny approach on the whole. I'd hate her to know I'm unprejudiced about women; she'd think I'd been frightened into it. So I'm looking for opportunities to annoy her. Today I congratulated her on her woman's intuition and told her she was looking pretty. That was so successful that I expect her to come in on Monday wearing a sack.

'Anyway, that's enough about me. I want to hear how things have been going with you two. Still enjoying the jet-set life, Ann?'

'No, I'm not,' said Ann starkly. 'Apart from anything else, I'm fed up with the kind of life Jim and I lead. We have hardly any time together. I'm a parasite, he's in a job that stinks, and I wish we could both get the hell out and do something worthwhile.'

7

Amiss hadn't been expecting this. 'I always thought you enjoyed your work.'

'Not any more. I'm sick of flying all over the world to seminars in identical hotels to learn some bright new statement of the obvious from some academic who never got his hands dirty, and come back here to incorporate into our consultancy service some new gimmick I don't believe in. After years in this business the only advice I have for British management is to scrap their self-indulgent perks and treat their employees like human beings. My only advice to employees would be to get a grip on reality, stop whingeing, be prepared to share jobs and stop demanding miracles. It's all happening gradually anyway because of the recession. And I haven't got right-wing. I'm sick of the ignorance of politicians as well.'

'How do you feel about all this, Jim?'

Milton shrugged. 'It's been coming for a long time.' He

looked over at Ann questioningly and raised an eyebrow. She nodded.

'That's not the whole of it, Robert. You won't have missed her crack about my job. Ann hasn't forgiven the Met since I was told in so many words that my promotion was being delayed because there was a general feeling that I was too much identified with the wets in the force. I think I should stay and fight. She thinks I should abandon ship.'

Amiss didn't feel he knew the Miltons well enough to come between husband and wife, and he was initially relieved when Ann broke in on his sympathetic murmurings. 'You're forgetting the main point. I don't care about the bloody police force any more except that it seems to be changing you for the worse.'

There was an uneasy pause. Milton clattered around with a decanter and filled their brandy glasses. He sat down again and looked across at Amiss. 'Ann was very upset by police conduct during the riots and after. Then something happened this week that made her think I'm condoning brutality.'

'And that was?'

Milton looked embarrassed.

'You're not sure you know me well enough to trust me with the story?'

'Oh, hell. What have I got to lose? You trusted me with your career last year. It'd be a relief to tell someone else about it. It comes down to a simple fact: last week I denied seeing one of my detective sergeants viciously hitting a suspect across the head during the course of interrogation.'

'And . . .?'

'I was lying. He hit him all right.'

'Why? You lying, I mean.'

Milton had been leaning forward tensely, but he now sat back in his chair and smiled. 'Thank you, Robert.'

'For what?'

'For asking why and not condemning me first.'

Amiss looked enquiringly at Ann, who was defiant.

'The why isn't central when it's a moral issue.'

'Maybe I'm more of an equivocator than you, Ann. I still want to know why.'

'Because Pike believed the suspect was a drug pusher and his own daughter is a heroin addict.'

'But if someone like Jim doesn't take an absolutist stand on coppers taking the law into their own hands, what hope is there for the police force?' asked Ann angrily. 'If he had told the truth when the solicitor lodged the complaint it would at least have showed that there was one honest man among them.'

'There are a lot of honest men among us, Ann,' said Milton evenly. 'You know that very well and you know why I lied. To save Pike from having his career shattered because, once, and just once, he lost his temper under circumstances of extreme provocation.'

'Pike is a decent bloke, is he?' asked Amiss.

'Salt of the earth. If he was a nasty piece of work I wouldn't have hesitated about shopping him.'

'And the fellow he assaulted?'

'Oh, he's a pusher all right. But it's not as simple as that. He's black, so anyone knowing the facts would assume that I've lied because I'm racist. Which I'm bloody well not.'

'What did you say to Pike?'

'That I would cover up for him this once, but that if I ever saw him raise a hand to a suspect again I'd do everything I could to have him fired.'

'And how did he react?'

'As you'd expect. Undying gratitude. It'll never happen again. He doesn't know what came over him. And I believe him. If he wasn't the kind of chap he is but one of the thugs, he'd resent me deeply for even criticizing him, let alone hesitating about lying on his behalf. He knows he did wrong.'

'What will happen if the allegation comes to court?'

'I'm pretty sure it won't. My wet reputation is a help. No one believes the story. But anyway, I've told Pike that if it does, I'll perjure myself. Now you really do look shocked.'

'I don't know what to think, Jim.'

Ann began to interrupt him. He got in first. 'No, I can't see it in your absolutist terms, Ann. I can't honestly say what I'd have done in Jim's position. Not everything is an issue of principle. I tend to be influenced by compassion towards the individual, and if Pike is as Jim says, personal loyalty would count a lot.'

'To the point of perjury?' she asked sharply.

'Christ, I don't know. Is perjury worse than lying to colleagues? Anyway, this doesn't change my opinion of Jim. He was a pretty remarkable copper when I met him and he still is.'

'Thank you, Robert.'

Ann look unhappily at Amiss. 'Maybe you're right. I've been married to Jim for fourteen years and I shouldn't start doubting his integrity now. And maybe your reaction to the story is another proof that I've been living in an ivory tower for several years and it's time I got a real job.'

'When you find one, will you make room for me? Jim's dilemma has been salutary for me too. I've been telling lies in defence of policies I didn't believe in for years. Maybe it's time I called a halt before my moral sense is eroded yet further. Tell you what, Ann: if they try to take paper purchasing away from PD2, I'll resign rather than fight on the issue.'

8

None of Amiss's colleagues had given him more than a passing thought that evening. Tiny Short was celebrating a 17–16 derby win over a neighbouring rugby team and was in better spirits than for weeks. He was sure that the captain would now have no excuse for acting on recent hints that it was time the over-35s made way for younger men. Tiny felt that the way he had converted his own try was sufficient proof that experience still counted for something. He was on his seventh pint when closing-time arrived, and was feeling beerily amorous.

By the time he had covered the mile between pub and home, with one stopover behind a hedge, he was feeling full of sexual confidence. Fran had been a bit caustic about his recent failures, but she wouldn't have anything to complain of tonight. Standing on the doorstep, fumbling for his latch key, he took a step back to examine the contents of his pocket in the light of the street lamp. There was a resounding crash as his right foot connected with a milk bottle. Cursing, Tiny picked up a few of the bigger pieces of glass and hurled them into a flower bed. He hoped she hadn't heard the noise: she'd accuse him of being drunk.

As silently as his heavy body would allow, he opened the door and crept quietly up to the bedroom. Fran was sitting up reading a magazine. Not even the sight of her glistening face and sensible pyjamas could put him off tonight. Launching into a description of his afternoon's triumph he began to undress hurriedly.

'I gathered you'd won,' she said icily. 'You'd have crawled home earlier otherwise.'

Tiny looked across at her pleadingly. 'Oh, come on, love. You know how it is. The lads all wanted to stand me one because of that try. It was one of my best ever.'

He propped himself against the dressing table as he removed his socks, thus guarding against the risk of staggering. Stripped to his underpants, he went over and sat down on the side of the bed. He couldn't tell from her expression what mood she was in. At least that meant she couldn't have heard the breaking glass. Leaning over, he kissed her rather clumsily, pushed her gently back on the pillows and began to murmur endearments. There were indications that, if not enthusiastic, she was at least being co-operative. As he shifted slightly to get himself into a more comfortable position, his elbow hit the glass of water on her bedside table and knocked it on to the bed. 'You stupid oaf!' she screamed, pushing him off her furiously. 'You just can't do anything without making a mess of it, can you?'

Without a word, Tiny left her to mop up the water unaided. He crept into his own bed, a recent innovation of Fran's to spare her contact with his night-time sweating. During the moments before beer and exhaustion claimed him for sleep, it flashed into his slightly fuddled brain that it would be days before she let him try again.

As soon as the children had gone to bed Tony Farson went to his den and addressed himself to the double glazing issue. Gloria had been nagging him about it ever since next door had had it done. It took a long time to translate all the pros and cons into figures: estimated savings in heating costs and increase in the value of the house had to be balanced against the reduction in his capital and investment income. He heaved a sigh of relief when the final calculation came out in favour of going ahead. That should shut her up for a while. The woman was possessions-mad. When he thought of the way she had persuaded him into buying that music centre, he went hot and cold all over. The capital outlay had been bad enough, but now she was frittering money on tapes and records.

He filed his papers away and let his mind stray back to his constant worry: Gloria just wouldn't give up on that insane idea of having another baby. Tony cursed the fashion for third children. He had worked out the costs of a child over a twenty-year period and had almost fainted when he found what the total was. He had estimated what her lost income would be. He had even read up on the dangers of late pregnancies and warned darkly of the likelihood of having a mongol. No argument had any effect. He was determined not to give in this time, but he had an uneasy feeling she might be taking the law into her own hands. There was no way he could check on whether she was still taking the pill. He didn't know what to do about that.

As Tony was morosely descending the stairs, Charlie Collins, fifty miles away, was smooching with Dawn to a Barry Manilow record. She was slightly high on rum and coke and giggled appreciatively as he murmured at her lasciviously. Their host had dimmed the lights and many of the couples moving slowly on the mock-parquet floor were discreetly feeling each other up. Charlie applied his tongue gently to Dawn's right ear: from her reaction he guessed he had located an erogenous zone. He move his head back a little and caught a glimpse of his wife draped around the newcomer from No. 42. Great. That should keep her out of the way for the evening, leaving him clear to concentrate on this superior piece of crumpet. He whispered a suggestion and Dawn indicated agreement. 'Only half an hour, though,' she said prudently, 'or someone might miss us.'

They were moving towards the door of the living room when the music abruptly changed to an aggressive track from *Saturday Night Fever*. The exit became blocked by a crush of erstwhile dancers who had yielded the floor to the extrovert minority – just one couple. Charlie and Dawn sighed resignedly. Flight would have to be postponed for a while.

Then Charlie saw that the woman strutting uninhibitedly up and down the room was Jill, led by No. 42 in ever more extravagant and space-consuming manoeuvres. Charlie waited for her breath to give out, but he had neither realized how much vodka she'd put back nor bargained for how No. 42's enthusiasm might augment her euphoric delusions. As the tempo grew more frantic, she seized a coffee table from against the wall and leaped on it unsteadily.

'That's it, petal,' called out No. 42. 'Give it to us, baby.' To Charlie's embarrassment, she began to undo the buttons of her blouse. Only his desperate lust for Dawn stopped him from intervening. Jill flung her blouse across the room to loud cheers. When her skirt followed it, the stretch marks on her belly and the spreading thighs were visible to all. Not till she began to grapple with the fastenings of her bra did Charlie accept that the party was over. Woodgrove might be a pretty permissive estate, but husbands couldn't abnegate all responsibility. It was his job – yet again – to stop the fun and take her home.

Graham Illingworth was at that moment happily putting the finishing touches to the bedroom of the doll's house he was making as a Christmas present for Gail. He fixed the handle to the door of the tiny wardrobe and placed it in the left-hand corner. Now it was complete. He could find no flaws anywhere. Even the matching bedspread and curtains that Val had grudgingly made were exactly right, and toned in prettily with the sample he had cut down into a perfectly fitting carpet.

He wondered if he had time to begin work on the fitments for the kitchen. Looking at his watch he was startled to find it was already 11:30. Val was late again: there must have been a lot of customers tonight. He picked up the doll's house and locked it in a cupboard. As he pocketed the key he heard a little voice crying 'Daddy'. He took the stairs in twos: as he entered the room, his arms were outstretched, ready to cuddle his little daughter.

Horace and Rita Underhill had watched television for the entire evening. They both felt a sneaking gratitude that neither of the children had stayed in. It was so cosy to be able to watch what they liked without anyone complaining. They looked at each other affectionately from time to time. Rita thought how distinguished Horace looked in the new sports coat she'd bought for his birthday. She wished he would stop using the Grecian 2000 and let his hair go grey, but he seemed certain that a youthful appearance was important for his promotion chances. Anyway, that new diet seemed to be doing his ulcer good. Horace noticed how pretty Rita looked in that blue jumper that matched her eyes. He'd buy her a whole new wardrobe as soon as Shipton retired. It couldn't be long now.

Bill Thomas had finished the ironing before nine o'clock and sat for a moment in a glow of achievement. The house was spotless and tomorrow was now clear for digging the left-hand flower bed and switching the position of the bird-table. They'd prefer it in the centre of the garden, now that next door was infested by cats. What a delight it was to be free to live his life the way he wanted, and no mother to contend with.

He went up to his room, took some seedsmen's lists from the bedside locker, and carried them downstairs to his favourite chair. He read for a couple of hours, occasionally writing notes on the appropriate reference cards in his indexed box. When he had replaced the card that listed varieties of brussels sprouts, he riffled absently through half a dozen other sections. His eye caught the section on leeks and he remembered something odd Melissa had said about phallic symbols. Frowning, he pushed the box away and reached for another catalogue.

Most of Henry Crump's evening had been peaceful. Having refused to accompany his wife on a visit to their married daughter, he had been able to eat his tea alone in the kitchen. When he pushed away his sweet-plate he rose, searched in a leisurely manner for a pencil and paper, wrote a note – 'CUSTARD LUMPY' – and dropped it on one of the dirty plates.

He found a can of beer and settled himself comfortably in front of the gas fire. He lit his pipe noisily, picked up his paperback and sighed with contentment. Two hours later, leaving Jackie Collins's heroine in another post-coital trauma, he turned on the television. He was hoping for something rewarding from the French film. The paper had said that this one had been considered very shocking in 1969.

By eleven o'clock he was feeling disappointed. There were more sub-titles than action. It wasn't a patch on last week's, all about a housewife who worked in a brothel in the afternoons. You could never predict what you'd get in a frog film. They had funny ideas about art. He was meditating on whether to give up and return to his book when the door opened and his wife came in. He looked up at her with his usual sense of revulsion. Tonight she was wearing a dingy old red raincoat and a bright blue woollen headscarf to depressing effect. Her feet were encased in sensible short fur boots, out of which rose thick legs, gnarled with varicose veins. She glanced over at the television as she began to peel off her outer garments. 'You're watching that filthy foreign muck again,' she observed. 'I don't know why you can't be your age.' Henry turned sharply and saw a closing shot of two naked bodies entwined. Bloody hell! The high-spot of the film and he had missed it looking at her. He turned off the set grumpily and steeled himself to listen to fifteen minutes of complaints about buses, weather and the uselessness of the doctor who was treating his grandson's cough.

By midnight Edna was in bed. Henry was sitting on the side of the bath gazing at a treasured picture which usually resided in his wallet. It showed two young women lying on a tiger-skin caressing each other. One of them had curly hair like Melissa's. From above looked on a lissom youth eager to join in. Henry was lost in a little world of his own. He was playing with himself.

Henry might have been surprised had he known that as he was working up towards his orgasm Melissa Taylor was living out at least a part of his fantasy. She was stretched beside her lover stroking her breasts. But in this room there was no man looking on.

Donald Shipton was asleep.

9

Dearest Rachel,

Many thanks for the marvellous long letter. Loved the story about Jeremy and the Rastas. He seems to have the same grasp of what's going on as your average high court judge. I only wish there was someone here I could tell it to.

I'm looking forward achingly to the weekend after this. It's only the thought of pleasures to come that's going to get me through the next few days. We're all off to the Twillerton conference centre at three this afternoon. No one wants to go except Horace. He's planning to write a report on the seminar for circulation to Authority so as to make same aware that under his leadership things are buzzing in PD. Of course he's secretly pleased that Shipton has gone sick. It's unbelievable what that layabout gets away with.

Not a lot has been happening. There's a general air of gloom and tension overlying all, which must, I suppose, mainly be Melissa's fault. Or maybe it's the thought of this weekend that is giving the lads a strained look. At least I'm getting on with them better now I'm no longer Public Enemy No. 1. Would you believe I haven't had a single practical joke played on me since she arrived? She has suffered at least one. I emerged the other day at about ten past five and saw her back view as she left the office. Stuck to her coat was the simple legend 'I am a dyke'. Regrettably, I am so coarsened by now that instead of pursuing her to point it out I gave Tiny a silent cheer. Or am I wrong and is this a new way of coming out? I thought they went in for lapel buttons.

Melissa's awfulness has made the awfulness of all the others pale into insignificance. I'm concocting a training plan for her that will send her touring regional offices and other parts of HQ to find out how they operate. I don't see why we should be the only ones to suffer. Did I tell you she's a proselytizing vegan? Last week she took it upon herself at lunchtime to tell Tiny he was eating cow sandwiches and Bill that his hardboiled egg was a chicken foetus. Tiny responded by saying that at least his cow was tastier than she was, but poor old Bill looked quite sick and pushed his egg away. He's apparently got rather a soft spot for birds. I heard him yesterday rather touchingly explaining to Tony how to attract robins to a garden – as if Tony would have food wasted on our feathered friends.

Anyway, I had some small revenge the following day. Cathy, our clerical assistant, complained that Melissa was giving her dirty magazines. It turned out to be a consciousness-raising attempt, with Melissa proffering *Spare Rib* as an alternative to *Woman and Home*. I summoned Melissa to my office and told her solemnly that if Cathy believed her vocation to lie in being a wife and mother, she, Melissa, should respect a Woman's Right to Choose. She couldn't decide if I was being serious or flippant so didn't have the heart to argue.

Horace is driving me to Twillerton, thus giving us the opportunity yet again to discuss how to make the party go with a swing. The others are all going in separate cars so they can collar the mileage allowance. Melissa is . . . guess! Yes – riding her motor bike. I hope it pisses down.

Enough for now. I'll continue this when I get a chance during the weekend. And may God have mercy on us all!

Sunday

Just when I really need you, your bloody phone goes out of order.

I needed to babble incoherently, and now I have to write it down instead. Where shall I begin? Yes, yes. I hear your trained mind calling on me to take it from the beginning. Here goes.

Friday

3:00–5:00 Unspeakable journey with Horace. I wish I'd known he hates driving in London. I could have ridden on Melissa's pillion. He is of the 'if-you-grip-the-steering-wheel-until-your-knuckles-turn-white-and-hunch-over-it-till-your-back-hurts-you-will-be-able-to-better-control-events' school of motoring. (Sorry about the split infinitive. I am not the purist I used to be.) Horace's eyesight is appalling. I had to yell warnings several times. Is the silly sod too vain to wear glasses? It wasn't until we got on to the motorway that he relaxed, but by then my nerves were in tatters and I could hardly make sense of his maunderings about creative confrontation, kicking ideas around to see where they led or alternatively throwing them into the air to see where they landed etc, etc. I gather some idiot sent him on a management psychology course three years ago and ever since he's been chewing over what he learned on it.

5:00–5:30 Unpacking and abluting. Layout of centre is roughly upon motel principle. (Mark this well. Its significance will become apparent.) Thus everything is at ground level: bedrooms come in square blocks of sixteen, built round a central courtyard, with a bathroom and exit in the middle of each side.

All fifteen of us then, snugly accommodated together in Block H. Horace chuffed: it makes for feeling of solidarity.

5:30–6:00 Tea in recreation block followed speech of welcome from small, fidgety centre manager. Listen to Graham and Tony arguing about the merits of their respective routes to Twillerton. Melissa the belle of the ball in ill-fitting denim boiler suit. Try as she does, she cannot avoid looking pretty. All over-forties wear nondescript sports jackets. Charlie hadn't been briefed on Melissa so shot over to her at first opportunity to try chatting-up. Returned crestfallen with flea in ear after three minutes.

6:00–7:00 Open session. Horace and self on dais as my plea to be allowed to sit with minions has been rejected as damaging to my authority. Horace read half-hour speech about essence of seminar being to decide what job we are doing and how we can do it more effectively. All stones are to be turned over and all worries fearlessly exposed. Peroration same as I got on my first day – about centralized purchasing being the rock on which success is built. Sat down and called for questions or comments. Silence. Self had anticipated this and had intelligent query re Buying British policy. Answered by Horace. No follow-up from rank-and-file. Glared at Charlie who responded nobly by making suggestion about how our approvals procedure might be streamlined. Horace tossed idea at audience where it fell like stone until picked up by one of his team who proved it unworkable.

Henry saved the day with a long tirade about the newfangled procedures contained in BC/P/4396 being contrary to the common sense displayed by the framer of BC/P/632. Even Graham slightly animated by that one.

Session ended. All balls-aching, of course, but Horace optimistic. Thinks that after an evening of communal fun the troops will have loosened up and tomorrow morning will see the fur really flying.

7:00–7:30 Pre-dinner drinks. Offered to buy one for Melissa and had head snapped off for being patronizing. Told her she looked even more beautiful when angry. Curried favour with Henry by asking for explanation about ambiguous point in BC/P/4396. He seems to know the whole canon off by heart.

7:30–8:00 Dinner. Large dining room with six long tables. PD clustered around one. Other tables occupied by massed rows of beery technicians on three-week refresher course. No contact between us and them. PD group identity shows signs of burgeoning.

8:00–11:00 Booze and recreation. Premises to ourselves. Technicians have gone off to nearby town. Parts of evening almost jolly. Tony beat the pants off me at table-tennis and admitted coyly to having been platoon champion. Graham played darts with considerable accuracy until he went flat and disappeared to bed. Session in bar with Henry and PD1 chap telling us stories of National Service. Some disgusting but not all unfunny. Tiny tried to organize poker game but got nowhere so we broke up at closing-time. Horace wasn't seen all evening. Presumably in his bedroom farting about with the agenda.

11:00–6:00 In own room asleep apart from one visit to bog. No, I'm not trying to do a *Ulysses*. Apparently insignificant details may prove important.

Saturday
6:00 Woken by fire alarm. Rushed into grounds where large crowd assembled looking for fire. No fire visible. Manager arrived and instituted thorough search. Still no fire. Nor anyone admitting to having sounded the alarm.

6:30 All head back towards bedrooms. Beat the rush to a bathroom. Have cause to regret this as loo-brush holder full of water falls on head as enter. Shout of pain and rage echoed by others around block: Tiny, Melissa and Charlie have suffered similarly, though Charlie has quicker reflexes and has escaped most of the deluge. All non-sufferers have fits of giggles except

Horace, who is distressed.

6:45–7:45 Get dry and doze a little. Dress and leave room. Notice large tea-urn on table near exit. Remember this is supposed to arrive at 7:30 each morning so conclude it's probably too stewed for me and go for walk.

8:15–8:55 Breakfast. Outbreak of sneezing. Turns out someone has laced the sugar on all the tables with sneezing powder. After a few chortles, everyone decides it's not funny.

8:59 Enter seminar room. Only self, Charlie and two PD1 chaps present. Horace arrives ten minutes late complaining of stomach upset. Turns out that's a euphemism for diarrhoea. Others roll in by degrees announcing same problem. Next hour spent in post-mortem on breakfast food interspersed with sufferers running in and out to bogs. Process of elimination demonstrates that the morning tea must have been responsible. None of four unaffected had sampled contents.

At my suggestion, seminar disbanded until 11:30 and Horace and self go to discuss with manager question of tea-urn. Manager says someone in block must have added laxatives. Sounds reasonable. Manager getting pissed off.

11:30 Reassemble, though four still absent. Horace shaky but determined to carry on. Distributes questionnaires about aspects of PD work that could be improved. All commence writing and Horace cleans blackboard preparatory to leading brainstorming, chalk in hand. Suddenly begins to scratch hands and arms furiously. You've guessed? Yes. Itching powder on blackboard duster. Horace goes out to wash hands and returns upset. Blackboard now unusable until major cleaning job is done. I suggest analysis of questionnaire be undertaken by him and self in bedroom and other ranks excused until after lunch. Point out that absentees will probably be well enough to participate then. Horace unhappy at waste of valuable time but gives in.

12:15–1:00 Read dreary answers to questions. Try consoling Horace for negative nature of same by saying people still not 100% and will probably amplify answers and be more positive after lunch. Interrupted by loud knocks on door. Distraught manager. Doors to recreation rooms have been glued up and TV indoor aerials are all missing. Maniac at large. Obviously from PD. No trouble during last two weeks with technicians. Won't take any further responsibility for us. We can all get the hell out as soon as we've eaten.

Horace in despair. Begs. Pleads. No avail. Tries pulling rank. Manager contemptuous. I eventually suggest Horace ring Shipton on sick-bed and ask for ruling on whether to fight or quit. He rushes off and comes back with the news that Shipton says quit. I always thought he was intelligent under all that fat.

1:00–2:00 Unhappy lunch. Several still toying with clear soup only. People glancing covertly at each other. Horace makes stumbling speech. I really feel for the poor bastard. He put so much work in. I had expected a farce but not a fiasco.

2:15 Enter car-park to find Tony and Tiny uttering little cries and wringing their hands over their cars. Turns out someone has let the air out of most of the tyres, motor bikes not exempt. Hardly anyone taking it philosophically. If it takes fifteen men – Melissa included – with three footpumps two hours to inflate forty-seven tyres, how long did it take one nutter to let them down?

Nightmare journey home with Horace. Steering wheel quivering under his hands.

And that, my sweet, is the full story. One of our little band has flipped. Horace spoke wildly about plots against PD by some technician ill-wisher, but ultimately admitted it was unlikely. It's a prankster from one of our team all right. Horace is being loyal to his lot and dropping dark hints about Tiny, but I don't think these events were Tiny-like. He's always been more boisterous than nasty. It could have been any of us who had come prepared and didn't mind sacrificing several hours of sleep. As far as I can gather, everything necessary could have been done during the hours of darkness except for meddling with the tea-urn.

I suppose there'll have to be an investigation. Personnel won't take kindly to footing the bill for a total cock-up. What's worrying me is whether, as Horace would say, this is a one-off, or whether it's going to go on. One way or another, I'm not looking forward much to next week. But unless some joker pushes me out of a window I'll be waiting for you at Heathrow at 7:00 on Friday our time. And I promise not to spend all weekend talking about PD.

Much love,
Robert

10

Shipton lay immobile throughout Horace's lengthy and confused account of the Twillerton *débacle*. When the witterings had ceased, he shifted himself slightly and said flatly: 'Call in Security.'

Horace's mouth opened in protest.

'No, Horace. It's no good. You know perfectly well we can't keep this quiet. In fact I'm not at all sure we shouldn't call in the police. The glueing of the doors must constitute criminal damage.'

This was the longest speech Amiss had ever heard him make. He admired its crispness and tactical sense. The mention of the police worked magically on Horace: his opposition to an internal investigation collapsed instantly.

'And, Robert, while Horace is telephoning Security I'd like you to draw up a time-table of the incidents. Oh, and provide them with a staff list and mark the names of those who were at Twillerton.'

Amiss nodded obediently and led Horace back to his office. He hoped this business would be sorted out quickly. Horace was looking ghastly and all the PD staff seemed subdued and jumpy.

He had just finished his notes when Shipton rang through to announce the arrival of the investigators. 'You and Horace can brief them, Robert. I've got a lot to do. They're using Room 510.'

Amiss collected Horace and went along to 510. His first reaction was one of disappointment. Whatever he had expected, it hadn't been the shifty-looking little Smithers or the large and benign Cook. As a team they bore a disconcerting likeness to Peter Lorre and Sidney Greenstreet, though it rapidly became apparent that for once Lorre was in command.

Lorre studied Amiss's papers and passed them over to Greenstreet without comment. Horace, sitting at the head of the leather and teak conference table, quivered with impatience as Greenstreet slowly read through the material, his lips moving in synchronization with his eyes. When he eventually looked up, Horace broke into impassioned speech. 'It must have been those young technicians. Our people are all mature and they'd all been looking forward to the weekend.'

Lorre was having none of it. 'We're not interested in opinions at this stage, Mr Underhill. All we want from you are facts. We intend to interview everyone who was at Twillerton last weekend and take statements.'

Poor chap, thought Amiss compassionately. He must be a frustrated policeman, banished for ever from Arcadia by the misfortune of being only five feet four.

'Yes, yes. Of course. But you will keep me closely in touch with your investigation, won't you? You'll need advice on how to handle my people. I don't want them upset.'

Lorre raised his hand in a silencing gesture. 'You must understand, Mr Underhill, that our findings have to be kept confidential until we are in a position to make a report. At this moment in time I regret to say that everyone – do I make myself clear? – *everyone* – in PD is under suspicion until proved innocent.'

'Except Mr Shipton,' said Greenstreet helpfully.

'Of course except Mr Shipton.'

'And the clerical assistant and the typist,' said Greenstreet, who had been studying the staff list carefully.

Amiss noticed Lorre's hand twitch as if it ached to land a blow on his moronic colleague's fleshier parts – but he confined himself to a quick grinding of teeth. 'Now, Mr Underhill. If Mr Amiss will leave us, we will take an account of your movements on the night of the outrages.'

Amiss melted silently away, but not before he had observed Horace's near-catatonia at the suggestion that he might himself have fouled up his seminar.

Summoned for his interview half an hour later, Amiss was amused to see that by now the furniture had been rearranged to more forbidding effect. There were now only three chairs in evidence. Lorre and Greenstreet shared one end of the table and the lonely chair at the far end was intended for the interviewee. No blinding lamp, alas. Amiss felt tolerantly disposed towards them. This case must be rather fun compared to their usual work. As far as he knew, Security usually had a pretty dull time organizing rosters for the guarding of BCC property and investigating petty theft. Why shouldn't they play Special Branch when the occasion presented itself?

He had to admit they were thorough. They led him efficiently through all his movements between arrival and departure and asked detailed questions about who had been in his company throughout the evening. As he finished, Greenstreet passed his notes over to Lorre, who scanned them quickly and nodded.

'Thank you, Mr Amiss,' said Greenstreet with a beam. 'You have been most helpful. We shall be coming back to you next week when we have completed our preliminary interviews . . .'

'Assuming we have not already identified the culprit,' broke in Lorre darkly.

'Oh, yes, indeed. Assuming we have not already identified the culprit. Then we will want to look for motives and consider the . . . er . . . psych-ol-og-i-cal dimension.' He smiled proudly and the interrogation was at an end.

Amiss's weekend with Rachel was a much-needed break. Although Lorre and Greenstreet had disappeared to Twillerton after two days in PD, they had left behind them an edgy staff who talked little and laughed less.

He was surprised to be called to Room 510 at 9:15 on Monday morning. They must have worked fast – presumably they got double time for the weekend.

He smiled brightly at them. 'Did you enjoy yourselves at Twillerton?' Then, recognizing from Lorre's face that that had been the wrong thing to say: 'I mean, did you have a productive time?' That wasn't successful either. Lorre glowered at him.

'We got the job done, Mr Amiss.'

'You mean you've . . . identified the culprit?'

'Let us say,' said Lorre, placing the tips of his fingers together, 'that we have considerably narrowed the field of suspects and are therefore closer to reaching a conclusion as to the perpetrator of . . .'

'The outrages?'

Lorre nodded grimly.

'Oh, well done,' said Amiss heartily. Christ, Lorre was

looking affronted again. 'How can I help you?'

Lorre leaned over the table and looked at him keenly. 'Acting on information received, we are now pursuing a new line of investigation.'

Amiss kept his face straight and tried to look encouraging. 'And that is . . .?'

'The sequence of practical jokes that has occurred over recent months in PD.'

'Oh, surely they're entirely irrelevant. They were all quite harmless.'

'That is for us to decide, Mr Amiss. Now, we know that you were a victim of several of them. We want facts. What happened and when?'

Amiss found himself dithering. How the hell could he protect Tiny without pleading the Fifth Amendment? He stalled.

'They were all so trivial. It's hard to remember them.'

'Try, Mr Amiss.'

Amiss stumblingly cited three or four of the most harmless. Lorre looked unimpressed.

'You can do better than that, I'm sure.'

'Perhaps it would be better if I went away and thought about it? Then I can write down what I remember.'

'Good idea,' said Greenstreet, clearly delighted to have his note-taking cut down.

Amiss thankfully got up to go. This would give him time to cook up an agreed story with Tiny. 'Just a moment,' said Lorre. 'We want to see Mr Short next. Kindly ask him to come here immediately. And Mr Amiss – no collusion. We shall be keeping Mr Short with us until your list is available.'

Shit, thought Amiss, stamping back to his office in frustration. They knew already. Who the hell had tipped them off? Now he was well and truly trapped. Presumably they'd get it all out of Tiny. And if not out of him, there would surely be plenty of others anxious to help. He'd have to come clean himself now. Otherwise he'd be seen to be obstructing them.

After passing the message to a worried-looking Tiny, he retired to his own office to begin his absurd list. He had made the decision to omit anything these clowns might regard as criminal damage to BCC property. His brief notes with approximate dates came to a page, which he put in an envelope and gave to Cathy to take along to 510. When he heard Tiny's voice again, he called him into his office and explained what had happened. Tiny looked astounded.

'But they told me they'd had a lot of useful information from you and of course I thought you'd spilled the beans.'

'Bastards. I never mentioned you.'

'Oh, Christ,' wailed Tiny. 'What was I supposed to think? Why should you cover up for me? I told them everything I could remember about any jokes I or anyone else has ever played here.'

Amiss groaned. 'I'll have to plead absence of mind, I suppose.'

'Well, if you didn't tell them, who did?'

'If we knew that,' said Amiss, 'we'd probably know who's responsible for the whole Twillerton mess.'

11

It was two days before Amiss was called to 510 again – two days during which relations among members of his staff had fallen to an all-time low. No one was prepared to talk about what he had told Security, and as no one was thinking about anything else it made normal intercourse almost impossible.

His interview started inauspiciously. Lorre was looking triumphant and Greenstreet unnaturally grave. Neither of them did more than nod a perfunctory greeting.

Lorre opened on a challenging note. 'Would you please explain to us why you omitted to tell us about the following occurrences? First, the placing of jelly in your briefcase.'

Amiss had already decided to stick to his guns. If he admitted he'd been trying to protect Tiny they probably wouldn't believe him and would seek some darker motive. Anyway the whole business was so idiotic he couldn't feel conscience-stricken about telling a few white lies. His mind flashed back to Milton and the contrast between their two moral dilemmas almost made him laugh aloud. As it was, he snorted slightly and then, seeing Lorre's face, wished he hadn't. 'I forgot.'

'And the upended pot plant?'

'I forgot that too.'

'And you will say the same, no doubt, about the drawing pins on your chair and the dirty postcard?'

Amiss felt self-righteous. Those two he had genuinely forgotten. 'Yes. Them as well.'

Lorre looked over at Greenstreet, who shook his head solemnly, shuffled his tidy pile of papers and selected a reference card. 'You are a graduate in History, Mr Amiss?'

Amiss was bewildered. 'Yes.'

'In other words, you have had an education which trained you to remember large numbers of facts?'

'No it didn't,' replied Amiss peevishly. 'It taught me to sift evidence and distinguish the important from the unimportant. That's probably why I don't have an encyclopaedic memory for japes and wheezes.'

'There's no need to be aggressive, Mr Amiss. I always understood history was about facts, but then I haven't had your advantages.'

Amiss winced. Another fucker with an inferiority complex.

Lorre maintained the initiative. 'Let us approach this from another angle. Did you form any opinion as to who was responsible for these outrages?'

'The PD ones? Here in the office?'

'Yes.'

He couldn't pretend ignorance here. Any imbecile, even a university graduate, couldn't have avoided guessing what everyone else knew. 'I wasn't sure, but I thought it was probably Tiny Short.'

'Did you take the matter up with him?'

'No.'

'Or with your superior officer?'

'No.'

'Why not?'

'I didn't want to cause ill-will among my staff. I was unpopular enough as it was. Anyway, I didn't really mind the jokes. They were all pretty harmless.'

'And why were you unpopular, Mr Amiss?'

Amiss was beginning to feel cross. 'Because they had all your affection for people with more advantages than themselves.'

'There's no need to get nasty, Mr Amiss.'

'Oh, I'm sorry, I'm just fed up with questions I don't see the point of.'

'You'll see the point all in good time,' said Lorre. 'We have established that you failed to act as a responsible manager and put an end to all this carry-on.'

'It is certainly possible to see it that way.'

'So you did nothing at all about it?'

'Nothing.'

'Why are you lying to us, Mr Amiss?' asked Greenstreet conversationally. 'We know about the obscene publication you sent Mr Short.'

Oh, no. How could he have forgotten about that? And how the hell had they found out he did it? They must have traced his cheque.

He looked at them wearily. 'You're not going to believe this, but I really didn't remember it.'

'You're quite right,' crowed Lorre. 'We're not going to believe it.'

'When you asked for a list, I was concentrating on the ones that were played on me. I completely forgot the only one I'd played myself.'

He could see they weren't impressed. 'Look. It was months ago and I was drunk at the time.'

Greenstreet looked shocked.

'Well, not exactly drunk, but pretty high. I spent a boozy evening with a friend and was telling him about the practical jokes. He showed me an advertisement for a publication called *Guys Only.* It seemed funny at the time to order a copy to be sent to Tiny at the office. I never heard that it arrived and it went right out of my mind.'

'Why did it seem funny to send obscene material through the mails?'

'It wasn't obscene. It was a catalogue of pouffy underwear. Tiny is aggressively heterosexual.'

'We have different ideas about humour,' said Lorre.

'Christ, we're not here to discover if we share a bloody sense of humour, are we? You haven't mentioned Twillerton yet. I thought that was what you were supposed to be investigating.'

'Would you kindly remain here for a moment while Mr Cook and I consult in the corridor?'

Amiss recovered his temper while they were out. After all, they couldn't help being a pair of bloody idiots landed with a job beyond their slender intellectual resources. He even managed a conciliatory smile as they re-entered and resumed their chairs.

'Let us explain to you, Mr Amiss,' said Lorre, 'why we have given so much attention to recent events in PD. For reasons that won't concern you, we have been able to rule out as suspects the entire staff at Twillerton and all the technicians.'

'So it's down to PD.'

'PD and Mr Charles Collins.'

'So?'

'You'll recall the sneezing powder in the breakfast sugar. Because of the short period in which the dining room was unlocked in the evening after the tables had been laid, we have been able to eliminate those PD personnel who have consistent alibis for the period 9:00–10:00. We are left with seven names: Mr Collins, Messrs Underhill and Sloan from PD1, and, from PD2, Messrs Farson, Illingworth, Thomas and yourself.'

Amiss was beginning to feel distinctly uneasy. He stayed silent.

'We have eliminated Mr Sloan because of his heart condition.'

Amiss couldn't quarrel with that. Poor old Sloan couldn't walk ten yards without difficulty.

'We are therefore looking at the remaining six for someone with a grudge. You wouldn't, I suppose, dispute that Mr Underhill had no possible motive to ruin his own seminar. Or that he is happy in this job?'

'No, I wouldn't,' said Amiss hopelessly.

'And would you also agree that Mr Collins's recent promotion also rules him out motive-wise?'

Amiss wasn't so sure that Charlie didn't still have it in for PD, but he wasn't about to rat on him. 'Yes, I suppose so.'

'That leaves four of you. Your three colleagues may have some resentment about poor promotion chances. You yourself have made no secret of your dissatisfaction with PD.'

Amiss was nettled. 'I think I've been very restrained about it really.'

'We know you complained to Personnel Division.'

'That was ages ago. I've settled down. Anyway, I'll be going back to the civil service within six months. Why should I screw things up now?'

'I thought you'd say that,' said Lorre smugly. 'And it might have counted for something if we hadn't had additional evidence against you.'

'In addition,' Greenstreet chimed in, 'to the fact that you concealed your practical joke on Mr Short.'

That again? 'Let's not argue about that now. What's the additional evidence?'

'You were seen at 1:00 a.m. walking down a corridor in Block H towards the exit door, wearing your overcoat.'

'I wasn't walking towards the exit door, you idiot,' yelled Amiss. 'I was going to the bathroom which is directly opposite it to get rid of some of the beer I'd been drinking all evening!'

'Wearing an overcoat?'

'Certainly wearing an overcoat. I didn't have a dressing gown.'

'Ah, ha!' said Greenstreet. 'The block is centrally heated. Why didn't you just wear your pyjamas?'

'I don't wear pyjamas. I sleep naked.'

This obviously shocked them more than his earlier revelation about drunkenness. Lorre recovered himself first.

'Well, why did you leave the bar for ten minutes at 9:15?'

'Because I had left my briefcase, containing the book I was reading, in the seminar room. I told you that before.'

'Your explanations are all very glib, Mr Amiss, but they don't convince us. The other people with opportunity and possible motive – people with no record of irresponsible behaviour – have all been very frank with us.'

'What about whoever tipped you off about the PD practical jokes? Wasn't that an attempt to point the finger at Tiny? Doesn't that look suspicious?'

'I am not prepared to discuss that with you. We shall be reporting to Mr Shipton now. I suggest you return to your office and wait to hear from him.'

As Amiss sat brooding at his desk he kicked himself for not having put up a better fight. He had annoyed them, patronized them and shouted at them. Of course they wanted him to be the villain of the piece: he was the one everyone would choose. And paltry as the whole thing was, and however leaky the case against him, it was going to make things very difficult here if it became known that he was the main suspect. Perhaps Shipton would suggest he sloped quietly back to the Department? That would look great on his career record: secondment aborted in suspicious circumstances.

When Shipton rang and asked him to come in, he walked slowly up the corridor trying to nerve himself for conflict. He wasn't surprised to see Shipton looking more animated than usual.

'Sit down, Robert. I've had the report from Security. They seem very convinced you're at the bottom of this.'

Amiss's heart sank. He might have known Shipton would want to go along with them. It would make life easier.

'You mean you believe them?' he said hopelessly.

'Of course I don't believe them!' roared Shipton indignantly. 'What do you take me for? I wouldn't believe those imbeciles if they told me Peter Sutcliffe was the Yorkshire Ripper.'

Amiss looked at him. The folds of flesh were fairly quivering. 'You mean you've told them to go on working on it?'

'I most certainly have not. I've told them they're a pair of bloody fools who've been wasting our time. Do you know they haven't even tried to find out who sent them the anonymous letter about Tiny's jokes? I've had enough. We'll have to let the whole thing drop. I've told them to clear off back where they belong and check the spoons. Evidence for the prosecution: "He claims not to wear pyjamas and doesn't like working in PD." If that's evidence, they should be accusing me. Get on with your work and forget all about it. I'll make sure no one hears about their report.'

He waved Amiss towards the door and settled himself back comfortably. As Amiss turned to thank him, he saw his eyes were already closing.

12

Amiss fretted in the departure lounge. It had been stupid of him to suggest meeting Rachel in a restaurant rather than picking her up at her flat. He'd be more than an hour late, whatever happened now. Could he ring the restaurant and leave a message? No. His fragile French would never stand the strain. Hell. She'd have left the embassy by now and her bloody phone was out of order again. Why didn't the frogs spend some of their ill-gotten gains from immoral arms sales on getting their stinking telecommunications right?

He bought himself another drink and tried to immerse himself in the novel he had just bought from the airline bookstall, but he had only got to page ten when a sepulchral voice announced the imminent departure of the Paris plane. Draining his glass, he began to hurry towards the departure gates. As he did so, he caught a glimpse ahead of a familiar-looking figure. After a momentary shock he realized he must be seeing things. If any of his staff decided to go abroad, it would be talked about for weeks. He was becoming obsessed with these people. This was a weekend for spiritual refreshment, not speculating on hallucinations.

By the time he reached the restaurant in Montparnasse, he was almost an hour and a half late. She was sitting in a corner, her feet propped on the chair opposite, reading with concentration. In front of her was a half empty carafe of red wine. He rushed over and apologized volubly. She looked at him with amusement.

'Good grief, Robert. Anyone would think I might accuse you of being late on purpose. Pull yourself together. You sound like a henpecked husband trying to blame British Rail for his night on the tiles.'

'Oh, God. I do, don't I?' He bent down, kissed her and handed his overcoat to a hovering waiter. 'I'm sorry,' he said, sitting down. 'It's catching. After last night's Annual Dinner Dance I expect all women to be unforgiving.'

'Take things gently. Have some wine and choose something to eat. Then when you've calmed down you can tell me all about the dinner dance. It sounds promising.'

Amiss gazed at her lovingly. After the sights of the previous night the effect was pleasant: short brown hair neither permed nor dyed; thin intelligent face not over-made up; clothes chosen neither to depress nor stun; unpretentious black glasses.

'You're looking particularly beautiful tonight, darling.'

'Nonsense, Robert. I'm looking the same as I always do. You're obviously suffering from overreaction to your colleagues' wives. Now shut up for a minute and concentrate on the menu.'

Amiss felt rather dashed. It wasn't often he made pretty speeches, and it wasn't pleasant to have them ruled out of order.

'I'm sorry. I didn't mean to bite your head off. It's just that you're carrying a whiff of suburbia with you. I'm surprised you're not bearing a placatory bunch of flowers.'

Amiss cheered up. That was another nice thing about Rachel. She didn't mind apologizing. He addressed himself seriously to the matter of food and ordered greedily.

'I don't know if I come to Paris so often because of you or the food.'

'That's more like the old Robert,' she said approvingly. 'Now, what's the matter with you? Tell me the latest.'

'Not yet. I can't do it justice till I've recovered from the trip and lined my stomach. You tell me about what you've been doing since your last letter.'

As ever, Rachel did the job entertainingly. Amiss munched on his endive salad, grappled happily with his *boeuf en croûte*, drank copiously of the house wine and delighted in the tales of diplomatic cock-ups and bureaucratic hassles. He almost choked over her account of the latest battle with the French PTT. It was a relief to be reminded that he didn't work in a uniquely silly outfit.

She timed her last story to finish as the coffee and cognac arrived. 'Your turn.'

'Are you sure you really want to hear?'

'Darling Robert,' said Rachel, whose most enthusiastic endearment this was, 'I've got too involved with this circus for you to start going coy on me now. You keep saying it's boring, but it seems pretty action-packed to me. What's happened since Lorre and Greenstreet departed in confusion?'

'Nothing much till last night. Shipton put the fear of God into Security. They wrote a formal letter to him – circulated to all the staff – saying that the enquiries had proved totally inconclusive.'

'So Shipton is no longer despised. You've found hidden depths in him.'

'Not half. Really, you know, not all these people are as bad as they seem on the surface.'

'Of course they're not. You judged them too harshly in the

beginning because you were suffering from culture-shock. You've led such a sheltered life. You knew nothing about how ordinary people live.'

Amiss felt injured. 'That's not true, Rachel. You know it's not. I come from a very ordinary background.'

'Spare me that shit about coming from the working classes. Your parents are as middle-class in their attitudes as mine – even if they don't have as much money.'

'Oh, all right. It's my automatic defence against allegations of privilege. Not that I admit that there's much in common between the household of a northern solicitor's clerk and that of a Jewish intellectual.'

She looked fixedly at him until he giggled out loud. 'OK, OK, I'm talking like a schmuck.'

'Well stop it and tell me what's been happening.'

'Things have been pretty good, really. Everyone was very relieved when the manhunt was called off. There seems to be a tacit gentleman's agreement to forget about Twillerton, and the plus point is that no one's playing any more practical jokes. And Tiny's being very nice to me.'

'So what was last night like?'

'Awful. Well, I admit I went to it apprehensively. All the married men had been griping about it for days, claiming they would never go if their wives didn't insist. Endless complaints about the expense of new dresses, the difficulties of finding babysitters, the cost of wives' train tickets, the problems of getting home. You can guess the sort of thing.'

'I can. But they came anyway?'

'Everyone except Melissa. I was surprised that Bill turned up. Apparently he never had before. But then he had to look after his mother until she died last year. He's branching out a bit now.'

'Where was it held?'

'In the largest conference room. BCC actually have four of these occasions every year to accommodate all staff and spouses. There must have been four or five hundred at ours alone.'

'It doesn't sound like a very festive venue.'

'They did try with Christmas decorations, but it was hardly the Talk of the Town. PD had two tables. I presided at one, Horace at the next.'

'Where was Shipton?'

'At a table for higher ranks.'

'Was there a band?'

'No. They used to have one in past years, but the recession's put an end to that. There were a lot of moans about that – hardly reasonable when you consider the whole thing was free. We had a disco with a DJ who specializes in catering for the over-forties, with an unrivalled collection of James Last records. You know the sort of thing – Bach, the Beatles, country and western, rock and roll, all brought down to the lowest common denominator and scored for quick step, waltz, fox trot – whatever you like.'

She sniggered. 'You must have been in your element.'

'Absolutely. I was the only one at the table who couldn't dance properly, having been brought up on the Do It Yourself method. Except for Bill, of course. That's another thing he doesn't like doing.'

'Don't keep me in suspense. What were the wives like?'

'Dreadful. Oh, not so much individually as collectively.'

'Come on. Do this in an orderly manner. Start with Henry's wife. I bet I know what she looked like – podgy and crimplene-clad.'

'That's our Edna all right. Though I have to say she's more fat than podgy. She was at my right hand during the meal. I was the young squire, you understand, and the placing was organized according to seniority.'

'Conversation?'

'Weather, grandchildren and television programmes.'

'Fair enough. Now the wife of the mean one.'

'Tony.'

'Yes, of course. My guess is rather dolled-up. There must be some reason why he's so preoccupied with money.'

'Right again. Gloria's hairdo must have cost buckets – all streaks and elaborate curls. She was on my other side. Conversation: a three-piece suite she's got her eye on; the job she's sick of; Tony's promotion chances. She's sure he's being pessimistic.'

'Is he?'

'No. He's OK at this level, but he doesn't have any of the qualities or qualifications that BCC want nowadays.'

'Poor devil. Right. What's his name? – Graham. The boring

one. Presumably a dowdy wife.'

'Nope. You're fallible after all. Val's quite a smart piece with a sharp tongue. Conversation: funny stories about the customers at the bar she works at in the evening – all malicious.'

'Who's left? Of course – Tiny. How could I forget him? No guesses this time except that his wife is probably a bit of all right.'

'Fran's not unattractive. But I really disliked her. Her main line in chat is mocking Tiny's clumsiness.'

'Did you meet Horace's wife?'

'Oh, yes – Rita. She's lovely. Plump, sweet and terribly proud of Horace. Completely deluded about him, but that came as a relief after the others. They didn't seem to have a civil word to say about their husbands. Oh, I forgot Charlie. He wasn't at our table, of course, but I went over to pay my respects and have one of the more manageable dances with his wife. She seemed OK. Quite fun, really. But like all the rest, anti-husband. It was a bit late by then and she'd had a few – kept complaining that Charlie was a kill-joy. That seemed out of character, but sure enough, I caught sight of him looking at us anxiously.'

'Maybe he's ferociously jealous.'

'Maybe. I doubt it, though. He knows about you. He was the one who warned me to stow the duty-free in my briefcase.'

'Well, so far it sounds boring, but not deadly. What was the problem?'

'Two things mainly. The social indignity of making a fool of myself on the dance floor, being bundled about by partners like Edna who really knew how to dance. Still, I didn't mind that too much. It's no harm to see the young master at a disadvantage. Good for marital relations. What shook me more was what I overheard of the women's conversation.'

'Complaining, you mean?'

'The nature of the complaints. I'm used to hearing the blokes at it. You know the kind of thing. "Women are unreasonable." "Women don't know the value of money." "The wife will kill me if I forget her birthday." It's almost a ritual: they stress their superiority and cement their macho relationship. They don't often make individual complaints. But the women! As soon as any two of them got together they were off comparing husbands' deficiencies.'

'Like what?'

'Oh, God. Let me think. Edna told Gloria that Henry didn't seem to realize that she was a grandmother, but whatever he said, she wasn't allowing any of THAT NONSENSE any more.'

'That explains a lot about Henry.'

'It sure does. And Gloria confided in return that Tony was as mean as hell and she – Edna – wouldn't believe the fuss he had kicked up just because she bought a new pair of shoes for the dance.'

'And the others?'

'Val said Graham seemed to think more of their daughter than of her and that she was properly fed up with it. Fran in return said she didn't have that problem with Tiny because he was sterile.'

'Christ!'

Amiss was pleased to see her looking rattled.

'How did you hear so much?'

'I was left at the table a lot of the time while various husbands tripped the light fantastic. And I moved my place several times and listened in. You know I'm insatiably curious about all of them.'

'It's bad enough that they talk to each other about these things. How could they do it within your earshot?'

'Oh, I expect they didn't realize I could hear. I was actually having a conversation with someone else and just keeping an ear open.'

'Don't take it too seriously, Robert. Now that I think of it, I once worked in a typing pool and it was the same story. Long descriptions of their husbands' failings in bed, their disgusting eating habits – everything. It comes of general discontent.'

'Maybe I'm a romantic. But not one of the couples at my table seemed to be happy. It's worrying. All these guys are bitterly disappointed by what's happened to their careers. If they haven't got anything at home to look forward to either, what have they got? And despite Shipton's injunction, I can't help thinking about that Twillerton business. And the anonymous letter about Tiny. Maybe most of them accept their lot, but one of them is turning nasty. It frightens me.'

'We'll talk it through tomorrow,' said Rachel abruptly, signalling for the bill. 'I think you're getting it out of perspective. I meant what I said about your sheltered life. At least I worked in grotty places during my vacations. You swanned off on VSO. That didn't equip you to understand how the failures survive in our society. Now let's go home to bed.'

'That's the nicest thing you've said all evening. Just promise not to tell the embassy women all about it on Monday.'

13

All through the weekend Amiss had dithered about whether to send Rachel flowers for St Valentine's Day. Well, why not? He loved her, didn't he? But wouldn't she think it suburban sentimentality? Well, why shouldn't he be sentimental if he wanted to be? But would she laugh at him? Or be touched by the gesture? But she was always playing down the romantic side of their relationship. But was that because she thought that was the way he wanted it? How did he want it anyway? Why were they both so frightened of talking about love? Because they'd both been hurt before? Or because they weren't properly in love? Or because neither of them was prepared to be first one to mention the word?

The dilemma was still unresolved on Monday as he sat leafing through *The Times* over breakfast. The page of St Valentine's messages finally decided him. If *Times* readers could address each other unblushingly as 'Tweety-bum' and 'Woozle-face', he didn't see why he shouldn't join in the general spirit of the thing. Live dangerously. He'd been turned sour by the coarseness of Tiny's comments on the festival and the moanings from Henry and Tony about having to waste good money on outsize velvet hearts.

He swallowed the last of his cereal hastily and grabbed his coat. What an idiot he'd been to leave it so late. Now he'd have hell's delight finding a shop near the office that could cope with getting flowers delivered to the Paris embassy before the end of the day.

He reached the office fifteen minutes late and was instantly dragged into Horace's command module for an interminable meeting about the pros and cons of holding another PD seminar. He didn't have the heart to condemn the idea out of hand, but he did manage to persuade Horace that it would be better to forget about it for a few months until memories of the last one had finally been erased. He hoped Horace wouldn't notice that he had a vested interest in its being postponed until he quit the BCC in May.

The rest of his day was routine: a mixture of tedious paperwork and coming the heavy with difficult suppliers, with enough time over to write a long letter to his parents.

Tiny poked his head through his door at two o'clock. 'I'm off to the dentist now, Robert. See you tomorrow.'

Amiss made noises indicative of fellow-feeling and returned to work. It was very pleasing that Tiny was so friendly now. Even the others were loosening up with him gradually. He wouldn't be surprised if they ended up quite sorry to see him leave. He couldn't say he'd really be sorry himself. He couldn't go on doing pointless work for ever. But he'd certainly become almost attached to his staff by now. The glimpse of their domestic sufferings had excited his compassion. He was even doing quite well with Melissa since he'd stopped goading her and had admitted to having read some feminist literature. That reminded him to return to her the book she'd just lent him about the treatment of women in pornography.

He called her in and managed to talk about the book without acknowledging that he thought its author had gone right over the top into paranoia. Melissa took it and smiled at him. She was clearly pleased with his progress.

'Would you like to borrow Dale Spender's analysis of sexism in language?'

He groaned inwardly. Trying to build bridges with Melissa was a taxing business. He certainly did not want to borrow Ms Spender's book, but there was no getting out of it. 'Oh, thanks. I read a few reviews of it and it sounded really interesting.'

'Good. I'll bring it in tomorrow.'

She got up to leave. A thought occurred to him. 'How do you view St Valentine's Day, Melissa? I mean ideologically.'

'Well, of course it's a real rip-off. But I don't object to it in principle. In fact, I sent someone a card myself.'

Amiss nearly asked if he'd sent her one and remembered just in time that in this case Dale Spender would have been justified in rapping him over the knuckles for insensitivity in the choice of the male pronoun. He couldn't quite bring himself to say 'she' so he compromised. 'Did you get one in return?'

'No. But I did get a box of chocolates this morning.'

'That's nice. I even sent a present to someone myself.'

She smiled tolerantly and withdrew. She didn't seem to mind heterosexuals any more. Maybe she was in love herself and was feeling more secure.

He was held up by Horace, who had had a new thought about seminars, and didn't manage to leave the office until half past five. He hurried home, nursing a hope that Rachel might ring him soon and indicate that he hadn't gone too far by sending with the roses a message saying 'I love you'. He'd stay at home for the evening in case she phoned. He had nothing better to do anyway and he had a promising-looking thriller to read.

As he walked into his living room, the phone was ringing. Already? That flower-shop assistant was more efficient than she looked. He ran across to it, trying to quell his nerves.

'Hello. Robert Amiss.'

It wasn't Rachel. It was a voice he couldn't recognize, even though its owner was saying 'It's Tiny.' Good Lord. What had the bloody dentist done to the poor fellow? He sounded as if he was choking.

'Sorry to disturb you, Robert. I'm just ringing to say I won't be in for a while.'

This was unprecedented. Even though they all had each other's private numbers, no one ever phoned a colleague at home. It would have been regarded as a frightful breach of etiquette. Amiss was puzzled, but he said encouragingly, 'Thanks very much for letting me know. Nothing much wrong, I hope. Is it your teeth?'

'No. It isn't my teeth.'

Amiss was seriously worried by now. Tiny sounded as if he was crying. 'What is it, Tiny?'

'It's Fran . . .'

'Is she ill?'

'She's dead.'

'Dead! My God. What happened? Did she have an accident?'

'I came home,' said Tiny tonelessly. 'She was lying on the floor of the lounge. I thought she'd fainted. When I tried to prop her up she was rigid. Then I realized she was dead.'

'But what had happened, for God's sake?'

'The police think she ate a poisoned chocolate.'

Amiss was gabbling incoherent sympathies when his mind made the connection. He set his teeth. 'I'm sorry, Tiny. It's awful to have to ask you this, but I must know. Where did she get the chocolates?'

'They came by post this morning.'

'Oh, sweet Jesus, Tiny. I'm really desperately sorry, but I can't talk any more. I don't think she's the only one. I've got to make a phone-call. Have you someone with you?'

'Yes. Don't worry about me. I'll be all right.'

Amiss felt wretched as he rang off, but then panic began to take over. He rushed to his desk and scrabbled for his list of PD numbers. Oh God. It had to be a coincidence, didn't it? If it wasn't . . .? As he dialled Melissa's number frantically another fear struck him almost speechless. He could hardly identify himself to her when she answered, despite relief that she was alive.

'Those chocolates. Have you eaten any?'

'No. I'm saving them for after dinner.'

'Don't eat any. Whatever you do, don't eat any. I haven't time to explain. I've got to phone the police.'

He slammed the receiver down and picked it up again almost immediately. No dialling tone. Oh God. Oh God. He jiggled the buttons feverishly until he got a line. As he dialled 999 he was trying to think of some way of explaining this sensibly. He almost screamed with impatience at the time the operator took to answer and put him through to Scotland Yard.

The policeman was soothing. Amiss realized he must sound like a madman. His frustration made him shout. 'I haven't got time to tell you why I think these women are in danger. You've got to get people ringing them now.'

'Of course, sir. But you must give me some more details first. You haven't even said who you are.'

Amiss's training reasserted itself. Pull strings, that was the thing to do. 'I'm Robert Amiss. Detective Superintendent James Milton of the Murder Squad will vouch for me. Now will you please take these telephone numbers and get to work.'

Milton's name had the effect he had hoped. The man became imbued with his sense of urgency and took down names and numbers in double quick time.

'And all you've got to say is if they got any chocolates

through the post they mustn't touch them.'

'Very well, sir. Now your number, please. We'll be in touch with you again shortly.'

Amiss rang off. Now what could he do? Start ringing himself? It would be a few minutes before the police could organize enough people to get on to all those in danger. Who should he start with? He couldn't make life and death decisions himself. He'd just work down the list.

Shipton: no answer.

Horace's wife was bewildered by his call. 'No, Robert. I haven't had any chocolates. What is all this about?'

'Can't tell you now. I'll explain later.'

No chocolates. Was all this a figment of his overstrained imagination? Please God it was. But if it wasn't? He'd concentrate on his own staff. Henry was next on the list. No answer. He wouldn't be home yet, but where was his wife? Out of the house or dead?

Tony: no answer.

Graham: same again. Would no one answer him? Only Bill left. But he doesn't have a wife. What has that to do with it? Why should this be directed only against women?

To his relief, Bill answered. Amiss had time now to speak at greater length. By now the Yard would have taken over.

'No. I haven't had any. It's dreadful about Tiny's wife, Robert.'

'We must just pray that she's the only one, Bill.'

'Of course. If there's anything I can do . . .?'

'There's nothing any of us can do except wait.'

'See you tomorrow, then,' said Bill automatically. He sounded as stunned as Amiss had been.

'Yes. See you tomorrow, Bill. Goodbye.'

He put the receiver back and gazed at the phone, willing it to ring with the news that he had been jumping to wild conclusions. Within a couple of minutes it began to ring. He snatched up the receiver.

'Your line's been busy. I rang to thank you for . . .'

'Oh God, darling. Something awful's happened.'

She listened as he poured out the story and then cut in. 'I'm coming over. You're not fit to be on your own. Stay put and I'll be with you as quickly as I can. I love you, darling. Try to be calm.'

As she rang off, Amiss had a moment of bitterness at the thought that the words he'd been waiting for her to say should come at such a ghastly moment. What could he do now? Should he try any of the numbers again? No. Keep out of it.

When Milton got through a couple of minutes later, Amiss had slumped exhausted into a chair and taken a large slug of neat whisky.

'What's the news? Are they all all right?'

'I'm afraid not, Robert. Brace yourself. One of Tony Farson's children is dead.'

'Anyone else?' asked Amiss dully.

'We don't know yet. All those we got through to hadn't received chocolates. The local police are sending cars to the other houses. I'll let you know as soon as there's any more news.'

'Melissa's all right. And Bill. It's only Graham and Henry's wives now. Or their children.' He could hear the unsteady note in his own voice.

'Have you anyone with you?' asked Milton sharply.

'No. Well, not at the moment. Someone's coming later on.'

'You can't be alone. Ann's already on her way. Just hang on till she arrives. I'll be over when I can.'

'Thanks, Jim. But don't worry about me. Worry about the others.'

'I am,' said Milton grimly, and rang off.

Rachel had made good time, but it was still almost ten o'clock before she rang the doorbell of Amiss's flat. It was answered by a dark-haired woman with a haggard face.

'Thank heavens you're here. I haven't known what to do with him. He's in a terrible state. Just drinking and crying.'

'So it's not just Tiny's wife, is it?'

'No. Tony Farson's son and Henry Crump's wife. That was bad enough, but we've just had another call to tell us . . .'

Rachel was already through the door of the living room. She flung herself beside Amiss, who clung to her in misery and despair.

'Did Ann tell you? Charlie too. And it's all my fault. I never thought of him.'

14

The alarm went at 7:15. Rachel snapped it off and looked anxiously at Amiss. Reassured by his complete immobility, she lay and contemplated her first job of the day. Unable in conscience to delay it any further, she climbed out of bed, found a dressing gown and went into the living room to hunt for his parents' telephone number. She blessed his poor memory when she found it written in the address book that lay beside the telephone.

She was relieved that the answering voice sounded neither angry nor panic-stricken at being rung so early. Amiss senior was clearly a phlegmatic type, who contained his astonishment at the news that his son was mixed up in a murder hunt to a brief 'What! Again?'

As she told the story, its sheer improbability struck her for the first time. Nor was it lost on her listener. When she finished rather haltingly by explaining how without Amiss's intervention the death-tally would have been higher, the flat northern voice commented: 'Well, lass. If I didn't already know you were a good friend of Robert's, I'd have said you were touched. As it is, I'll confine myself to asking what I can do. I gather he's not in a state to talk?'

'Not for a while.'

'Tell him not to worry about ringing us till he's sorted himself out. Should his mother or I come down?'

'I don't think that'll be necessary. He's going to have a lot to do over the next few days. It'll be better for him to keep active.'

'You sound like a sensible young woman,' said Amiss senior approvingly. 'And a thoughtful one. I'm very grateful to you for warning us before we saw it in the newspapers. Don't let him wallow in it or he'll fall into a depression and it'll be days before he comes out of it. Get in touch if you need any advice on how to handle him.'

Rachel felt a wave of relief as she put the receiver down. In similar circumstances she'd have had to keep her own mother away by physical force. She cast a look around the room and shuddered. At what stage during the evening had Robert kicked over the remainder of the whisky? Its stink was even more pervasive than that of tobacco. He had managed to get through two of the packets of cigarettes he had sent Ann Milton out for. He'd be back on them now with a vengeance – after three years of abstention. She found the energy to pull back the curtains and open the window and then crept gratefully back to bed.

She was asleep when the phone rang a couple of hours later. She ran to it, hoping to get there before the noise penetrated Amiss's semi-coma.

'May I speak to Robert Amiss, please? Donald Shipton here.'

'Would you mind if he rang you back? He's asleep at the moment.'

'Lucky devil,' said Shipton with feeling. 'Yes, of course. How is he and who are you?'

What an admirably direct man, she thought. Presumably he liked to conserve his energy. 'He's having a good sleep, so I expect he'll be OK when he wakes up. As you can imagine, he was very upset last night. I'm a friend of his – Rachel Simon.'

'Well, Miss Simon. I'm not surprised he's upset. I've been in a right state myself. And now I've got the press after me. They seem to think I'm running some kind of slaughterhouse.'

Rachel uttered some commiserating words.

'But you've got enough on without listening to my troubles. The press know about Robert. Some idiot mentioned his name to them, but I don't think they've got his number yet. It's only a matter of time. You'd better be ready for them. They're quite up to going through the Amisses in the telephone directory.'

'Thank you for the warning.'

'Now, tell him to forget about the office for the rest of the week. I've arranged compassionate leave for him and all his staff, but Bill and Melissa have come in anyway. I don't think we'll crack under the pressure.' He gave a cynical snort and said goodbye.

Rachel sat by the telephone for a couple of minutes with her head in her hands, assessing the likely demands of the day. After making a call to the embassy, she took the phone off the hook and headed for the bathroom and a contemplative shower. Twenty minutes later she was sitting at Amiss's desk scribbling a few sentences for the benefit of the press. Shuddering at the inevitable fatuity of the final draft, she replaced the receiver. It took only two minutes for the first journalist to strike.

'Sorry. He's not here. He's staying with friends.'

'Can you tell me how to get in touch with him?'

'I'm afraid not. He's incommunicado. But he's given me a press statement.'

Dammit, she thought defensively, as she attributed to the hapless Amiss such phrases as 'deeply shocked and appalled', events like this generate only banalities. As she finished off with 'I regret that I can cast no light on this terrible tragedy', she had the comfort that the journalist seemed perfectly satisfied.

Four tabloids later her equanimity was beginning to crack. When she answered the telephone yet again her voice sounded harsh and abrupt even to her own ears.

'It's all right, Rachel. It's Jim Milton. I infer that you've been having a tough morning.'

'On top of a tough night, Jim. But no doubt it's been worse for you.'

'All in a day's work,' said Milton wearily. 'How is he?'

'Hasn't woken yet. But he was pretty bad until he finally got to sleep at about 4:00 a.m. After you'd gone he just went on and on about his stupidity in not thinking of Charlie.'

'I wish I could help,' sighed Milton. 'But it's no good trying to pretend that Charlie couldn't have been saved if we'd had his name. But doesn't he realize that he saved the lives of Melissa Taylor and probably one of Graham Illingworth's family as well?'

'It didn't seem to be any consolation.'

'But no one else thought of Charlie Collins. He'd been gone from PD for over three months.'

'Well, I wish you'd point that out to him, Jim. He's likely to be more receptive now.'

'I'll call in when I get a chance. I'll have to take some kind of statement from him anyway.'

'You're not free for lunch by any chance?' she asked.

'I don't know. I'm up to my eyes, but I could come if you think it's important to see him soon.'

'I just think it might help if he was forced to face up to the full story now that he's sober. He might get things more in perspective.'

'Lunch at your place or in public?'

'Oh, here, I think. I don't think he'll be fit to go out.'

As her mind flashed to the one egg that appeared to be the only food in the flat, Milton said, 'I'll bring lunch. And my Detective Sergeant, if you don't mind. He's a good bloke, Sammy Pike. Mention his name to Robert. He may remember my telling him a story about him a few months ago. See you 1:00-ish.' As Rachel went to the kitchen to make tea, her heart went out to this domesticated policeman.

Two hours later she was feeling a sense of achievement. She had cleaned up the flat, fobbed off the local newspaper and a London radio station, and Amiss had been persuaded to get up, shower and dress. Though he was hardly light-hearted, he was showing more resilience than she could have hoped. The promise of Pike's visit had awakened his interest and he had shown some animation in telling her of the dispute over the Milton dinner table concerning Milton's lie about Pike's aberration. She had expressed no opinion on the issue. The moment was not propitious for the luxurious exploration of moral dilemmas.

She tried to look incurious when Pike arrived. He was a placid-looking man in his early forties. Where he might have looked solidly comforting in uniform, in his plain clothes he looked like a man in search of anonymity. What distinguished him from any other deferential subordinate was the doglike devotion he displayed towards his boss and his obvious anxiety to adapt to the informality of the occasion. Immediately after introductions had been effected, he gathered up the packages that he and Milton had been carrying and headed off towards the kitchen, where he cheerfully refused all offers of help and set to buttering bread and making complicated sandwiches as if that was what he voluntarily did for a living.

Amiss began shamefacedly. 'I'll ring Ann this afternoon and apologize for being such a trial to her last night.'

'You'll do no such thing, Robert. She specifically told me to say that she was delighted to be able to help and you're not to ring her up unless you want her. All this is bad enough without you falling into a state of abjection because you showed the weakness of a normal human being.' He turned to Rachel, who was emanating approval of this robust approach. 'How long are you staying?'

'Till Sunday.'

'And your plans, Robert?'

'I'll stay away from the office until Monday. Apart from anything else, I've got to go to four funerals, if they don't clash.'

'They won't,' said Milton, tossing across a piece of paper. 'Chaps from the local forces have been liaising with the families to make sure they'll at least have the consolation of as big a turn-out as possible. If you look at that list you'll see that you can make all of them between Thursday morning and Saturday afternoon.'

'You're getting through the post-mortems pretty fast, then.' The choking note in Amiss's voice caused Milton and Rachel to look at each other in alarm. They were thankful at the interruption caused by Pike's arrival with bottle and glasses. As he poured the wine Amiss said, 'Not for me, thanks. I made enough of a fool of myself last night.'

'Robert,' said Milton evenly. 'I came here because I thought you might be able to help me. I did not expect that you were going to indulge yourself by acting like a cross between chief mourner and self-flagellator. I have on my hands two widowers, one widow and a pair of bereaved parents. Additionally, I have to contend with co-ordinating the work of three separate police forces, dealing with a popular press that has gone delirious with excitement and incidentally trying to find the reptile responsible for this mayhem. I understand your distress, but I need you to rise above it and give me the kind of support you gave me when we first met. I want information – not remorse.' As their eyes met, Rachel looked on and wondered whether this tactic would prove to be kill or cure.

Amiss's eyes dropped first. He leaned back in his armchair, stretched out his legs, pushed his hands through his hair and looked at Milton again. 'It's Charlie,' he said finally. 'I can't get him out of my head.'

'I know you were fond of him. But no one else thought of him either – even those who had worked with him for a damn sight longer than you. It was the most natural thing in the world to think this whole nightmare was confined to PD. Think of how you'd be feeling if you hadn't made the connection in the first place. Or made it and been too self-doubting to risk making a fool of yourself. You must realize that ninety-nine people out of a hundred would have thought the idea too far-fetched and would have let the whole thing go.'

Pike, who was standing by with two plates of sandwiches, intervened unexpectedly. 'That's right, sir. That Information Officer. He thought you were daft at first. Would usually have taken a lot more convincing, but said you seemed to know what you were talking about.'

'Middle-class confidence,' said Rachel.

Amiss smiled wanly and stubbed out his tenth cigarette of the morning. 'I'm grateful to all of you and I'll try to be positive.' He reached forward, helped himself to a glass of wine and raised it in the direction of Milton. 'To another successful collaboration.'

'That's the spirit,' said Milton approvingly, as they all drank the toast. 'I'm only on this case because of you. It took long enough to persuade the local forces that the Yard had to direct this, and my superiors only put me on it because they were impressed by what you had done and I admitted to being a friend of yours. My Chief Superintendent has helped by being out of action with a broken leg.'

'What have you established so far?'

'The preliminary pathology reports indicate that all four victims died of a massive dose of strychnine. It's a super-toxic poison and about 100 milligrams is the normal lethal dose. Our murderer doctored each chocolate on the top layer of the six boxes of chocolates with about 150 milligrams. They were very sweet chocolate cream that disguised the bitter taste of the strychnine.'

'Thorough chap,' said Amiss, putting down the sandwich he had begun to eat and reaching for a cigarette. 'Sorry. Melissa's indoctrination is slipping. Thorough person.'

Milton realized the effort behind Amiss's attempt at a joke. He said gently, 'I've got to tell you now the worst thing, Robert, because I don't want you to find out from anyone else. It's one of the most vicious poisons there is. Once it begins to affect the central nervous system it causes breathing difficulties and convulsions, and gives rise to intermittent spasms of extreme pain.'

'How long does it take to die?'

'It varies, but roughly an hour.'

Amiss sat silently for a few moments and then suddenly rose and rushed to the bathroom. They could hear the sounds of violent retching. Rachel followed him and returned quickly.

'He says he'll be all right when he's had a couple of minutes on his own.'

He was back before their uneasy silence had been broken. 'I'm sorry,' he said. 'That was just too much on top of my last night's excesses. Nothing against your sandwiches, Sammy.'

Rachel felt a rush of affection towards him deeper than any she had previously experienced. He looked over at her and smiled.

'All this will make a man of me yet. If a wet like Jim can become impervious to grisly deaths, so can I. Carry on, Jim. How was it done?'

'All the parcels were sent first-class letter-post on Friday from the main post office near the office. There were six in all – one each for Melissa, Edna Crump, Val Illingworth, Gloria Farson, Jill Collins and Fran Short.'

'So why didn't they arrive on Saturday?'

'Each one had a typewritten note stuck on saying "Please don't deliver before first post Monday 14 February, St Valentine's Day." The Post Office, bless their romantic souls, obliged and kept the parcels back.'

'Smart murderer.'

'Very smart. That way he ensured the women were on their own when they received the chocolates and assumed they were from their husbands.'

'Why didn't any of the wives . . .?' asked Rachel. 'Sorry. I've thought of the answer.'

'I bet you were going to say "Why didn't any of the wives ring up and say thank you?",' said Amiss.

'I was. But they just weren't given to phoning their husbands at work.'

'Right,' said Amiss. 'That's the cruel thing about it. All these guys were either careful about money or hard up. Phone-calls from far distant homes during peak hours were only made in emergencies.'

'To continue,' said Milton, looking anxiously at his watch. 'Tiny's wife succumbed to the temptation first, and she died sometime mid-morning. Thank heavens Tiny had that dental appointment and was home earlier than usual. If he hadn't phoned you, it could all have been much worse.'

'I wondered why he did phone me. It wasn't necessary.'

'He says it was because he thought you'd give him some support. He likes you. Or so he told the officer who took his statement.'

Rachel was relieved to see that the impact of this was not lost on Amiss. He looked almost happy for a moment. Then his face became serious again. 'And the others?'

'No one else touched the stuff until late afternoon. Gloria Farson was surprised to get a present which she could only assume came from Tony. She thought they should celebrate his uncharacteristic generosity by opening them together ceremoniously.'

'So what happened?'

'Their seven-year-old son arrived home from school at four o'clock. He had his tea and wandered alone into the living room. He was a greedy little chap, apparently, and when he saw the box he ripped it open and took one. By the time she heard him screaming, called the ambulance and tried to comfort him, it was too late to get in touch with Tony. The office was empty.'

'Edna?'

'She was on a diet, but she obviously couldn't resist having one at afternoon tea-time. She was on her own, and wasn't discovered until the police arrived and saw her corpse through the living room window.'

Rachel looked anxiously at Amiss. She had to ask it for him. 'Charlie?'

'Charlie and his wife had been having a bit of a coolness, so though she assumed the chocolates were from him, she wouldn't open them. I think she wanted some kind of reconciliation scene first. He came home, saw the chocolates and shouted out, "What's this, then? Something from one of your boyfriends?" Pulled the wrapping off and took one. He had the best chance of survival of any of them. He was the biggest, and the ambulance got to him within fifteen minutes. But his heart was none too strong, and the strain on it so great that he was dead on arrival at the hospital.'

Rachel took Amiss's hand and squeezed it. 'And the others?'

'Melissa you know about. Graham Illingworth's wife, it seems, was also either working up to or recovering from a tiff with him. So she didn't open the chocolates either. He's beside himself with relief over it. Especially since he heard about Tony's kid. Keeps going on about how it could have been his little Gail.'

Amiss looked up. 'That rings a bell. Something from the dinner dance.' They looked at him hopefully. 'No. It's no use. I'm too befuddled still. Can't think clearly. It'll come to me.'

'Robert, we haven't come here to grill you. Have we, Sammy?'

Pike shook his head sympathetically. 'Mind you, sir, I'm noting this down as a preliminary interrogation, but saying that Mr Amiss was in bad shape and couldn't be of much assistance at this time.'

'Quite right. Sammy and I can't stay any longer. We've got a meeting this afternoon with the relevant officers from the three forces. I'm going to interview the main *dramatis personae* myself in due course, but I'm getting the local people to take care of relatives, neighbours and so forth. My Chief Inspector will be in charge of the routine investigations of sources of supply, checking with post office staff and that kind of thing. Motive's the real bugger. We haven't got anything yet. It's either a lunatic, or someone who so hated one of the women in question he was prepared to sacrifice six or more people just to spread the risk of being discovered.'

'Sounds like a lunatic either way,' said Amiss.

'Have you any nominations?'

'Not at the moment. I don't know what you remember from what I told you a couple of months ago, but you should be aware – though it sounds treacherous to say it now – that none of them seemed to me to be happily married. Frankly, I wouldn't have been stunned if any of them had strangled his wife or any of the wives had poisoned her husband. I can't see any of them doing this, though. Can we meet tomorrow? In the meantime, I'll try to get my thoughts and memories into some sensible order.'

'Lunchtime again. Here? And tomorrow you two can go out in the morning and buy it.'

'Done,' said Rachel. 'You'll be coming too, Sammy?'

'I expect so, miss.'

Milton and Pike gathered their belongings and moved towards the door. As Rachel saw them out she said, 'Thanks, Jim. That helped a lot. He's got something to occupy him now.'

'I'm fond of him too,' said Milton. He bent and kissed her. She walked quickly back into the living room and stood for a moment looking at Amiss, who was stretched out with his eyes shut.

'Come on,' she said, affecting her Margaret Thatcher voice. 'Pull your socks up and get cracking. You've got four letters of commiseration to write and a number of phone-calls to make. I'm going to order the wreaths and plan our next few days.'

He looked up and tried to blink away his tears. Then he grinned. 'I knew I shouldn't have taken up with a Jew,' he said. 'You're all such bloody achievers.'

15

Wednesday, 16 February

Amiss lay in bed listening to Rachel's breathing and trying all the tricks he knew to get to sleep. Come on, he urged himself. Try to work through the detailed plot of the last film you saw. Shit, it was a thriller and I can't think of a soothing alternative. Focus on an imaginary black velvet curtain . . . ugh, as black as the grave I'll be looking into tomorrow at Edna's funeral . . . How about Latin verbs . . . *amo, amas, amat* . . . Rachel . . . she's being wonderful . . . *amo*, certainly . . . she's pulled me through the worst of this already . . . without her I wouldn't be able to think calmly about Charlie . . . Charlie . . . If I hadn't got him promoted, he'd have still been in PD1 and would have been saved in time . . . no, no . . . Rachel argued me out of that . . . you're not responsible if you inadvertently kick a stone and start an avalanche of boulders . . . back to the sleep-inducers . . . Purchasing Instructions . . . BC/P/5293, Horace's most bewildering . . . try to remember its provisions again . . . 1) This instruction should be read in conjunction with BC/P/4396 . . . how did that begin? . . . I can remember Henry quoting it at Twillerton . . . Twillerton . . . I haven't been there since I drove away leaving Charlie pumping up a flat tyre . . . don't think about Charlie, think about nailing his murderer . . . funny how personal knowledge of the victim makes one vengeful . . . but not vicious, really . . . I don't want whoever did this hanged, but I can't feel very forgiving . . . still, today Jim sounded more liberal than I did . . . talking about the fellow responsible maybe being mad and not to be blamed for his actions . . . fellow? maybe it was some lesbian friend of Melissa's? . . . Jim says her lover had access to her list of PD1 names and addresses . . . an old one with Charlie's name on it . . . wouldn't that be better than knowing one of my staff could have done it . . . couldn't be Tiny . . . I like Tiny . . . not as much as I liked Charlie . . . stop it . . .

He looked at the clock and saw it was almost midnight. He got out of bed and went into the living room, poured himself a large whisky and lit a cigarette. He might as well think sensibly about the information he and Jim had exchanged today. The estimate was that among all the chocolates, over seven grams of strychnine had been used. How the hell did anyone get hold of any strychnine, let alone that much? Jim's people hadn't come up with any answers. Preliminary advice suggested that only those with easy access to a chemical laboratory could lay their hands on that amount. Or someone with criminal associations. But how could any of these blokes consort with criminals? None of the married ones had had enough time to call their own to enable them to make the right kind of contacts. Only Tony and maybe Tiny had the money. Bill had both but he had no motive. Unless he was a psychopath. And there were several others in PD – and maybe outside it – who had access to the same list. Maybe someone in PD2 was responsible? Or Horace? Or Cathy? Or Shipton? Impossible to imagine any of them as mass murderers. Poor Bill had even burst into tears this morning when Jim mentioned Tony's son. Is that because he's soft-hearted? Or because he meant to kill Gloria and was upset because he'd got the wrong person? Nonsense. It would have been impossible not to know he was running that risk. And that rules Tony out too, doesn't it?

Graham's out of it too, for the same reason. No one could be more devoted to his child than Graham is to Gail. Charlie didn't commit suicide. That left only Henry, Tiny and Melissa's friend. He refused to believe Tiny was capable of such cold-blooded callousness, even if he had a motive. Henry? He was a ghastly, selfish lecherous old bastard, but surely . . . That was the rub, of course. How could he believe that anyone he knew could do something like that? Yes, selfishly, it would be best if it proved to be Melissa's friend. Jim said that he had got no information worth the name out of Melissa last night. He only found out she had that list at home by snooping and finding it stuck inside the telephone directory.

So far, so bad, he thought. If all he could come up with for Jim was the time-honoured advice that it must be someone other than those he knew, he might as well throw in his hand as an unofficial helpmeet. He wouldn't go back to bed until he had thought of something useful. He had nothing to add to the character analyses he had given Jim today. Or rather, yesterday, he observed, seeing that it was now well after midnight. That was a smart idea of Rachel's, he thought, ringing her flatmate Helen to ask her to send over his letters in the diplomatic pouch. It was rather an invasion of privacy, but Jim had promised that only he and Sammy would read them. He had seemed very interested in the Twillerton business. Maybe there was a link. Some of the things that happened there had been downright unpleasant, even if laxatives were a long way from strychnine. Jim should be able to sort out Lorre and Greenstreet and come up with an answer to that one.

He poured himself another, smaller shot, lit another cigarette and considered it thoughtfully. All the agony of giving up had been wasted. He'd never have the heart to go through it again. What a bore he'd been on the subject of how he could now take them or leave them. Of how he took an occasional cigarette at moments of pressure but used his iron will to ensure that he never went beyond three a week. Indeed he had had a long conversation about that with poor Fran Short the one and only time they met. She was a reformed smoker herself. Edna had confessed that her one and only passion was chocolate. And Val Illingworth had said – good God, yes – she had said she liked it too, but wasn't it funny, Gail wouldn't touch the stuff. Unnatural in a child, they had all agreed. But Val had said it was because Gail once got so sick from over-indulgence in Easter eggs that she couldn't bear the smell since.

His job, he considered, was not to ponder the implications of this remembered information any further. It was for Jim to decide whether this put Graham seriously into the running as a likely murderer. He looked around for the book most likely to put him to sleep, a search concluded when his eyes lit on C.P. Snow's *The Masters*, a novel he had greatly enjoyed on first reading. Everything is a matter of perspective in the end, he thought to himself as he reached for it. How could I ever have cared whether one set of wankers succeeded in pushing their candidates into the mastership of a college in the face of the machinations of an opposing set of wankers? At this rate I won't even think it matters if I don't become a Principal next May.

16

Inspector Romford glowered resentfully at Milton. 'We're doing the best we can, sir,' he said plaintively.

'Well, then you must do better,' responded Milton, wincing as he recognized the absurdity of the injunction. He stopped pacing up and down his room, sat down at his desk and tried to recover his temper.

'Look, Romford. I know I'm asking a lot of you. I know you're without a Chief Inspector. I know you're new to the job. I know – believe me, I know – that sifting reports from three police forces, all trying to outdo themselves in keenness, is an appallingly difficult job. I know you're short-staffed because Chief Inspector Trueman has borrowed one of your sergeants to work on the London end. But you cannot really think it reasonable to present me with this two-feet-high pile of paper and tell me I should read it all because it is all potentially significant.'

'Well, sir. If you'll forgive me saying so, you're the one who's been telling me that everything is of potential significance.'

'Dear God.' Milton did not notice Romford's lips purse at this blasphemy. 'I said that *you* must regard everything as of potential significance, and exercise *your* judgement in deciding what was promising enough to bring to *my* attention.'

He pulled a piece of paper from the top of the pile. 'What is promising about a report from the Essex force that Charlie Collins incurred a parking fine for leaving his car on a yellow line in Chelmsford last December?'

'It might be near a well-known area for drug pushers, sir. I think it should be followed up.'

'Collins was one of the victims, Romford.'

'Well, sir. For all I know he wanted to commit suicide. Or maybe he didn't recognize the chocolate box as the one he'd sent. Anything's possible in this case. I can't see any reason why anyone should have done this. All these men had safe jobs and nice houses and I can't see why they should have wanted to poison anyone. As far as I can see, their wives looked after them all right. It's as likely that one of them should have wanted to kill himself as that he would want to get rid of a good wife.'

Milton leaned back in his chair, closed his eyes and thought for a couple of minutes. 'Romford,' he asked when he looked at him again, 'do you understand about hate, loathing, vengefulness, passion – madness?'

'A bit,' said Romford. 'I know that I think that child-killers should be strung up. And I suppose that's a kind of hate, though the Bible does say an eye for an eye.'

'I'm talking about what makes an apparently ordinary person commit a crime that to us seems unspeakable and to him seems justified.'

'You mean wickedness, sir.'

'I mean putting yourself in the murderer's shoes and trying to understand his motives. I mean looking for reasons that might make a particular individual plan and execute a crime like this. I mean searching for evidence of betrayal, cuckolding, lust, greed and hatred of a human being.'

They looked at each other helplessly. 'I'm not a psychologist, sir,' said Romford finally.

You're not, thought Milton. You're a decent, thorough and conscientious policeman who is being asked to demonstrate an imagination he hasn't got. He picked up the pile of paper and passed it across the desk.

'Carry on with checking discrepancies and building up composite reports on each suspect. Select from among your staff the person whom you most frequently have to reprimand for showing too much curiosity about things that don't concern him and the affairs of other people. He should also be bright. Tell him he's got till tomorrow morning to give me a selection of reports that bear on motives in this case and to come up with any ideas – however mad they seem – that look worth pursuing.'

Romford made a mighty effort at concentration. 'There's

young Ellis Pooley, sir. He's always at it. Dreadful gossip. And reads too many detective stories, if you ask me. He was saying only yesterday that this was just like Agatha Christie's *The A.B.C. Murders*, where some chap wanted to kill some other chap whose surname began with a "C", so he first murdered people whose names began with "A" and "B" so it'd look as if there was a maniac at large. I had to tick him off for being fanciful. He doesn't seem to know the difference between these books and real life.'

'Does our murderer?' asked Milton. And seeing that Romford was preparing himself to give a well-reasoned response, he added hastily, 'Pooley seems just the man for the job. Well done, Romford. You can go now.'

Mollified by the compliment, Romford went off in search of Pooley. Maybe there was more to the impudent young whipper-snapper than he had thought. He wondered yet again what Pooley had meant when he said *sotto voce* that Romford reminded him of Inspector Lestrade.

Milton had already opened the file marked 'Twillerton'. Robert had insisted it might be only a red herring. But one way or the other, it was time to clear it up.

17

Saturday, 19 February

'I've never much minded one way or the other about being Jewish,' remarked Rachel, as they trudged up the hill towards the crematorium. 'But after the last couple of days I've decided I'm lucky.'

Amiss turned his attention from the trickle of rain down the back of his neck. 'What's brought about the change? The sausage rolls after Edna Crump's funeral?'

'No. Bad as they were, I prefer them to gefilte fish. It's the apparently complete absence of any tradition among this particular set of gentiles to cope with death and grief.'

'What do you mean? Family support and that kind of thing?'

'To some extent. I was thinking more of attitude to the mourners. Do you know about *shiva*?'

'No.'

'I've only sat *shiva* once – for my orthodox grandmother. The whole family was very upset when she died and she got the full works. A seven-day period of formal mourning – that's *shiva* – when the family sits together at home, friends visit and everyone talks about the dead person. You can get the worst of the sadness out of your system and everyone thinks it quite proper if you want to cry or reminisce.'

'I see what you mean. I didn't have much experience of funerals myself until now; and even I've noticed the predominance of the stiff upper lip. A general terror on the part of all present that someone might say something to cause the bereaved to behave embarrassingly.'

'Mind you,' said Rachel reflectively, 'from all you've said, seven days talking about poor Edna could have been too much of a strain for anyone to endure. But it might have helped the Collinses and the Farsons.'

'I don't know about the Farsons, considering those of us outside the family didn't even get invited to the baked meats.'

'I have to admit to being grateful for that. The other two occasions were agonizing enough. Do you think we'll have to stay at Tiny's for long?'

'The poor devil seemed very insistent when I spoke to him yesterday.'

'Well, as long as we get away in time to have our last evening together. Is it very selfish of me to feel I've had enough of this? Where the hell is this bloody crematorium, anyway? I thought it was only a few hundred yards.'

Amiss, who had been holding his head bent in the face of the wind, raised it and peered ahead. 'It must be just around that corner. The chap at the station said left at the top of the hill.'

As they began to cross the side-road that lay between them and their destination, a figure in a heavy grey raincoat leapt out of a car parked dangerously near the corner and called to them vigorously.

'Who is it?' asked Rachel. 'I can't see a thing.'

'It's Sammy Pike. And he's waving us over to join him in the car.'

'Get us out of the weather for a couple of minutes. We're early anyway. Nice to see you, Sammy,' she said as they got into the back seat. 'Where's Jim?'

'He's interviewing the BCC security men, miss.'

'What?' said Amiss. 'On a Saturday? They'll claim double time. What are you doing here?'

'The super couldn't get hold of you this morning, sir, and he had an urgent message for you.'

'Sammy,' said Rachel. 'You wouldn't consider substituting "Rachel" and "Robert" for "miss" and "sir", would you?'

'Do you mind if I don't, miss? I've always found it easier to keep a line between my private and official lives. Not that that's easy with the super. This message is strictly off the record.'

'And it is . . .?'

'I think you'd better read this first. It's the gist of a report from a Woman Police Constable in the Kent force.'

'You read it first, Rachel, while I find a fag.'

She read without expression and handed it over without comment. Amiss scanned the three paragraphs and exploded. 'This is a hell of a thing to read just before we meet Tiny to see off his wife's corpse. It's evil-minded tittle-tattle from some nosey old bitch.'

'I'm inclined to agree with you, sir. But you know we can't ignore any leads.'

'Well, what does Jim want us to do about it? Find this Miss Nash among the mourners, always supposing she's there, and chat her up? I'd be more inclined to lay her out with one of the urns.'

'It's more a case of trying to find out if there's any truth in it, sir. He thought you might get a chance if you stay on long enough at Mr Short's house to elicit some confidences from him.'

'In the unlikely event that I stayed on and that he poured out the information that his dead wife had intended to divorce him on grounds of impotence, can you tell me why that should be suitable grounds for suspicion of murder? Couldn't they have done it quietly?'

'We're a bit short of motives, sir. And our Detective Constable Pooley reckons that what with his being a rugby player and what with all Miss Nash says about Mr Short's violent behaviour at home, maybe it's a macho thing. Trying to save his reputation with the lads.'

'Tiny would have throttled her, not poisoned her. He's far too clumsy to have managed all that stuff with grains of strychnine, needles and razors.'

'Well, you might be better able to find out the truth than we could in a formal interview.'

Rachel broke the silence that followed. 'It's all right, Robert. Forget about our going out this evening. I've thought of something useful I can do instead. You go on to Tiny's house on your own and I'll meet you back at the flat whenever.'

Amiss emitted a sound half-way between a sigh and a groan. 'I don't know who to resent most, Sammy. That smart-ass DC Whatshisname . . .?'

'Pooley.'

'. . . Pooley. The slanderous old bitch, Miss Nash. Jim for his moral blackmail. You for so efficiently finding us. Or this woman for publicly granting me the freedom to get lumbered with a shitty job.'

'It's difficult to choose, sir.'

'Goodbye, Sammy. You may tell Jim from me that only the debt of gratitude I owe his wife prevents me from telling him to take a running fuck.'

'I shall make a note of it, sir,' said Pike, as he got out to open for them the near-side car door.

They walked silently for a couple of minutes, until Rachel stopped and faced him. 'Robert,' she said, 'have I ever told you you're beautiful when you're angry?'

He made a valiant attempt to narrow his eyes, tighten his mouth and look severe. His failure was apparent to them both. 'All right, you cow,' he muttered affectionately. 'I only hope you've got something spectacularly awful lined up for tonight.'

'It may come to nothing, so I'll keep it a surprise.'

They rounded the corner to see the arrival of the funeral cortège. Gathered in the car-park was a small group of wet and miserable people and, for the fourth time since Thursday, Amiss found himself nodding at Shipton, Horace, Graham, Bill and Melissa. As on every previous occasion, he could not repress his astonishment that Melissa had elected to do the simple, decent thing.

Supplemented by family and friends, they stood by unhappily until the coffin had been carried into the crematorium chapel by Tiny and five strong men who looked like stalwarts of the rugby club. As the mourners shuffled into the chapel, Amiss looked around for Rachel and saw she had moved back to join Melissa.

She's distancing herself, he thought. Making sure that she can make a clean get-away afterwards. If Melissa stayed true to form, she would be the only PD member who didn't trail back to the house for the food and drink.

At first, during the brief religious service, Amiss could keep neither his eyes off Tiny nor his mind off the accusations of Miss Nash. Could he really be the brute she portrayed? Surely he was merely an oaf with a quick temper. He tried to wrench his mind away to listen to the vicar, who was making it abundantly clear that he wouldn't have known Fran if he had met her in the street. The unctuous voice flowed over the congregation, making bland utterances about 'the natural goodness she displayed in the conduct of her daily life', and that 'though not outwardly apparently a religious person' (code for never going to church), 'she was possessed of an instinctive spirituality' (code for promising that St Peter would do his bit without any quibbles). Nothing of course about the nastiness of her death. Don't upset the listeners. Just like the anodyne services for Tommy Farson and Charlie. Hadn't Edna's service been preferable? Even though that Baptist minister had rather overdone the Old Testament angle, banging on about her slayer, he had at least known something about her and cared. It had been a bit surprising to find that Henry was a pillar of the congregation. Unlucky for him to have been born a Baptist. He'd have been better off a Roman Catholic. At least he'd have got a kick out of confession.

This service, Amiss was thankful to see, was going to be briefer than any of the others. 'Abide with Me', he sang along with his neighbours, as a sub-standard type of organ music played in the background. The coffin began the slide down the rollers, with a squeak that suggested the maintenance staff might lack the sense of duty befitting their position. His teeth ground in sympathy with those who were really mourning Fran. Was there no way to be disposed of that didn't have these ghastlinesses? He flinched at the memory of the heart-stopping moment on Thursday when one of the ropes had slipped and Edna's coffin plummeted down into the grave with indecent haste. No. Panic was unnecessary this time. Despite the squeak, the coffin was making a stately progress along the decline. It was only seconds before it vanished, the curtains fell back together and the sing-along tape indicated that a few verses of

'Jesu, Joy of Man's Desiring' would put an end to the proceedings. He sneaked a covert look at his watch. A quarter to five now. Allow about a quarter of an hour to get to Tiny's house. What then? Was he supposed to hang around the whole evening in the hope of getting Tiny to himself? There were bound to be relatives staying. If he once realized there would be no opportunity for a *tête-à-tête*, surely he could get away within a couple of hours. As he joined the procession from the chapel, he looked around for Rachel to tell her that he'd ring her about seven o'clock and let her know if their evening could be salvaged after all. She was nowhere in the car-park. He looked about in bewilderment and then caught sight of her moving away in the direction of the railway station. She was talking earnestly to Melissa.

18

'Would you like some of my tea wine?' asked Melissa. I should not, thought Rachel wistfully. I can think of nothing more loathsome. What I'd really like is a large gin and tonic, with plenty of ice, and the promise of more to come.

'Oh, yes please,' she said. 'That sounds great.'

Melissa hung their coats carefully in a cupboard concealed by a long green felt curtain festooned with badges. As she left the room Rachel took the opportunity to scrutinize the display. Many of the messages were predictable. Only a couple of hours of Melissa's company had led her to expect that she would be for abortion on demand, the environment, reclaiming the night, alternative living, positive discrimination, the IRA and international socialism. It was no surprise either that she appeared to be against capitalism, urbanism, female circumcision, pornography, rape and other varieties of male oppression. Rachel even felt a collector's delight in actually seeing rather than reading about badges proclaiming 'I am a lesbian' and 'I am menstruating'. The only legends that occasioned a wrinkling of the forehead were those concerning, on the one hand, 'wimmin' and, on the other, 'wommin'. She knew about the liberationists' rejection of the anti-female overtones of the word 'women'. But now it seemed as if there was a split about the proper alternative. Or was 'wommin' a misprint? And why not 'wimmon' – or even 'wummin'?

Better not distract Melissa by raising the issue, she concluded, and returned to the sofa to which she had been directed. She had worked hard to get this far. It would all prove a tiresome waste of time unless she could get hold of the information she needed for Jim. As Melissa reappeared from the kitchen carrying a bottle and two glasses, there was the sound of a key turning in the lock of the front door.

A tall, slim fair-haired woman of about thirty came swiftly into the room throwing her anorak energetically into the far corner. Rachel just had time to note the grim expression and to learn from her chest that she was in favour of 'WOMANPOWER' and against the bomb when Melissa said, 'This is my lover, Angela Perry. Angela, this is Rachel Simon. We travelled together from the funeral.'

Angela nodded a distracted welcome, threw herself into an armchair and began a discourse that impressed Rachel with its fluency and spread of invective. Angela was angry. The peace demonstration had been thinly attended; there had been rain throughout; the police had been heavy; they had acted roughly in removing some of the women who had lain down in the middle of Whitehall; and Angela had a large bruise on her upper arm to prove it. She seemed if anything crosser with the women (including Melissa) who had failed to turn up than with the police, who were behaving true to their porcine form. Melissa was sympathetic and soothing, but impressed Rachel by her refusal to apologize for electing to honour Fran on this occasion rather than to enter her protest against cruise missiles. 'You must see, Angela,' she said firmly, 'that when violence against women occurs in one's own vicinity, one must express solidarity.'

'Oh, I suppose so,' said Angela grudgingly, 'but I still don't see why you went to the funerals of the man and the boy.'

'I told you,' said Melissa patiently. 'They were the incidental victims of violence intended for women.'

This line of argument struck Rachel as being short on logic. Surely Charlie's death in particular should have been the cause of rejoicing that an anti-woman plot had boomeranged back on a representative of the collectively guilty male sex? It struck her that Amiss's view of Melissa was probably correct. She could not in practice live up to the harshness of her theoretical views. With a hard-liner like Angela she sought to cover up her wetness by ideological obfuscation. Angela was forceful but simple-minded. Melissa's office braggadocio was put on to cover more open-mindedness and intellectual uncertainty than she would like to admit.

'Since two of the four who died were male, you don't think there's any chance that it was not violently intended against women, *per se*?' As she asked the question, Rachel saw nervously that Angela's expression became hostile.

'Whose side are you on?' she demanded.

'I just meant that maybe one of the men wanted to kill his wife and didn't mind who else – of either sex – suffered in the process of obscuring the real target.'

Angela looked thunderous. 'God, you're so naive,' she began.

Melissa cut in swiftly. 'You're not seeing this clearly, Rachel. The motive behind this is simple. This was as straightforwardly designed to kill women – and only women – as it would have been if the murderer had gone out into the streets and stabbed the first six women he saw.'

'And which of your colleagues would have wanted to do that?'

'Any of them,' said Angela firmly. 'Every man wants to violate women in some way. Any of them could have had so much aggression in him that he wanted to destroy as many as possible. It's an inevitable consequence of living in a capitalist patriarchy.'

Rachel took her first sip of tea wine and heroically controlled the grimace that fought its way nearly to the surface. 'So there's no point in speculating about the specific motives of any individual?' she asked.

'None whatsoever,' said Melissa vehemently. 'This is just one more expression of the backlash against the women's liberation movement. If the police had any brains they'd be looking for whichever of those men feels most threatened by us.'

What would that mean in practice? wondered Rachel. An opinion survey? A check on their propensity to buy pornography? A psychiatrist's analysis of their sexual fantasies? This paranoid drivel was getting her nowhere. She had to steer them round to giving her the facts she wanted. Without thinking, she took a fortifying gulp of wine. The wave of nausea that hit her sent her rapidly to the bathroom. Through the partition she could hear Melissa talking rapidly. She returned to the living room trying not to look self-conscious. Angela challenged her at once. 'So you want to join the women's movement?'

'Well, I feel I should be doing something about it. I was asking Melissa what kind of activities I could get involved in – when I'm transferred back from Paris.'

'Rachel's got a rather decent job in the embassy there,' interpolated Melissa.

'Foreign Office tokenism,' snarled Angela. 'If you're really serious you shouldn't be shoring up aggressive imperialist institutions but working for the movement itself.'

Rachel assumed her most guileless expression. 'I've been rather out of things over there. I can always think about changing my job when I get back.'

'She wants a run-down on the local groups and that kind of thing.'

Rachel's heart warmed to Melissa. It was disarmingly trusting of her to take a known heterosexual time-server at face value so readily. She suppressed a spasm of guilt and prepared herself for dissimulation on any political or social issue they cared to throw at her. Angela's first question was unexpected. 'You're Jewish, aren't you, with a name like that?'

'And a nose like this,' responded Rachel frivolously. 'Yes, I am.' She now recollected nervously that there was an anti-Zionist badge pinned to the green felt.

'So where do you stand on Israeli fascist expansionism?'

Rachel let herself into Amiss's flat just before midnight. Mournfully she realized it was empty. She poured herself a treble measure of gin, topped it with tonic and took a large mouthful before locating the ice. After a momentary dither, she looked up the Miltons' home number. She was greatly relieved when it was answered immediately.

'Rachel Simon, Jim. I wouldn't have rung you so late if you hadn't insisted you didn't mind, and if I hadn't put in a frightful evening on your behalf.'

'Where? At Tiny Short's?'

'No. That, I imagine, is where Robert is. I've been doing my bit by sussing out whether the feminists of North London might have been gunning for Melissa.'

'What results?'

'You're not going to get off as cheaply as that,' said Rachel grimly. 'I have come away from there feeling, as Angela Perry would no doubt put it, "marginalized" to an extreme degree. I have been abused for my sexual preferences and my racial origins. I have had to betray some of my relatives by agreeing finally that the simple wish to see Israel survive is morally wrong. I have eaten a meal of lentils and brown rice washed down with tea wine. Worst of all, instead of being able to incriminate one of that bunch of lunatics, I have to tell you that for all practical purposes you can forget them. Angela Perry is innocent.'

'Who the hell is Angela Perry?'

'Melissa's lover. You told us you were trying to find out if anyone in Melissa's circle with access to the PD list had reason to murder her.'

'If you've managed to eliminate that lot, I am more than grateful. Melissa wouldn't tell me a thing.'

'Right. Here is the gist of what I picked up as a result of six hours of self-sacrifice, lying and taking advantage of Melissa's and Angela's desire to make a convert . . .'

Milton listened intently for the next few minutes. When Rachel finished speaking she awaited a response.

'You're laughing, damn you,' she said.

'I'm sorry. It's just that, given all that polemic about male oppression and police brutality, it seems funny that I've just spent two hours ironing. Ann needed a wardrobe for the conference in the States she's going to tomorrow, and I thought I might as well do a week's shirts at the same time. To be serious, let me summarize what you've said. Angela has been Melissa's lover for the past year – in other words, since long before she came to work in the BCC. You are absolutely convinced from their description of their lives that no one but Angela knows anything about Melissa's work or colleagues. Therefore, only Angela could know which of them were married.'

'Right so far. And since no chocolates were sent to Bill's non-existent wife, only Angela could be a suspect.'

'How can you be so sure that Melissa didn't chat to others?'

'Because she admitted that she associates socially only with a fanatical women's group that won't allow any man's name to be mentioned.'

'And you say that Angela's alibi is uncontrovertible for the period between the last post on Thursday the tenth and the first on Friday the eleventh.'

'You wouldn't doubt it if you'd had to listen to her rundown of everything that happened at the consciousness-raising group on the Thursday night. Melissa had been at it too, so she wasn't making it up. And why should she? She didn't know I was a spy. She could never have got to the letter-box six miles away, because by crafty questioning I discovered that they went back to Melissa's afterwards for a nourishing whole-food meal, went to bed together, and by nine o'clock the following morning Angela was opening the proceedings at a seminar for social workers ten miles away in the wrong direction. Besides, they're a very happy couple.'

'Well, it's always cheering to be able to make a straightforward elimination. DC Pooley will be disappointed, though. He suggested this afternoon that a feminist enemy of Melissa's might have decided not only to get rid of her, but to eliminate several housewives as well on principle.'

'I suppose that's no sillier than Melissa's view that one of her colleagues simply wanted to kill women as a form of revenge on the whole sex.'

'It's harder to rule out that possibility,' sighed Milton. 'Sensible motives are a bit thin on the ground.'

'Any luck with the Twillerton wrecker?'

'We're working on it. Those BCC idiots were so convinced Robert was the miscreant that they didn't bother to complete the routine investigation. We're hoping to sort it out during the next few days.'

'Where will you be tomorrow, if Robert has anything to report?'

'At the Yard, I expect, shuffling paper and bullying subordinates.'

'Good luck. I won't see you for a while. I'm going back to Paris tomorrow evening.'

'Of course you are. I'm sorry. I'd forgotten. I've been the cause of ruining your last evening in London. Don't think I'm not grateful for your help. I wasn't looking forward to coming the heavy with Melissa and her gang. I only hope Robert's time has been spent as usefully as yours. I'm afraid he's probably had it rotten, too.'

'Well, at least it's better than ironing. Goodbye, Jim.'

19

'I didn't mean any harm. You know that, don't you? They were only jokes. Only for the sake of a bit of fun. Livened things up. I'm sorry if they upset you.'

Tiny was sitting perched on the edge of a small armchair that could only just contain the spread of his backside. What had possessed Fran, wondered Amiss yet again, to choose furniture which made her husband look ridiculous and ungainly? Only the sofa was big enough to offer him any bodily comfort, and that he refused to sit in. Nothing was too good for his friend Robert, he kept reiterating – 'my only friend', he added in his more depressed moments.

'Tiny! We've been over this again and again. I wasn't upset. Honestly. Please stop apologizing.'

'You're too good to me. Knew you were a good bloke when you wouldn't shop me to those security bastards. You're a true friend, a true friend.'

Tiny crumpled into an abject posture, edged himself back into his chair and tried to adopt a foetal position. The wooden arm caught his knee a painful crack, his arms flew out sideways as he attempted to right himself and a glass ornament on a side-table crashed to the pine floor and shattered. He jumped up with a look of panic. 'Must clear this up. Fran'll be furious.' Then, as reality forced its way through his alcohol-fuddled brain, he sank down unsteadily, buried his face in his hands and said: 'No, she won't. She's dead. Wait till I find the bastard who did this. I'll kill him.'

Amiss looked miserably at his watch. One o'clock in the morning. He'd been in this room now for eight hours. He couldn't blame Jim for this. Once he'd discovered that Tiny had no one to stay with him he would have felt bound to offer his own services, Miss Nash or no Miss Nash. He hadn't expected when the last stragglers left two hours earlier that Tiny's brave front would so quickly collapse. At least he could feel he was being useful. Tiny had a lot of misery to get out of his system and he didn't seem to know anyone else with whom he could let go. I suppose it's a form of *shiva*, he thought.

For a moment he thought that Tiny had fallen into a restful doze; then there was a stirring of the massive frame and Tiny clambered to his feet. 'I'm not looking after you. Have some whisky?'

'Just a little one.'

Tiny located the bottle and began to slosh its contents vigorously into Amiss's glass.

'Plenty, thanks.' He noted with resignation that Tiny had yet again succeeded in spilling a fair quantity over the arm of the sofa. Amiss topped up his glass with water to the brim. Tiny eschewed any such adulteration. He raised his half-full tumbler to his lips and swallowed half of it.

'Cheers,' he said heartily.

'Cheers,' responded Amiss with some embarrassment.

'You never know who your friends are till you're in trouble.'

Tiny embarked once again on the circular conversation about the nature of friendship. Wearily Amiss made yet again the correct-seeming responses to Tiny's monologue about how he hadn't seen his old pals, his true pals, since he and Fran moved down south. How the rugby club fellows were all very well, but only good for talking over games. How he didn't know the neighbours, because in the south there wasn't the memory of hard times shared to bring people together. How the blokes at the office were decent enough, but not like pals, real pals.

'Except you, Robert,' he said, making an affectionate lunge, the purpose of which was to pat Amiss on the arm but which succeeded only in knocking his ashtray on to the floor.

'Did Fran have friends?' asked Amiss, hoping to break the cycle.

'How would I know?'

Amiss hoped the belligerent note in Tiny's voice didn't presage trouble. If Tiny proved to be as violent as Miss Nash claimed, Amiss doubted his ability to overcome him. A thoughtful expression crossed Tiny's face.

'She used to talk to a few of the neighbours. And there were the women at the kindergarten she helped out at in the afternoon.'

This was a new one on Amiss. 'Fond of children, was she?'

'Cracked about them.'

Nothing ventured . . . thought Amiss. 'Couldn't she have any of her own?' He looked nervously at Tiny. There was a brief silence.

'No, she couldn't.' He seemed to have sobered up somewhat, observed Amiss with surprise. Emboldened, he continued.

'What was the trouble?'

'S'posed to be my fault, first. Then s'posed to be her fault. Then they said it was both our faults.'

Amiss felt a swimming sensation in his head. He topped up his glass with more water and said, 'Sorry, Tiny. I don't quite understand.'

'I can tell you this. Couldn't tell any of the other fellows. 'Cept my old pals. But never see them.'

'You can tell me.'

Tiny's eyes closed tight in concentration. 'When we were looked at first, ten years ago, they said I'd a low sperm count.' He looked up anxiously. 'That doesn't mean I couldn't do it. I'm as good as the next man.'

'I'm sure you are.'

'Had to get fit. That's why I took up rugby again. You'd think she'd have been grateful, but she wasn't. Then we had to be careful when we did it. Only the times they said she'd ovulate. Kind of took the fun out of it.'

'And that didn't work.'

'Bloody didn't. Next thing they say she's got something wrong with her hormones as well. Injections. All that carry-on. Then, a few months ago, another bright bloody medico said we'd both probably be all right with someone else. Something about a chemical antagonism between my sperms and her secretions. Is this getting too difficult?'

'No, no. I think I follow. Didn't they have any suggestions?'

'Only one was that she might get artificially inseminated by some other fellow.'

'How did you feel about that?'

'How do you think I felt about that?' Tiny's voice had risen to a bellow. He stood up and shouted, 'That'd be just like her having a bastard! Wouldn't it? How would you feel?'

'But would it really make any difference?' asked Amiss hesitantly. 'It would be like adopting, wouldn't it? Except that it would be half hers.'

'That's what she said.' Amiss was relieved that Tiny had sat down again, and his voice had dropped. 'But I couldn't see it that way. Kids are a bloody nuisance, really. I don't see how you can like them if they're not yours.'

Pooley had a point, thought Amiss – even if he had got hold of the wrong end of the stick. Tiny certainly was afflicted by inhibiting macho attitudes.

'Did she mind a lot?'

'Did she hell! She said she'd divorce me. I expect I'd have given in. I couldn't have stood her carry-on much longer.'

'You didn't want a divorce?' Amiss hoped he wasn't pushing his luck, but Tiny seemed calm enough to take the risk.

'I don't know. Marriage. I often wondered what the point of it was. We got married first because we thought she was pregnant. Good joke, that. Or maybe she pretended. I often wondered about that too. I don't suppose either of us enjoyed being married much. She couldn't have the kids she wanted. I couldn't do anything I wanted. Couldn't even have the kind of house I wanted. Bloody stupid jerry-built crap-house full of rubbish.' He picked up a Hummel figurine. 'See that? Do *you* like that?'

'It's not my kind of thing, I must admit.'

'Not mine either. But I had to work in that cruddy job to pay for stuff like this. Not any more, though.' He looked at the ornament with intense dislike, and in a sudden movement, hurled it at the wall. It met a china vase head-on, and the fragments of both fell into the mock fireplace.

Amiss looked with awe around the living room. At this rate of progress, between intentional and unintentional destruction, Tiny would have laid it waste within a couple of days. He lit another cigarette and picked up the ashtray. There didn't really seem now to be much point in clearing butts off the floor. He observed with interest that when Tiny again rose to do the honours with the whisky he succeeded in grinding ash into the rug with his left foot and fragments of ornament into the floorboards with his right.

'Did anyone know you two were having these infertility

problems?'

'I didn't tell anyone. Fran must have told some of them something. She probably blamed me. She couldn't stand people thinking she was barren. Women are bloody stupid. It's nothing to be ashamed of.'

Amiss didn't pursue the question. He couldn't himself see much difference between the respective hang-ups that plagued Tiny and Fran, but there was no point in trying to mediate between a suspect and a corpse.

'You wouldn't have minded her blaming you?'

'No . . . Well, not much . . . I could take it. The important thing is to know you're a real man. Have I told you about that try I made a couple of weeks ago?'

Twice, thought Amiss. 'No,' he said.

'I went through them like a dose of salts. There I was, mid-field, and Johnny Chadwick snaps one back from the ruck . . .'

A couple of minutes later, the triumphant climax to the story woke Amiss up. He applauded vigorously. 'Are you going to go on playing?' he asked.

'Not here. I've had enough of this dump. And the BCC. I'm getting out as soon as I can.'

'Where to?'

'Kenya.'

This promise of adventurousness almost took Amiss's breath away.

'Kenya?'

'Yes. I've got a brother there with a big farm. He always said he would find a job for me on it. But Fran wouldn't hear of the idea.'

Motive for murder? wondered Amiss. Surely not. Tiny could just have upped and gone. But he hadn't, had he? Not till she was dead.

'When are you thinking of going?'

'As soon as I've got rid of this house and everything in it. And I'll not be going back to the office. I told Donald this afternoon that I wanted to give in my notice. He seemed to think that what with the leave I've got saved up, I won't have to turn up again. I don't think I could face it, anyway. Imagine me, Tony and Henry – and the others – looking at each other wondering which of us had done this.'

Amiss couldn't imagine. All he knew was that he would have to turn up on Monday and try to behave normally.

He assumed his most hearty tone. 'I think it's a great idea, Tiny. Here's to it.' They both raised their glasses and drank.

Tiny got to his feet. 'I'll miss you, Robert. You've been good to me.'

Fearing a return to the well-furrowed discussion of friendship, it was with some relief that Amiss saw Tiny's knees buckle under him. He finished the contents of his own glass at one swallow and prepared to try to heave Tiny to his bedroom.

20

Amiss gripped the receiver tighter. 'Come on. Say something. Don't you think this rules Tiny out?'

'I have to agree that it very much weakens any case against him.'

'Surely, Jim, it demolishes it completely. If they had gone on with the divorce he'd have buggered off to Kenya, so what price the issue of his reputation in the rugby club? Anyway, she wouldn't have been divorcing him for impotence. The old rat-bag next door must have got the story muddled. Doesn't my account of last night prove she's not a reliable witness?'

'Well, it does sound as if the alleged violent orgies of destruction were probably Tiny repeatedly falling over his feet.'

'Can you take him off the list of suspects?'

'I'll have to check out his story with doctors, friends and relations, but I'm inclined to believe it.'

'You won't quote me, for God's sake, will you?'

'No, no. We're a bit more discreet than that. I'll get Sammy to have a chat with Miss Nash first off. If she's a very impressive witness, we'll have to consider the possibility that Tiny was cunningly pulling the wool over your eyes. But, as I say, that seems unlikely to me. How was he this morning?'

'Distinctly under the weather. I don't think he's used to drinking spirits. He didn't seem to regret having talked to me – though I doubt if he remembers quite what he said. He went so far as to repeat his protestations of undying friendship on the doorstep this morning. We even managed an awkward manly embrace.'

'I'd like to have seen that. Right. Many thanks. You did your job nobly. Ann was touched by the message you passed on via Sammy. She sent her love to you both and departed this morning telling me to look more closely at Bill.'

'Why Bill?'

'The Melissa theory seems to fit him better than anyone else.'

'Poor old sod. You can't be a bit of loner nowadays without everyone deciding you're a nutcase. Anyway, aren't there a couple of equally peculiar blokes in PD1?'

'Didn't I tell you? They're all ruled out. Absolutely rock-solid alibis. I won't give you the boring details, but there's no doubt about it. The credit mainly goes to Horace Underhill, who had called an ideas meeting with them for 8:30 on the Friday morning. Your lot straggled in at various times and could all theoretically have made it to the post office before work.'

'Hell,' said Amiss, stubbing out his cigarette furiously. 'What about any of PD1 sneaking up from home to push their parcels into the box after the last collection on Thursday?'

'Believe me. Between witnesses, railway time-tables and information from British Rail, we are absolutely certain that only your people are in the running. There is no doubt about it. Chief Inspector Trueman is thorough to a fault. Pooley remarked that the exercise was conducted in a manner worthy of Inspector French.'

'Who is this Pooley?'

'A rather engaging, desperately keen, detective constable. He's becoming rather a pet of mine. Makes an interesting contrast to some of our stolid cynics. He likes making comparisons with cases he has read about – real and fictional. He's been going on rather about famous strychnine cases – have you heard of Cream and Palmer?'

'This Pooley strikes me as too much of an antiquarian. I didn't think the young read Freeman Wills Croft any more.'

'That's what I like about him.'

'Jim. Much as I'd like to chat to you all day, I have things to do. I'm going to buy Rachel the best lunch I can find.'

'Enjoy yourselves. I am shortly heading off for Hertfordshire to try to force a confession out of Graham Illingworth.'

'It's impossible to force as much as a stapler out of Graham Illingworth unless you've got the appropriate requisition slip.'

'I think I have. The fact that his daughter doesn't like chocolates makes him now our leading suspect.'

'Did your predecessors get Cream or Palmer on such flimsy evidence?'

'I don't know. I'll have to ask Pooley.'

Amiss's spirits began to sink on the tube to Heathrow.

'Maybe I should move in with Tiny for a week or two. It'd be better than being on my own.'

'You're not serious, are you?'

'No. I suppose I'm not. From what I've seen of Tiny as a housekeeper, I'd turn into the nagging partner of *The Odd Couple*. I'm just feeling ill-equipped to be on my own.'

'You couldn't stay with Jim?'

'That would go down well with my staff, wouldn't it?'

'Sorry. Silly idea.'

Amiss looked with dislike at a gaggle of German tourists whose Aryan beauty and muscular frames made him feel prematurely aged.

'I really must do something about getting fit,' he muttered. 'It's disgraceful, at my age, that I can't run upstairs without panting.'

'You could take up a sport.'

'I hate sports.'

'So buy yourself a little pair of blue satin shorts and jog to work every morning. Or give up smoking. And drinking. I don't care. Just shut up whining.'

Amiss took on an injured tone. 'I thought you'd understand how dreadful I feel about facing work tomorrow.'

'I understand. Of course I understand. Haven't I been putting on a convincing imitation of a ministering angel all week?'

Amiss leaned over and kissed her. 'I'm sorry. It's a combination of lack of sleep, general horrors and the fact that you're going.'

'I'll be back in six days, for heaven's sake.'

'That's the trouble with you modern women. You're as bad as Ann Milton. You think it's normal to conduct a marriage – or in your case, a courtship – in the occasional intervals between pissing off around the world.'

'On whom would you have me model myself?'

'I don't know. Any good housewife. Edna Crump?'

'A few days ago, I'd have found that a singularly tasteless remark. But I've been discovering the truth in that ancient adage about laughing so that you won't cry.'

'That's just as well. I should think you'll be getting a fair share of hysterical giggles down the phone during the week. At the moment, I'm returning to cheerfulness at the thought of what Jim is likely to be going through with Graham. If he thought Melissa was a stone-waller, he hasn't lived until now.'

Graham was sitting primly on a hard-backed chair in his tiny dining room. As he had explained to Milton, the living room was in use by Gail, who was watching an old film on television. Her joyful snorts of laughter occasionally punctuated the difficult conversation next door. Milton had been struck by the fond expression that crossed Graham's face every time he heard her. He thought briefly of asking if she could be persuaded to turn down the volume a little, but thought better of it. Graham was clearly so besotted that the request would alienate him permanently.

Milton sipped the tea that Val had provided with such bad grace. He couldn't spin the preamble out any longer. He had been given confirmation of Graham's movements between leaving work on Thursday and arriving in on Friday. He could prove he had caught a train home that left London before the last post on Thursday. He looked after Gail all evening until Val came home from work at midnight. What he could not prove was whether he had, as he said, missed the 7:35 train to work and had to wait for the 7:55. The former would have given him ample time to make the detour to the post office.

'I fear, Mr Illingworth, that you do not have an alibi.'

Graham sat up even straighter in his chair. He had to raise his voice to drown out the sound of singing from next door. 'I have to say that I resent your scurrilous inference that I might have wanted to murder my wife.'

'I am making no such implication,' said Milton. 'You will surely understand the need to carry out the appropriate police procedures . . . Without fear or favour,' he added as an afterthought.

'Just as long as you understand that I know my rights. I won't put up with any bullying.'

'Neither the constable nor myself is here to bully you, Mr Illingworth. I am here to put a number of straight questions to you. I would be grateful for straight answers. Detective Constable Pooley is here to make a record of our conversation, a copy of which you will be asked to read and sign.'

'In that case, I hereby make a statement for him to write down.'

'Please do so, Pooley,' said Milton with due gravity.

'My . . . wife . . . and . . . I . . .'

Observing the agonized expression on Pooley's face, Milton cut in. 'It's all right, Mr Illingworth. You may speak at your normal speed. The constable uses shorthand.'

Graham cleared his throat and spoke at a pace which made Milton realize he had learned this off by heart. 'My wife and I are a united couple. I have never wished to perpetrate any injury upon her. I repudiate totally any imputation whereby I might have tried to poison her. Such allegations are an insult to her and I. At this moment in time I wish it to go on record that I shall have to seek legal advice if there is any police harassment of my family.'

Milton adopted a conversational tone. 'Could you explain to us now why you lied about your daughter being in danger from the chocolates?'

'I dispute the factuality of that statement.'

It took ten minutes – during which Milton had to read out the relevant parts of statements from the two policemen who had been to the Illingworth household on St Valentine's Day – before Graham reluctantly admitted that he might have said Gail could have been poisoned by a chocolate. Milton was relieved that at least he was not mug enough to claim she did eat the stuff. Even Graham could grasp that both wife and child were readily available to be interrogated about this.

'Who's been talking to you about our business?' he demanded.

'That is none of yours,' said Milton. 'I want to know why you sought to deceive police officers into thinking that your daughter was vulnerable.'

'I forgot.'

'Forgot what?'

'Forgot she didn't eat them.'

Nothing could shift him from this position. Fifteen minutes later, Milton recognized that he was beaten.

'I will leave it at that for the moment, Mr Illingworth. But I must warn you that I am not satisfied with your answers. I shall need to talk to you again.'

'I hope you will confine yourself to visiting me at the office. I resent having the privacy of my home invaded, particularly on a Sunday.'

'Sometimes I resent having to work on a Sunday. But perhaps my priorities are different from yours. I attach more importance to saving lives than to suiting my own convenience. Perhaps it has not occurred to you, Mr Illingworth, that this murderer may strike again.'

As they walked down the front path, Pooley said approvingly: 'That will have rattled him, sir'.

'Only if he's innocent. I was letting off steam rather than being clever.'

'I don't know how you kept your temper, sir. Whether he's innocent or not, he told a lie to try to deflect suspicion from himself. He reminds me of a man I once read about who . . .'

'Not now, Pooley. I've got some ideas I want to dictate to you. Get in.'

Pooley sat behind the wheel, making copious notes of Milton's instructions. At the end he looked up in excitement. 'Shall I get on to the Hertfordshire police force myself, sir?'

'No, Pooley. I don't think they are ready for such a level of egalitarianism as you propose. The instructions will have to come from me. But you may draft them for my signature.'

Pooley looked rather crestfallen as he started the car. Milton had a sudden recollection of being snubbed as an over-zealous young policeman. 'Ellis,' he said, 'you may now tell me about this man Illingworth reminded you of.'

Making a brief appearance, the sun lit up the highly polished silver on Miss Nash's sideboard. Sammy Pike looked at it critically, and concluded that at least the poor old soul had been accurate when she said she was used to better circumstances.

Shabby-genteel was the only description you could apply to the rest of her room. The chintz was faded and the carpet worn. He felt sorry for her. If even Mr Amiss was here now he'd realize that she wasn't malicious. Just a bit confused. Her generation and class couldn't be expected to understand the changes in the world around them. It wasn't fair of Mrs Short to have told her all that stuff about infertility. No wonder she thought Mr Short was impotent. She didn't sound like the sort who'd grasp fine distinctions.

'Thank you, madam. I will take another slice of your delicious cake.'

Pike prided himself on his ability to win the hearts of old ladies. Ten years on the beat had made him an expert. Miss Nash continued to witter on in ever-greater excitement.

'You must be careful, ma'am. It is really very unlikely that Mr Short was responsible for his wife's death. You could get yourself into trouble saying so.'

'But what else can I be expected to think, officer? Poor girl. All that violence she had to put up with.'

'Did she ever complain to you?'

Miss Nash twisted one ankle round the other. 'Well . . . not often. She was very brave.'

Pike knew enough to interpret this as never. The violence was clearly a myth. He looked at his hostess with compassion. She must have a boring life. Sitting here all dressed up in her Sunday best waiting for someone to call. You couldn't blame her for getting a bit carried away with the drama.

'You'll miss her, then.'

'Oh, yes, officer. So much. I went to her cremation, you know, but I couldn't bring myself to go into his house afterwards. I was glad I didn't. Can you believe . . .' She lowered her voice. 'Last night he had some kind of drunken party. The poor girl laid to rest in her coffin, and that very night he's shouting and fighting in her house.'

'Fighting?'

'Yes. I could hear them breaking things.'

Pike repressed a grin. The walls looked thin enough, but she must have stayed up late to hear what was going on in the living room in the middle of the night.

He finished his cake and made a move to go. Miss Nash waved at him in a distracted manner. Her little angular face turned pink. 'Please, officer. I haven't told you the worst.'

Pike's interest was aroused. 'Well, tell me now.'

'I couldn't bring myself to speak of this if you weren't a policeman.'

Not half, thought Pike. You seem to have talked pretty freely about your neighbours' sexual habits.

'You must look upon me like a doctor.' That always got them, he reflected complacently.

'The thing is . . . I understand now why he couldn't give dear Fran a child.'

Clamping his hands on his thighs, Pike leaned forward in fascination. 'Do tell me.'

Miss Nash's faded eyes gazed frankly at him. She paused briefly for effect. 'He's a homosexual, you see. Of course I know they don't lock them up for that any more, but it's a motive, isn't it?'

Pike was riveted. 'How do you know this?'

She lowered her voice this time to such a confidential level that he had to strain to hear. 'He had a young man staying with him last night. I heard them. They shared the bedroom.'

'Maybe there wasn't a spare bed made up?' suggested Pike. He was beginning to savour the joke.

'Oh but officer, I saw them this morning. The young man – I mean you'd know he was one of them. They hugged each other on the doorstep. Imagine. At nine o'clock on a Sunday morning. They didn't seem to mind who saw them. It was disgusting.'

She looked up at him expectantly. He got to his feet. Mr Amiss had been right. She was indeed a nosey bitch. He felt a strong impulse to tell her so. No, he thought. I know what frustration does to people.

He sat down again and put on his kindest voice. 'Ma'am,' he said, 'for your own sake, I think I'd better tell you something about the laws of slander.'

As the gentle homily went on, Tiny was lying on his bed next door. He was leafing through a picture book of Kenya, rescued from the attic to which Fran had consigned it.

21

It was already a quarter to twelve and Milton's headache was getting worse. 'It'll be better soon,' said Pike. 'Just take those aspirins.'

Milton swallowed the three tablets and drained the glass of water. Sammy is beginning to sound more like a batman than a sergeant, he thought. Am I letting standards of discipline slip? Demonstrating favouritism? Romford seemed upset that I took Pooley with me yesterday. Oh, the hell with it. Things are bad enough without pandering to the kind of prejudices that lose us hundreds of bright young coppers every year. If the only people I can talk freely with about this mess – and get a useful response – happen to be Sammy, Ellis and Robert, then so be it.

'Bad meeting, sir?'

'Pretty grim. There are noises being made about the amount of police time being spent with nothing to show for it.'

'That doesn't seem a fair criticism, sir.'

'It doesn't, does it? I don't think there's really much conviction behind it. It's inter-force jealousies mainly, I think. The local chaps feel they have to put in the effort but that we'll take the credit. The higher echelons of the Yard feel they've got to meet the criticisms by making sure I don't turn into a megalomaniac.'

'I'd have thought that with the noise the papers are making, no one would be thinking much of economy.'

'Don't mention the papers. That press conference this morning was awful. I can't tell them anything without pointing the finger directly at our small band of suspects.'

'Coffee, sir?'

'Yes, please.'

Pike returned a few minutes later bearing a paper cup. Milton sniffed it incredulously. 'This hasn't come from the canteen, has it? It smells too much like the real thing.'

'I popped out and got it round the corner.'

'You're like a mother to me, Sammy.' He took out a

pocketful of loose change. 'Here, take it out of that.'

Pike hesitated for a moment, and then picked up thirty pence. Poor devil, thought Milton. It's awful to be so fearful of corruption allegations that you can't stand your superior a cup of coffee. And in Sammy's case it could be interpreted as bribery, if anyone ever found out the truth about that drug pusher. He grinned at him. 'You can buy me a pint, Sammy, if either of us gets a promotion out of this.'

Pike grinned back. 'Gladly, sir. Anything else I can do, or will I get back to those phone-calls?'

'Try and set up a meeting for half past two with Chief Inspector Trueman and all the inspectors dealing with the case. I want to be brought up-to-date with everything they've got.'

'Right, sir.'

The throbbing had somewhat subsided. Milton had another apreciative swig of coffee, then took a handful of small sheets of paper out of his drawer. He wrote a name on each of five of them. Then he put them in his order of choice: Graham Illingworth; Henry Crump; Bill Thomas; Tiny Short; Tony Farson. No. There was no case against Tiny. He shouldn't be in the pile at all. Nor was there a case against Tony Farson. No father would take the risk of killing his kid. He tore up the sheets that bore their names.

His outside line rang.

'Hello. Jim Milton.'

'It's Robert. I've heard something that is probably of no significance, but here it is. Gloria Farson is pregnant.'

'Which makes it even less likely that he'd have wanted to murder her.'

'Not necessarily, I'm afraid. I heard her telling Edna at the office dance last December that she would like another baby but Tony was dead against it.'

'You think he might have thought of this as the only way to bring about an abortion?'

'I don't think anything. I feel like a traitor. I've just been congratulating him about this while trying to sympathize about Tommy and now I'm sitting in Shipton's room passing on gossip.'

'You should try to take a pride in it – like Miss Nash.'

'You're supposed to be the straight man. I'm the comedian. Incidentally: I've been worrying about it ever since you rang last night. What was it about me that she thought was homosexual?'

'Probably your high heels and handbag,' said Milton and rang off feeling pleased with himself.

He looked at his pieces of paper. Taking another blank one, he wrote Tony Farson's name again. Under it he put 'When did he know?'; 'How much did he mind?' Then he wrote 'Tommy'. He swivelled round in his chair and looked at the scene in the office across the street. Four male heads were bent industriously over their work. Through the other window, he could see a man and a woman laughing. He tried to speculate about what was going on in their heads. Secret discreditable thoughts? Or just common enjoyment of a joke? Was he much better than Romford really? Could Tony Farson . . .? No. It was as stupid an idea as that Charlie had committed suicide.

He turned his chair around and tore up Farson's name for the second time. He shoved the other pieces of paper into his desk and pulled towards him the bulging in-tray he had cleared the night before.

'Let me summarize the findings once more from the beginning. And interrupt me if I've got anything wrong. The wrapping-paper could have been bought in any one of a hundred or so shops in London – let alone the provinces. The sellotape was the standard variety. The string, being coloured, gives a terrific lead. It could have been bought only in about forty London shops, most of which are self-service. The chocolates were carefully selected for their size, sweetness, popularity throughout the British Isles and the fact that the box they came in was small enough to go through the large letter-box outside the post office. The stamps were just stamps. The only lead is the typewriting on each parcel, which the experts are pretty sure was done on a cheap portable that last year sold in excess of ten thousand in England alone. We are told that the typing was either done by an expert who exerted even pressure on each key or by a one-finger typist who achieved the same effect. Where can we go from there?'

'Nowhere, sir,' said Trueman.

'We have finally rejected any idea of taking the suspects' photographs around typewriter shops other than those within

easy reach of their homes. No dissent from that decision?'
There was silence.

'We have four people working full-time on trying to trace the sources of the strychnine. Their preliminary conclusion is that it will prove impossible to trace. No thefts have been reported and no link can be made between legitimate sales and any of the people involved in this case. It looks almost certain that it must have been acquired through criminal means. But no one can think off-hand of any criminals who deal in such a relatively cheap and unpopular commodity. It would be a substance easy to acquire abroad also, but here we are stumped for ideas. Apart from the Crumps' holiday in Majorca last summer, no one admits to having gone abroad during the last two years. Majorca seems unpromising, but we are investigating it anyway. Our conclusion is that once the team checks out Majorca and confirms its preliminary report, we will abandon this hunt also, simply leaving it to officers to keep their ears open to anything promising that comes in from the usual grasses.'

Silence again.

'There is no shadow of doubt that the list of suspects is down for all practical purposes to five, although we cannot rule out the possibility that someone of whose existence we know nothing got hold of the list of staff, knew Mr Thomas was unmarried, and had the means, motive and opportunity.'

'Five, sir?' asked Romford. 'I make it six.'

Milton looked impatient. 'We've ruled out Melissa Taylor's girlfriend, don't you remember?'

'Yes, sir. But . . .' He consulted his notes. 'I still make it six: Amiss, Crump, Farson, Illingworth, Short and Thomas.'

'Amiss? But he saved the lives –'

'Yes, sir. I know. But that could have been because he thought it would look fishy if he didn't.'

'Motive?'

'The same as Thomas's, sir.'

When this is over, Romford, thought Milton, I will have you transferred to Traffic Division. Meanwhile, I must be patient.

'Technically, I cannot fault you on that, Romford. I confess that I excluded him because I know him well and consider him sane. But for the sake of propriety, I shall add him to the list.'

Milton looked round the table at the seven faces of his

subordinates. He caught the flicker of a smile on Trueman's face. There was a brief pause. Then he collected his wits and said, 'Sorry, gentlemen. I lost my thread for a moment. We have six suspects, three of whom look distinctly unpromising. We have been through the reasons why Farson and Short cannot be taken very seriously. And if Inspector Romford will forgive me, I cannot put Amiss high up the list either.'

Romford was too pleased with the flexibility of mind he had just exhibited to press the point. He nodded his agreement.

'We will therefore put tails only on the top three. I realize that it is almost certainly a futile exercise, but I think it is worth the investment in manpower.'

They proceeded to technicalities. It was almost six when the meeting finally broke up. Pike, who had been taking notes in the corner, looked up at Milton once they were alone.

'Are you going to tell Mr Amiss that he's on the list, sir?'

'Oh, I am, Sammy. I am. It's time he realized he isn't the only comedian around.'

22

'That's a nice thing to ring me with at this time of night.'

'I'm sorry I'm so late. But I've only just arrived back from a visit to Henry. You aren't taking it seriously, are you? I thought it was funny.'

Amiss put his feet up on his desk and contemplated his toes intently. 'It's funny as long as *you're* handling the case . . . I suppose. I wouldn't be very amused if your pal Romford took over from you. I feel a bit like the suspect they discover so late in the book that he has to be the murderer.'

'Don't,' groaned Milton. 'I've only just parted company with Pooley. He ventured to admit that I reminded him of Adam Dalgliesh. I think he's suffering from hero worship. I've never written a poem in my life.'

'I've written some letters, though.' There was a thoughtful note in Amiss's voice. 'You did promise, didn't you, that you wouldn't show them to anyone except Sammy? I'm just beginning to remember various indiscretions that might convince Romford I was trying to put all my staff out of their misery by murdering their encumbrances.'

'Oh, Christ!'

'You did, you bastard.'

'Not to Romford. But I got carried away yesterday afternoon and showed them to Pooley. He's filtering all the regional reports, you see, and I thought it would help if he knew as much as possible about the people we're investigating. I'm very sorry. I should have asked you first. It didn't occur to me that you'd mind.'

'I probably wouldn't have minded yesterday. Pooley indeed. I expect he's already making comparisons between me and the narrator/murderer in *Roger Ackroyd*. I can't understand why you've picked up this court jester, Jim. But no doubt you have your reasons. All right. I'll overlook this breach of confidence if you now spill the beans about Henry.'

'Not a lot to tell, really.'

'Don't you dare fob me off. For a start, what's it like, *chez lui*?'

'Horrible enough. I suspect that given the opportunity, Henry would have decorated his home in the manner of some American red-neck.'

'I would have expected him to do it more in the manner of Hugh Hefner.'

'Well. A combination of the two. Let's say ideally lots of guns interspersed with explicit pictures of exotic women. As it is, the objects of his choice are in a minority compared to those of Edna's. There is the occasional picture of a bull-fight or a battle-scene; there's what looks like a stoat's head grinning at you off the wall of the hall; and there's the odd bit of cheap foreign touristy nude women sculptures. All these nestle in the midst of a plethora of china from Margate and plaques saying things like "There's no place like home" and "All my love to the best grannie in the world".'

'You're depressing me.'

'You'd have been more depressed if you'd seen it. It's already looking neglected and dirty. Henry doesn't seem capable of looking after himself at all. I would guess that Edna worked on the principle of making herself indispensable. I don't think the poor fellow could have known at first where to find the saucepans.'

'Aren't his children keeping an eye on him?'

'I rather gathered he's holding them at arm's length. He talked a bit about wanting to be independent. Maybe he means free. In any case, his daughter lives quite a distance away and she's tied down by kids.'

'Did you get anything out of him?'

'I don't know if there's anything to get. He's got no alibi and obviously he's admitting no motive. He's bemoaning Edna's loss and for all I know he may be genuine. I can hardly arrest him for behaving like a dirty old man in the office.'

'Nothing helpful from gossip?'

'Only that he's active in the church, plays bowls in the summer and otherwise has little to do with his neighbours.'

'You've got nothing on anyone, really.'

'All I can do is go on digging until something presents itself. I'm going to see Bill Thomas at home tomorrow night. It's worth the travelling to see these people in their own lairs.'

Amiss was too tired to be helpful. 'I suppose there's nothing on Twillerton?'

'Not yet.'

'I'm going to bed. I'm knackered. I don't know how you keep going.'

'I sleep well. It comes of not being emotionally involved. Though I daresay I might toss and turn a bit if it turns out to be you.'

'That's not funny. Greenstreet and Lorre would probably pin it on me tomorrow.'

'Didn't I tell you? On Saturday they said that, in their view, it would be too great a coincidence if the Twillerton demon wasn't the PD2 murderer. Goodnight, Robert.'

'Goodnight, Jim.' Amiss replaced the receiver, got up and began to wander distractedly around the room. He was beginning to feel his sense of humour couldn't withstand much more. What would his lair indicate to a psychologist? Functional furnishings provided by the landlord. No effort made to stamp anything with his own personality. His books and records were those of someone with wide but undisciplined interests. Odd, he realized for the first time, that he possessed not one picture or ornament of his own. The place was neither clean nor dirty, tidy nor untidy. I suppose it's a fair enough indication of what I really am, he thought. Rootless, easy-going, intelligent and reasonably well-informed. And without any firm convictions or sense of purpose. Other people have families, hobbies, jobs that preoccupy them. I don't even have greed or ambition. I just stumble along trying to make life pleasant for me and those around me. What would a preacher say about me? 'An amiable chap who wanted to be liked'. Is that the only epitaph I want?

He switched the light off and went through into his bedroom.

'Can you spare a few minutes, Donald?'

'Now?'

'Preferably.'

'Come along.'

Amiss left his cubby-hole and walked towards the door. As he passed by his staff he looked at them sideways. Tony was staring sightlessly at a staff memorandum. Graham sat beside him, his cheek propped on his left fist, clearly trying to work up enough interest to open the file with the red 'URGENT' sticker that lay before him. Opposite Tony, Bill was mechanically ticking off items on a supplier's list. The seat beside him was vacant, as it would be until Melissa returned in a few weeks from her training period in the Midlands. Three of the four desks situated behind Bill were completely clear. Two had been so since before Amiss's arrival at the BCC. The third had been Tiny's. Henry sat alone in his glory reading the *Sun*. No one looked up.

As he walked down the corridor to Shipton's room, Amiss rehearsed his argument. It seemed irrefutable. He sat down uninvited.

'I've got two proposals to make, Donald.'

Shipton looked encouraging. 'Go on.'

'The first is that I be released from my secondment now. The second is that PD be reorganized. Either PD1 and PD2 should be integrated under Horace, or the staff should be switched around, the numbers in the two sections evened up and a new PD2 appointed.'

'You've had enough?'

'It's insupportable.' There was no point in not being honest. 'You must have guessed that I've hated the job since the beginning. But I'd have stuck it out until May if it hadn't been for all this. We can't go on as we are – as a ghetto of sad and frightened people. And if the switch-round is made, it would be absurd to put me in charge of new staff when I'll be leaving within three months anyway.'

Shipton looked at him thoughtfully. He heaved himself up in his chair, leaned his elbows on the desk and rested his chin on his crossed hands. 'First, let me say that I have never doubted that whoever sent you here played a dirty trick on you. You were far too intelligent for the job. I am too intelligent for my job, but I was exiled for other reasons and have to make the best of it.'

You've certainly done that, you lazy sod, thought Amiss affectionately.

Shipton altered the position of his body to the one he usually affected at meetings: body comfortably back in his chair and arms resting on the sides. 'Second,' he said, 'I understand that the present position must be intolerable for you and your remaining staff.'

'Then you agree with me?'

'*I* agree with you that those unhappy people should be mixed in with their colleagues. Unfortunately others don't.'

Amiss saw the prison-gates closing again. He said feverishly: 'But surely no one with any heart would block this change?'

'I don't know if he's got a heart, but I know he's got a brain.'

'Who?'

'Superintendent Milton.'

'What's he got to do with it?'

'I rang him this morning to check that I would be causing him no inconvenience if I made the changes you propose. I had already concluded that integrating the staff under Horace would be in everyone's interest - including yours. The unions would wear it as a temporary measure.'

'And . . .?'

'He said . . . let me recollect his precise words . . . he said, "I'm sorry Mr Shipton, but I'm afraid it is imperative that they all be left there to sweat it out." '

23

'Come in,' called Milton.

The lanky form of DC Pooley inserted itself through the doorway. His reddish-fair hair was in disarray and his bright blue eyes shone with excitement. He sped over to his superior's desk and slapped a piece of paper down in front of him. 'I think we've got something here, sir.'

'From Hertfordshire?'

'No. From Essex. A WPC's report on a conversation with Tony Farson's mother-in-law.'

Milton waved him to a seat and began to read. He stopped and reread a sentence in the middle and then skimmed the rest.

'We've been idiots, Pooley.'

The young man grunted non-committally.

'I've been allowing myself to get diverted into too many problems of public relations. I haven't been thinking hard enough about the circumstances of the people involved.'

'You can't be expected to think of everything, sir. I should have thought of this possibility.' Milton felt unhappy at this new evidence of devotion. Am I beginning to encourage sycophancy? he wondered uneasily.

'Well, let's leave the question about my culpability out of it. I want you to do something for me.'

'Anything, sir.'

'I'm going to take Pike to see Bill Thomas tonight instead of you.' And, as Pooley's face fell into utter dejection, he added hastily: 'Because I want you to do something much more important.'

Pooley's whole frame tightened with anticipation. He looked rather like a red setter whose master was flourishing a stick preparatory to throwing it.

'I'm going to stick to my schedule and wait to see Farson until tomorrow evening. In the light of this new piece of evidence, I'd like you to spend the evening looking at everything we know about Farson, chasing up any outstanding reports from his area and preparing a few lines of questioning for me. Keep it brief.'

Pooley jumped to his feet. He was fairly quivering. 'Right, sir. I'll just finish up what's on my desk and get down to it straight away.'

As he darted for the door, Milton said idly: 'If by any chance you've got any time over, you might come up with a few wild ideas about the others.'

'I'll do my best, sir.'

Pooley was half-way through the doorway when he turned around. 'Please, sir. Do you think you could take me with you to the Farsons' tomorrow night?'

'Have you no ambition to lead a normal social life? I fear you're cut out to be a serious policeman. Yes, you can come.'

Pooley rushed out, apparently too overcome with emotion to speak. Milton hoped he wasn't actually panting.

It was with relief that Milton followed Bill into the garden. The previous hour had been so tedious that he had doubted if he would come through it without screaming. Only a dogged determination to get to know something about the man had kept him sitting making polite conversation long after they had run out of questions relating to Bill's alibi. The garden might keep them going for another few minutes. Then, short of asking his host if by any chance he happened to be a psychopath, he would have to leave.

As Bill led them through the french windows, Milton and Pike exchanged glances. Milton was no gardener, but Pike was an enthusiast, and it was clear that they shared the same awe at the beauty Bill had created in this unpromising rectangular suburban plot. The lawn was lush and even, and the daffodils and crocuses covered large areas of it with a naturalness and profusion that made the senses dance.

'I'm afraid it's not at its best,' said Bill apologetically. 'It's nicer in June when the azaleas and rhododendrons are out.'

'It's magnificent,' said Milton, meaning it. Even to his untutored eye it was clear that early summer would see the high circular wall of shrubs bursting into almost indecent glory. How peculiar that so apparently dull a man could create something like this. He had an artist's eye for the importance of contrasts and irregularities.

As Pike clucked knowingly over the precise and flourishing

little vegetable patch that lurked discreetly behind a honeysuckle-clad fence, Milton tried desperately to draw some conclusions from this unexpected facet of Bill's personality. Did he want to murder ugly women for some distorted reason? No, hardly. Melissa, Gloria and Val were definitely nice to look at, and Fran Short and Jill Collins well up to the average. Anyway, why not ugly men? Then he remembered a point that arose from one of Amiss's letters. He led into it gently as they went back indoors.

'I believe your mother died quite recently. Was she a gardener too?'

'Well, not much in recent years. She was eighty-five, you know. But she took an interest. She loved flowers, Mother did.'

'You must miss her.'

'Oh, I do. We were very close, Mother and I.'

'She didn't get difficult the way old people can? I know from my own the way they can get rather demanding.' Milton repressed a spasm of guilt at the thought of his lively, independent mother.

'No. I'm thankful to say that Mother stayed sprightly to the end.'

No joy here, thought Milton. Though I suppose it's worth trying to find out if she was a fearful old devil who turned her son off women for life. But I won't find out from Bill.

'We'd better be off now, Mr Thomas. Unless you've anything left to tell us.'

'I can't think of anything. Though of course I'm happy to oblige any time you want to ask me questions.'

'I wish more of the public were like you, Mr Thomas.' Milton was glad he had brought Pike. He couldn't have borne to have Pooley hear him talking like this.

'If it hadn't been for that garden, Sammy, I'd say I'd finally met someone who didn't exist.'

Pike swung the car left to get into the correct lane for the on-coming roundabout. 'I know just what you mean, sir.'

'Every view he expressed was qualified. Did you notice?'

'You mean the way he kept saying he didn't much like this or quite liked that.'

'Precisely. He quite liked his colleagues. He thought their

wives seemed quite nice. No. I must enter an exception here. He did say he thought the murders were dreadful. But he didn't mind his job. He even said that all in all he thought British Rail was doing quite a good job. Tell me, have you ever in your life met a commuter who didn't complain vigorously about public transport?'

'I can't say I have, sir.'

'And he didn't go out much because he was quite happy at home. Quite liked housework, didn't he? And the neighbours were nice enough. Still. He seemed genuinely to miss his mother. That's some kind of emotion. And the garden shows he's got one passion in life.'

'Do we keep him on the list?'

'Can we afford to cross him off? I don't want to eliminate everyone bar Robert. Anyway, my wife said when she rang last night that if it was a psychopath we were looking for, he would be an introvert. Mind you, I knew that already. Still, we mustn't lose sight of that line of investigation. I could do with a psychologist in the Yard to talk it over with.'

'Would you call Mr Crump an extrovert, sir?'

'Yes. It's a point in his favour. And Illingworth and Farson seem to be introverts. Oh, bloody hell. I can't imagine any of them doing it.'

Pike spoke uncertainly. 'Sir. I can't swallow the psychopath theory myself.'

'Why not?'

'Because say if Mr Thomas is a psychopath, he could have been almost certain of not being found out if he had simply sent chocolates to women at random. Whereas if it was one of the husbands aiming just to get rid of his own wife, he'd have been a suspect anyway.'

'I've thought of that, Sammy. I've got a counter-argument. If it was Bill Thomas, he might have wanted to kill women he'd met. Mind you, it's unfair to describe him as the only possible psychopath because he had no apparent motive. In my book, someone prepared to kill others like this to cover himself must come into the same category. One way or the other, we're not looking for anyone you could call normal.' The car began to slow down. When it stopped Milton opened the door. 'Care for a quick one, Sammy?'

'Thanks, sir. But I've got to get home. My wife's getting a bit fed up with the hours I'm working.'

As Milton walked up to his dark house, he felt a great longing for Ann. Then he heard the telephone, and broke into a run.

'If I'd had any strychnine with me, you'd have been next.'

'I'm sorry you've been so upset. But even if you'd told me you were hoping to leave, I have to admit I'd have tried to stop you.'

'I've got nothing to tell you.'

'But you might pick up something. Anyway, that's not the real point. The important thing is to keep the suspects together in the hope that the strain may ultimately make the guilty one more likely to crack.'

Amiss said nothing. Milton began to feel seriously worried. Was he about to lose yet another friend through the demands of his job? 'Robert,' he said. There was an uncharacteristically pleading note in his voice. 'Don't let this screw things up between us.'

'You were just doing your job. Is that it? And friendship comes second.'

'It has to.' Milton felt miserable.

'I know it bloody has to. And I'm not as cross as I sound. I'd already worked out that you didn't really have any choice but to ask Shipton to keep the *status quo*. I just wanted you to sweat it out for a bit too.'

Milton grinned with relief. 'All right, you bugger. I did. Honours are even. Now do you want to hear about Bill?'

'Hang on a moment.' Amiss put down the receiver and fetched his cigarettes and lighter. 'OK,' he said. 'Fire away.'

24

Wednesday, 23 February

The expert seemed confident. 'There's little doubt about it. The typewriter is Amiss's and Illingworth typed this note. Of all the suspects, only he typed with all his fingers. Hence the lighter type of the letters depressed by the weak little finger. Do you want to compare the note with the samples?'

'No thanks,' said Milton. 'I believe you.'

The expert received his thanks and left.

Milton looked at Romford. 'Fill me in,' he said. 'How did you get hold of these samples of typing?'

'From Mr Amiss, sir.' Milton looked blank. Romford consulted his notes. 'On Saturday you asked the BCC security men to let us have the anonymous letter about Mr Short and his practical jokes. At the time, you said you bet it had been done on a BCC office typewriter. So over the weekend I got someone to take samples from all the PD machines and when the note arrived on Monday our man said it had been written on Mr Amiss's. Yesterday I rang Mr Amiss and asked him if he'd be able to give us samples of the typing of any of the suspects without them knowing. These arrived this morning.'

'When did you ask him to do this, Romford?'

Romford tried to guess the possible relevance of the question. He concluded that he would never understand the inscrutable way the super's mind worked. 'Just before lunch, sir.'

A couple of hours after he heard from Shipton that I'd scuppered his break for freedom, thought Milton. He favoured Romford with a beatific smile. 'You didn't fear he would give you forgeries?'

'No,' said Romford seriously. 'He could be found out too easily, couldn't he? And that would be incriminating. Although if you want me to check . . .?'

'No, no. Of course not. You've behaved very sensibly. It's much better that none of them knows about this.'

'Does this mean Mr Illingworth is behind all that nonsense at Twillerton?'

'I think so. Yes. I definitely think so.'

'And does that mean he's the prime suspect over the poisoning?'

'I don't know, Romford. Don't forget that the murderer was clever enough to make his typing untraceable. Still, this certainly adds to my interest in Illingworth. See that someone goes round all the likely joke shops with his photograph. As soon as possible.'

Romford withdrew. He's coming on, reflected Milton. Maybe he's not so bad. Perhaps not Traffic Division.

'Do you think there's anything in my ideas, sir?' Pooley took his eyes off the road for a moment and looked hopefully at Milton.

'I'm sorry, Ellis. I'm only getting down to reading your stuff now. I haven't had a minute today, between meetings, phone-calls and preparing a progress report for tomorrow's session with the Assistant Commissioner.'

'I've dealt with Farson on one page, sir. But I've written down some general thoughts as well.'

Milton saw to his alarm that the memorandum headed 'Some possible lines of enquiry' covered six sheets of foolscap in crabbed handwriting.

'I'm sorry it isn't typed, sir. I did it in the middle of the night and I haven't got a typewriter at home. I thought you'd want to see it first thing this morning.' He sounded rather hurt.

'I appreciate the hard work you've put into this. Why don't you come in for a drink when you drop me home, and I'll read it and we can have a chat about it. If you've got time, that is. I'd like to concentrate on what you've said about Farson now.'

'Oh, sir! I'd love to,' said Pooley fervently.

A couple of minutes later, Milton closed the file and returned it to his briefcase. 'You're wasted in this job, Ellis,' he observed.

Pooley looked at him warily. With the experience of a young man too often rebuffed, he asked, 'Do you mean all my possible motives are too far-fetched?'

'Not all. Though I must admit the one about a concealed pools win he didn't want to share with his wife is stretching my credulity rather far. I meant it as a compliment. You obviously have a remarkable imagination that can't get much expression in your normal work. However, enough of that now. I think one of your ideas is a beauty. The life insurance one.'

A deep flush of pleasure crept over Pooley's fair skin. 'That's my favourite too, sir.'

'Good. Now leave me in peace for the rest of the journey. I've got to think about how to make use of it.'

For a mean man, he lives in unexpected opulence, thought Milton. This house must be worth at least £80,000. But I suppose he sees it as an investment. He must have done some clever cashing in on property booms to afford this on his salary.

114

He looked appreciatively around the landscaped housing estate as he waited for someone to answer the door. As such developments went, it was very well laid out.

'It's like one of those neighbourhoods where they go in for wife-swapping,' said Pooley.

'I should think Farson probably charges for his,' said Milton. As the door opened to reveal Gloria, he felt conscience-stricken about this coarseness. The woman before him, vulgar though she might be, was a bereaved mother. She bore the signs of it too. Her hair, though apparently expensively dyed and permed, looked neglected, as if she hadn't bothered to do more than pull a comb through it. Her jeans fitted her superbly, but there was a large brown stain on the knee. As she led them into the living room he saw that her bottom bore the legend 'Gloria Vanderbilt'. She was certainly taking the loss of Tommy hard. No woman vain enough to throw away money on a label would have normally allowed herself to appear like this.

She went in search of Tony, allegedly working in his den. Milton looked curiously at the decor. He would have expected Tony to save on items with a low re-sale value, yet the room was well if rather garishly furnished. It was only as both Farsons entered that he realized that even though they clashed, the carpet and the furniture had one thing in common. They were all hard-wearing. Gloria might have chosen the colours, but Tony had been around to make sure that what she got would need no replacing for years.

'Would you like a beer or a whisky?' asked Gloria.

Milton wondered if he was imagining an expression of instant resentment on Tony's face. What misery must it be to love money so much that you grudge a stranger a can of beer? Every day must bring Tony several moments of exquisite agony. Well, he thought, I'll start him off in a good mood. 'No thank you, Mrs Farson. You're very kind, but we're on duty.'

'Tea and biscuits?'

'No thanks. We couldn't manage a thing. We've just eaten.'

His stomach reminded him sharply that it had that day consumed a bowl of cornflakes and a ham sandwich, but he had his reward in the relaxation of Tony's face. He sat down opposite the policemen as Gloria left the room and said abruptly, 'I hope you've come here to tell me you've caught the man who murdered my son.'

'Not yet, I'm afraid.'

'I've always known that the tax-payers' money was wasted.'

'Actually, our salaries come out of the rates, Mr Farson.'

'Very high salaries they are too.'

'Look, Mr Farson. I haven't come here to discuss the level of our recent pay increases. My job is to find the person who was responsible for Tommy's death and bring him to justice. For that I need your help.'

Tears gathered in Tony's eyes and began to trickle down his face. He hastily wiped them off with a crumpled handkerchief. Milton suppressed his compassion. There wasn't any doubt that Tony regretted Tommy's death. The question was: would he have regretted Gloria's?

He decided to eschew the routine introduction and questioning. If the man had no time to recover from his emotional state, so much the better. 'Mr Farson. When I spoke to you last week you did not tell me that the children were due to be picked up from school on February the fourteenth by your mother-in-law.'

'What if I didn't?'

'We understand from her that they would have been away from home until the following afternoon, as the circus she was to take them to – the one that was cancelled – would have ended late and she thought it better they should go straight home to sleep at her house.'

'So?'

'So you believed they would have left the house before the first post on Monday and not have returned until mid-afternoon on the Tuesday.'

'So?'

'So had you – to put it crudely – wished to murder your wife, you could have been sure your children would run no risk.'

As Tony's face assumed an expression of fury, Milton added, 'Please, Mr Farson. Don't tell me I've no right to make any such suggestion. You know as well as I do that I have to ask unpleasant questions whether you like it or not. It's only by getting the truth from the innocent that I can identify the guilty.'

He was pleased to see the mollifying effect of this platitude.

'All right, then. If I had wanted to kill my wife, which I didn't, I suppose I could have known my children would be safe.'

'Why didn't you tell me this when I saw you last, Mr Farson?'

'Why should I? I don't have to do your job for you.'

'No. You don't of course. Although I should have thought you might consider it in your own financial interests to assist in saving police time.' The jibe seemed to go over Tony's head at first. Then he glowered.

'You're wasting your time with me anyway. Why would I have wanted to kill my wife?'

'I don't know. Quite possibly you didn't. But I should like to put a few specific questions to you. If you wish to be left in peace, I suggest you co-operate.'

The sullen silence lasted some seconds, then Tony said, 'Oh, all right. Go on.'

Thank God he's a bit more intelligent than Graham Illingworth, thought Milton. Resting his elbows on his knees and clasping his hands, he leaned closer to Tony. 'When did you learn that your wife was pregnant?'

'Some time in the middle of January.'

'Were you pleased?'

'You can't have the right to ask me questions like this. I'll complain.'

'Complain away. I have the right. Perhaps I should put them to your wife instead?' He watched Tony closely. He could see the facial signs of his mental struggle. He would have to come clean. He couldn't trust Gloria.

'If you must know, I was a bit put out.'

'This baby was not planned?'

'No. It was an accident. Or so she said.'

'How much did you mind?'

'I said I was a bit put out and that's what I meant.'

'Did you want her to have an abortion?'

'She thinks abortion's wrong, so there wasn't any point arguing with her. I'm glad now anyway. It might take our minds off Tommy.'

Milton sat back on the sofa, crossed his legs in a relaxed way and then said suddenly, 'Why didn't you want a baby, Mr Farson? Most men would have been pleased.'

'I'm getting a bit old for all that crying at night. But I didn't mind that much. I mean I might have got a bit cross, but I was getting used to the idea.'

You're lying, thought Milton. But I doubt if I can prove it. Gloria is unlikely to rake over the dirt at a time like this.

'If you're saying I tried to murder Gloria because I didn't want the kid, you must be daft. How could I afford to hire someone to do the work Gloria does?'

The fellow's a monomaniac, thought Milton. He sees everything in terms of money and thinks everyone else does as well. Still, it's convenient that he's set up this opening. From the corner of his eye he could see Pooley, aware of what was coming and tense with anticipation. 'Have you not got life insurance on your wife, sir? I should have thought that a responsible man like you . . .?'

The colour drained out of Tony's face. He stared at Milton with loathing. 'You don't mind what you say to people, do you? Have you forgotten my son's only been dead nine days?'

Milton decided to treat that question as rhetorical. 'Have you or have you not taken out life insurance on your wife?'

'Some.'

'For how much?'

'Not a lot. Only about £20,000 or so.'

'Can you show me the policy?'

'I'll get it now.'

While he was out of the room Milton observed, 'That's no motive, I'm afraid. It's just not enough.'

'But sir. Maybe he's got more than one policy.'

Milton cursed himself for a fool. He was beginning to miss the blindingly obvious. When Farson returned and handed him the policy he looked at it perfunctorily.

'I want you to think carefully before you answer my next question, sir. You should know that I will be able to go if necessary to all the insurance firms in the country and check with them. Have you any other policies covering your wife?'

About half a minute later Tony muttered an assent.

'May I see them, please? All of them?'

Before he returned, Milton said, 'Ellis. Would you please wipe that grin of triumph off your face? You are supposed to be invisible.'

'Sorry, sir. But . . .' He relapsed into silence as Tony stormed into the room and handed Milton one of the two files he was carrying.

'They're all there. I took the other two out over the past few years. But I was only being prudent. I'm heavily insured as well.'

Milton examined the contents of the file. 'You, I note, are insured for £50,000. Your wife appears to be insured for eight times that amount.'

'I thought you'd get the wrong end of the stick. First, she'd have my pension. And look at this. This is how much she'd cost to replace.'

Milton blinked at his choice of word but took without comment the newspaper article Tony had pulled out of the second file.

'You see. It says that taking all the costs into account, you'd need about £10,000 a year to pay housekeepers and babysitters and laundries and so on. And her part-time job brings in £3,000.'

'Even accepting these inflated figures, a capital sum of £130,000 would cover it.'

'Not if interest rates go on dropping the way they are,' said Tony darkly.

He's mad, thought Milton. But is he bad as well? He looked down at the floor where Tony had placed the second file and observed that it was labelled 'FAMILY'. He lent casually over, picked it up and opened it. 'I must say, sir, you have a very tidy mind. Do you file in date order from front to back or vice versa?'

As he flicked through the papers inside apparently in search of an answer to this fatuous question, he came to a heading that made him pause. 'Goodness me, Mr Farson,' he said. 'I never realized that bringing up children was so extraordinarily expensive.'

25

'If you've finished, we'll go in next door.'

Pooley jumped up. 'Let me clear this up first, sir.'

Milton waved dismissively at the fish and chip wrappers and the empty plates. 'Don't bother. It's not worth doing now. Come on.'

He led the way inside and switched on two reading lamps. 'You can get the drinks if you like. You should find all you need in that cupboard. I'll have a neat brandy. And make it a large one.'

He sat down and began to read the memorandum. Pooley passed him his drink and sat down in the opposite armchair with his own whisky and soda.

'I know you're driving, Ellis. But that looks too weak to taste. You're not just being polite, are you?'

'Oh no, sir. I drink very little. I like to keep in condition.'

'I commend you,' said Milton solemnly. 'I like my men to be fit.' He took a long enjoyable swallow, reached over to his side-table and selected a cigar. As he lit it he saw Pooley's eye upon him. He could not repress his chuckle. 'It's all right, Ellis. I'm only an occasional sybarite. Now I must get down to this. Find yourself a book and put on a record if you like.'

A couple of minutes later he heard the opening bars of a Fats Waller number. He looked up and saw that Pooley was sitting down with an anthology of *New Statesman* competition winners. Milton felt pleased. Pooley wasn't such a prig after all.

When he finished reading, he took a thoughtful pull on his cigar. 'Ellis,' he asked, 'have you any idea what all this would cost?'

'But that doesn't matter, does it? Not in a murder case.'

'Not in one sense. If it could be shown to be necessary, no one would quibble about undertaking the projects you outline here. But I would have to be able to make out a good case, and frankly, for most of this, I couldn't. Now don't be disheartened. There's some good stuff here. Let's go through your paper in detail and find what I can justify. But first give me a refill.'

It was just after eleven when Milton got rid of Pooley and was free to ring Amiss. He was unable to resist describing the meeting with Tony at considerable length.

'You're sounding pretty pleased with yourself.'

'Do you blame me? It's the first real break I've had. Although much of the credit goes to Pooley.'

'So where does this leave Tony?'

'With far and away the best motive to date. If his figures are right, the death of a pregnant Gloria would have made him overall about £400,000 better off than if she had stayed alive and produced the baby.'

'Where do you go from here?'

'Plodding on trying to find some circumstantial link. Motive isn't enough without something to back it up. Of course, I'm not neglecting the others. Let me fill you in on the Twillerton development. Friend Illingworth is the central character . . .'

'Rotten sod,' said Amiss, when Milton had finished. 'Fancy trying to pin it on Tiny.'

'Well, I suppose if he wasn't responsible himself he might have merely intended to be helpful. But from what I know of him, I think he was. There was a caution and lack of imagination behind the tricks that seem to me to smack of Graham Illingworth.'

'God knows how you're going to get an assistant in a joke shop to remember someone like him after three months.'

'Even the most tentative identification will do. I only want to be able to frighten him. There's no chance of this coming to court.'

'Anything on the others?'

'They're all lying low. Their tails have nothing to report.'

'I never saw the point in tailing anyone. They're hardly likely to be rushing out to get hold of more strychnine.'

'It's just in case they act out of character in some way. We've got so little to go on, we're trying desperate measures. By the way, I've had to put shadows on Tiny also. My Commander rather fancies him as a candidate. Thinks he might make a break for Kenya and doesn't like the idea of extradition proceedings. But don't worry, I still believe him to be in the clear. Have you seen him recently?'

'No. But I've talked to him on the phone. He seems to be getting on OK. I'm taking Rachel down to meet him at the weekend. We can have an evening in the pub. I feel it's the least I can do . . . Well, unless you've anything else to report, I'll be off to bed.'

'You might be interested in what I've been talking over with Pooley. He believes that we should be taking action on two new fronts. One is to go into the past lives of all the suspects in case we come up with a trace of any abnormal behaviour. The other is that since we've drawn a blank at home we should be looking to places abroad for a source of supply.'

'But they never go abroad.'

'Certainly only Henry admits to any recent travel. He hated the dagoes, you'll be surprised to learn. Thought the women disappointing, the food fit only for natives, and objected to their jabbering in a foreign language.'

'In Majorca? I didn't know they had any Spaniards left.'

'Too many for Henry. I suggested Gibraltar next time, but he said he's never setting foot outside his own country again. Anyway, to please Pooley, I'm going to check on whether any of the others have passports. He's preoccupied with the mechanism for getting false ones spelled out so helpfully in *The Day of the Jackal*. This led him to propose that if any of the suspects denied having a passport, we should check his photograph and physical characteristics against those on application forms of the last two years. Then we should follow up any apparent resemblances and find out if the applicant actually existed.'

'That would certainly keep you out of mischief for a while.'

'It would probably keep the whole of the Met out of mischief for weeks. Can you imagine how many Illingworth look-alikes we'd find? No. It's an attactive theory, but I'd never get authorization.'

'What about the past lives idea?'

'Same problem. It would take weeks and would involve sending teams around the country asking how they all performed at infant school. And we'd almost certainly be no better off at the end. But I did take up his idea of checking on their National Service backgrounds. Maybe one of them got a dishonourable discharge for some nasty offence that didn't warrant a criminal charge. We're clutching at straws, but I'm in the frame of mind to do just that.'

'Pooley seems a bright fellow.'

'Very. You'll be amused to hear that he's an ex-civil servant. He went into the Home Office straight from university, full of reforming zeal. Left after two years and came in on our graduate entrant scheme. I hope he doesn't give up through frustration.'

Amiss lit another cigarette. 'Jim,' he said. 'If he survived two years of the Home Office he's a better man than I am. Let me tell you the story of the one time I had any dealings with them . . .'

'I doubt if he'd be prepared to swear to it, sir.'

'I don't want him to. It's enough for me that he considers it a probability.'

'Oh, he certainly does, sir. He told the sergeant the incident stuck in his mind because the customer bought so much sneezing powder. And he seemed so nervous and out-of-place. Not at all typical of the usual clientele. He might well be able to confirm his identification if we held a parade.'

'No thanks, Trueman. I've got enough with this, unless Illingworth has more nerve than I give him credit for.'

'Good luck, sir.'

'Thanks.'

Trueman turned to leave and Milton called after him. 'Will you ask Romford to have Pooley ready with the car at seven? And tell him not to make any appointment with Illingworth. I'd prefer to turn up on his doorstep without any advance warning.'

26

That the night was relatively mild was a considerable relief to DC Ollie Richmond of the Essex force. He had already sat for three nights on the trot and for hours on end in an unmarked saloon car fifty yards from Henry's house. The change in the weather at least meant that he was not now in actual discomfort. But he'd only been on the job an hour and the best part of the night stretched before him.

Around eight o'clock he was reflecting bitterly yet again on a recent advertising campaign for police recruits. ' "DULL IT ISN'T" my arse,' he muttered to himself. Pounding the bloody beat in the middle of the night was boring enough, but there was always the chance of a drunk or a villain to keep you on your toes. It had been heaven compared to this job. It would have been all right if he'd been allowed to do a bit of reading in the car, but the inspector wouldn't hear of it. He mimicked his high-pitched peevish tone to himself. 'I never heard of such an idea, Richmond. Are you anxious to make yourself visible to the whole neighbourhood? Really! I am horrified. Horrified!'

Bloody old woman. This fucking neighbourhood was dead. Stone dead! What was it that killed people and left buildings standing? Neutron bomb, that was it. Maybe they'd let one off without telling him. Might account for the change in the weather, too.

What about this old Crump geezer then? He'd only seen him once when he was sent to lurk early on the first evening. Fat old slob in a grey tweed coat climbing up the hill with a plastic carrier bag, packet of cornflakes sticking out the top. He didn't look like a cool callous poisoner. Didn't look like anything really except a tired old man. Must be fifty-five at least, thought Richmond, who was twenty-three and still believed life ended at forty. He began to feel pity for this decrepit object of police attention. It's not fair, he thought. All the poor old bugger does is sit at home all evening – watching the telly, I suppose – and off he goes to bed at ten or eleven o'clock. He's probably very upset about his wife. He shouldn't be spied on like this.

Richmond was beginning to work himself up into a state of righteous indignation when he saw the front gate of the victim's garden open and a portly figure step briskly into the street. He wheeled to the right and strode off downhill. Richmond scrambled out of his car, locked it and set off in pursuit. He's probably just out for a constitutional, he thought. He was happy with that prospect himself.

Ten minutes later he realized that Henry was almost certainly heading for the railway station. Richmond checked his watch and tried to remember the train times he had studied on the inspector's instructions. The only train due during the next quarter of an hour was the 8:35 to Liverpool Street. That was the wrong direction for this to be a family visit. Maybe he was going to call on some old friend up the line? Shit, thought Richmond, all I need is to have to stand outside someone's house for two or three hours. It's not only colder than sitting in the car, it's fraught with the danger of being spotted. He wouldn't get much sympathy from the inspector if that happened. He imagined the reaction: 'Slipshod! Slipshod, Richmond. I will not tolerate my men being slipshod in their work.'

Henry turned into the station and Richmond followed cautiously. When he saw him safely through the barrier, he quickly purchased a return ticket to London. He was pleased that he timed his entry on to the down platform to coincide with Henry's absence from view as he crossed the covered bridge that led to the up platform. Richmond shot over to the bridge and waited out of sight at the opposite end until he heard the train pulling in. Peering cautiously around the edge he saw the now familiar form climbing into a carriage half-way along. Richmond catapulted himself from his cover and managed to leap into the adjacent carriage just as the train began to move. He wiped his brow. Dull it isn't, he thought as he sank back into his seat. This is bloody nerve-wracking.

He was grateful to fate for making him the solitary occupant, for he could check on whether Henry was alighting only by peering out the window at each station. It was a relief when they got to Liverpool Street and he saw his quarry again. All the way up the platform, through the barrier and across the concourse, Richmond prayed that he would not be faced with a taxi pursuit. He had never had to do one yet, but he had heard too many stories for comfort about mocking drivers, changing traffic lights and stranded detectives. He let out a sigh of relief when he saw that Henry was headed for the tube. Then he began to fret. What if the old bastard uses a season ticket? He could get out of reach while Richmond was queueing at the ticket-office. Then he remembered that he had automatically equipped himself with plenty of change to meet such emergencies. But suppose the machines were out of order? That often happened.

He was beginning to sweat again as he followed Henry towards the Central Line. When he came level with the boxes, Richmond jammed two fifty-pence pieces into the £1 machine, grabbed his ticket and speeded up until he could see Henry now proceeding rhythmically down the escalator. But would a £1 ticket be enough? What would he do if they ended up at one of those stations where the London Transport busy-bodies had set up excess fare offices? Could he flash his warrant card at the collector?

Listen, he said firmly to himself. Just get on with it and worry about the problems as they come up. He focused his attention on Henry's disappearing bald patch and narrowed the gap between them to ten yards. He's going west, he thought. That means probably into the West End. I hope he's off to the pictures. I couldn't half fancy a couple of hours at a decent movie for a change.

Richmond managed to get into the tube unseen without any difficulty. Looking sideways through the window between his and Henry's carriage he could see him sitting staring straight in front of him. Just after Holborn, Henry began to rise and Richmond got up and waited by the exit door to alight at Tottenham Court Road. He was grateful that Henry had to turn right for the exit, so sparing him the need to hide until he had passed him by. His luck continued to hold. It became clear that this was Henry's destination, so there would be none of the aggravations of changing trains and Richmond's ticket would more than cover the journey.

He emerged from the station only five or six yards behind. There were crowds enough to make him invisible. For the first time in his life he was grateful for being neither tall nor striking-looking. He walked after Henry down Oxford Street and took the first left after him. He looked up at the street name and suddenly realized where they were headed. The dirty old devil, he said to himself. He's going to Soho, and I bet it's not for the food.

At that moment he realized that he had almost cannoned into Henry, who had stopped at the end of the street and was surveying Soho Square, his head turning from right to left apparently in search of something. Richmond dodged into a doorway and watched with interest. Henry pulled from his pocket what looked like a street map and bent over it under a street lamp. Then he slammed it shut in a purposeful way and turned left. Richmond followed him around two sides of the square and then into Greek Street. He speculated busily on where they would end up.

The next half hour was one of the worst of Richmond's life. Had he not had his watch he would have claimed that he spent two hours trailing Henry through the crowds and the web of narrow little streets – almost losing him several times. Henry, he realized, had not a clue about Soho. He wandered aimlessly and kept stopping to feast his eyes on photographs of huge mammaries. Occasionally he would allow himself to be engaged in conversation by a pimp or a club doorman, but then he would abruptly dart away until he came to the next arresting set of pictures. Richmond was almost faint from tension when Henry at last stopped dead in front of a cinema and marched inside.

Richmond hastily looked at the poster display and realized that there were three separate films on show. Through the glass doors he could see that Henry was at the box office. He waited till he disappeared from view and then entered.

'The gentleman who just bought a ticket from you is a friend of mine,' he said to the unsavoury olive-skinned youth dispensing tickets. 'I'll join him. Which film did he choose?'

'*Submissive Virgins*,' said the youth in a bored voice. 'That'll be five quid.'

Richmond blushed to the roots of his hair, shoved his money through the aperture and set off in search of Henry.

An hour and a half later, feeling he had had enough erotic stimuli to last him the rest of his life, he left the cinema, wondering how Henry was proposing to get home. The silly old sod had made them both miss the last train, and it would be a hell of a job for either of them to persuade a black cab to take them such a distance. He was feeling hungry, thirsty and cross. Then he realized that Henry was showing no interest in taxis. He was conducting negotiations with a doorman touting for customers for what purported to be 'An all-nite extravaganza of sexy strippers and friendly hostesses'. Henry was apparently satisfied with their chat and duly vanished inside.

Richmond gave him five minutes to settle, paid the exorbitant membership fee and was ushered into a small room furnished with candle-lit tables for two and red plush chairs. At the far end was a small dais, presumably for the sexy strippers. Even to someone as unsophisticated as Richmond, the predictable tawdriness was evident. He sighted Henry at a table commanding an excellent view of the stage and chose for himself an unpopular table at the back. Henry was already being tended by a friendly hostess. Richmond decided to stay on his own and drink beer.

He was approached within moments by a girl of about his own age who offered to keep him company. Richmond explained his wish for solitude.

'I'm sorry,' she said sweetly. 'I'm afraid it is a club rule that gentlemen should be accompanied by a lady. If you'd prefer to be with one of the other girls, that would be quite all right.'

He looked at her and then at the row of smiling women sitting at the back. Like them, she was wearing a low-cut dress and was made-up and coiffed more elaborately than he would have wished. But rules were rules, and she had a nice smile.

'Please join me,' he said, with as much enthusiasm as he could muster. 'Would you like a drink?'

'Yes please,' she said. 'I'd like champagne.'

He gulped apprehensively. He had read about places like this.

She smiled again and said, 'All of us girls only drink champagne.'

'A glass?'

'A bottle would be handier, wouldn't it?'

Richmond picked up the wine list and saw that a bottle of champagne cost £90. He put it down again.

'The club takes credit cards,' she said. She made a signal to a passing waiter who appeared magically with an ice-bucket before Richmond could open his mouth.

The woman leant towards him until their shoulders touched. 'My name's Zara,' she confided in a soft voice. 'Tell me yours. And then tell me all about yourself.'

Richmond looked over at Henry's table. He too had an ice-bucket and a nestling woman. Hell, he thought. I won't often have the chance to do this on expenses. Might as well enjoy it. He smiled at Zara for the first time. 'I'm Ollie,' he said, 'and I'm rather a lonely soul.'

27

Friday, 25 February
Milton's hand reached out to the tiny stack of paper on his blotting-pad. He reshuffled it. Tony Farson – definitely the front runner. Graham Illingworth? Yes, even after last night he was still a fair each-way bet. Henry Crump and Bill Thomas well behind, with Henry perhaps ahead by a nose. Tiny Short's name had been added in once again at the Commander's insistence, but despite his early burst, he seemed now to have lain down permanently in the middle of the track.

Pike knocked and came in quietly. 'Morning, sir.'

'Morning, Sammy.'

Pike sat down in his usual chair. 'The meeting didn't take long.'

'No. After the one with the AC yesterday, everyone today seemed happy to leave me to get on with things for a while without interference.'

'I had a brief word with Pooley earlier, and he said you were a bit disappointed with the way things went last night with Illingworth.'

'Yes and no. Or rather, no and yes. We got no nearer finding a motive for murder, but on the plus side he caved in and confessed over Twillerton. That at least shows he's capable of acting crazily. Though it's a long way away from killing people.'

'Did he give in easily?'

'What do you think?'

'I'd guess he held out as long as he could.'

'You're dead right. I had a horrible feeling he was going to call my bluff over the salesman's identification, which I claimed was firm. He went on and on stubbornly repeating that he didn't, he hadn't and he wouldn't – to an extent that would have led a lesser man to clout him one . . . Oh my God, I'm sorry, Sammy. It was only a figure of speech.'

Pike smiled gently at him. 'Don't worry, sir. I know you weren't getting at me.'

'Where was I? It wasn't until I promised him immunity from prosecution that he showed any dawning signs of mental activity. He asked a couple of "Supposing I had, though mind you I'm not admitting anything" questions. Then he brooded for a while until I put the boot in by telling him I'd be arranging pronto for him and a number of his colleagues to take part in an identification parade. He cracked up completely then. Admitted the lot.'

'Did he tell you what made him do it?'

'He claims it was just frustration over not being called to the promotion board. He had visions of spending the rest of his working life in PD and he wanted to get back at the BCC somehow. He panicked afterwards – hence the anonymous letter. He claims to be ashamed of that now.'

Pike's forehead wrinkled. 'It doesn't sound like a good enough reason to me.'

'I don't know. You've read Robert's letters. Don't you think the prospect of staying for ever in that ghastly dump could give you a kind of nervous breakdown? Pooley and Robert seemed to think so.'

'If you'll forgive me saying so, sir, I'm not sure I agree with you. The three of you are maybe a bit too intelligent to put yourselves in Illingworth's shoes. He sounds dim enough to me to put up with the sort of boredom you couldn't stand. He had quite a soft option there really.'

'But he was very upset about the promotion board. There's no doubt about that.'

'I know, sir. But I've known chaps like him in the force. They complain a lot and pretend they think they should get promotion, but they don't really believe it themselves, and a couple of days after they've been turned down they've got over it. It adds a sort of interest to their lives.'

Pike was warming to his subject. It was the longest speech Milton had ever heard him make. 'You see, sir, from what I've heard about Illingworth, I'd say it was only his private life that really mattered to him. He would see work just as a way of supporting his family. And I can't see him taking the risk of losing his job and putting his child's future in jeopardy just because he was going to stay stuck as an APE. I bet something at home had upset him a lot.'

Milton scratched his head vigorously. 'You may well be right. In fact, you probably are. But what the hell was it? I've had the local police tailing his wife to see if she's carrying on with anyone, because I thought that was the most likely motive for attempting murder. She doesn't look to me like the faithful type and when we were there last Sunday she was ratty with him. But they've drawn a blank so far. She's been arriving home promptly from her bar job every evening and they haven't picked up any gossip about her. Even Pooley can't think of any other reason he might want to kill her, except that she might have been battering that bloody kid he goes on about *ad nauseam*.'

There was a loud rap on the door and Romford entered in what for him was an unceremonious manner. He was wearing what Milton privately called his Mary Whitehouse expression. He thrust a couple of sheets of paper in front of Milton and said grimly, 'I think you'd better read that at once, sir.'

Pike got up but Milton gestured at him to stay. He preferred not to be left alone with Romford in a censorious mood. As he scanned the first few paragraphs of the report his lips twitched. By the end of the first page he was grinning broadly. When he came to the concluding paragraph he burst into roars of laughter, which halted abruptly when he caught sight of Romford's scandalized face.

'I beg your pardon, Romford,' he said with as much sincerity as he could muster. 'I realize it's all very squalid and reprehensible, but I can't avoid seeing the joke.'

'I wish I could see some humour in it, sir,' said Romford. His heavy-handed delivery indicated that he would consider his soul to be in danger if he did. 'But quite apart from anything else, I find it disgraceful that police funds should be used in that way. And now, if you'll excuse me, I have work to do.'

Pike looked at Milton in bewilderment as his inspector closed the door loudly behind him. 'It's a report from the Essex DC who does the second shift watching Henry Crump. Henry has broken out at last.'

He watched Pike hopefully as he began to read. It was with relief that he saw his face begin to contort as he read slowly on. When he turned over the page he emitted a loud snigger.

Good old Sammy, thought Milton. And now what *am* I going to do with Romford? I wish the Vice Squad was still in existence.

28

When the last of Amiss's staff left to begin the long journey home he dialled Milton's number.

'Jim? Robert. I'm ringing now for two reasons. First, I'm off to meet Rachel at Heathrow and we'll probably be out too late for you to ring me tonight, so I thought I'd ask for news of the day. Second, I want to know if someone has been duffing up Henry.'

'Did you know you still talk like a civil servant at times?'

'Cut out the insults and answer my question.'

'What makes you think we've been duffing him up?'

'He rang up mid-morning to say he wouldn't be in because he was feeling very ill. He certainly sounded it. Naturally I thought you'd had one of the heavy mob trampling on him since we spoke last night. Graham isn't in either, but I expected that after what you told me.'

Milton decided to save up the Henry story. 'This must be putting a lot of work on to you, Robert,' he said, hoping his amusement was not evident in his voice.

'You're not kidding. Between us, the remains of PD2 today did at least six hours solid work each. I took on Henry's, Tony did Graham's and Bill's doing Melissa's in any case. If you can arrange for one of us to be arrested, you will finally have eliminated over-manning here.'

'It certainly adds a whole new dimension to the concept of natural wastage.'

Amiss looked suspiciously at the telephone. 'You sound to me as if you're in a rather skittish mood. Is it something about Henry? Have you caught him with his socks stuffed full of toxic substances?'

With considerable relish, Milton commenced the account of Henry's night out. When he got to the scene in the night club, Amiss was laughing so much he almost fell off his chair. A thought struck him. 'Hang on a minute, Jim.'

He went to his door, looked around the office and came back. 'Sorry. I just had to check that the workaholics of PD1 have all gone. Some of them occasionally stay for an extra ten minutes. Go on. How long did Henry stay?'

'Until the club closed at five o'clock, by which time Richmond had been obliged to buy four bottles of champagne. He alleges he had no option. His expenses claim is going to be a beauty.'

'What was Henry doing all this time?'

'What you'd expect. Leering at the strippers and pawing the hostess. You haven't heard the best bit yet.'

'Don't keep me in suspense.'

'Well, reading between the lines of the report, Richmond was rather the worse for wear and Henry was extremely drunk. He didn't cause any trouble over the bill – probably because he couldn't read the figures. Tendered his credit card like a gentleman, embraced his hostess and left like a lamb. Richmond followed him out and hung around within a few feet of him, reckoning that Henry wouldn't be able to remember anything the next day. He didn't realize why Henry was

132

standing outside the club until he began hammering on the door shouting for Twinkles.'

'Twinkles?'

'Yes. History does not record whether that was her given name, her professional name, or a nickname bestowed upon her by Henry. Anyway, it became clear that Twinkles had promised to take Henry home in gratitude for the champagne and a £50 present, handed over in cash in the club.'

'And she had in fact vanished?'

'Of course. And no one within the premises was prepared to answer the door to Henry. He was making such a racket that Richmond, sloshed, forgot he was a detective rather than an ordinary copper and began to remonstrate with him.'

'How did this go down?'

'Badly. Henry hit him and he had to get him in an arm-lock to prevent further damage. As Henry began to quieten down, a patrol-car came cruising down the street and two uniformed bobbies joined in. Richmond was afraid to reveal his identity in front of Henry, lest the struggle had sobered him up, so they were both taken to a police station.'

'They weren't charged?'

'No. Richmond managed to square things with the sergeant at the desk and so instead of being done for Drunk and Disorderly, Henry was put in a taxi and sent home.'

'It was lucky for Henry that Richmond was about, all things considered.'

'Not so lucky for Richmond. I'm afraid he'll be in trouble.'

'He didn't do anything terrible, did he?'

'In my view he did well, apart from the one minor lapse. But there is a school of thought that he should have waited outside the club for Henry rather than sampling the flesh-pots within. He'll have to be taken off this job anyway, just in case Henry recognizes him. Whether he gets put back on the beat depends on whether he's got an understanding inspector.'

'I wish him luck. Now where does all this leave Henry? Have the odds on him shortened or lengthened?'

'No change as far as I'm concerned. He hardly behaved like the grief-stricken widower he claims to be. But that's balanced by the fact that he was so much an innocent abroad that it's difficult to think of him fraternizing with the criminal fraternity.'

Amiss looked at his watch. 'I've got to rush, Jim. Any chance of seeing you this weekend?'

'Possibly. I'll be working late tonight and all day tomorrow in the hope of having Sunday clear to spend with Ann when she arrives back. We might give you a ring and suggest an early evening drink.'

'Good. See you.'

'Goodbye, Robert.'

Milton reached out for his in-tray and picked up the file on top. It was labelled 'Thomas', and he saw with alarm that Pooley had marked it 'Urgent'.

29

Saturday, 26 February
Sammy Pike bade a loving farewell to his wife and set off on the drive to Surrey. He regretted having to leave her alone again, but he reckoned he should be back within three hours. Sue would keep herself busy in the garden. As he often did, he thought with admiration of how she'd coped over the last couple of years since they found out about Jeannie being a drug addict. Some mothers would have gone to pieces, but not Sue. It was silly really that she'd taken it better than him, what with him being a policeman and everything. But she'd always been stronger. Look how she'd consoled him when their first baby died all those years ago. Poor little Jeannie. Who'd have thought all those dreadful things could happen to her? She always seemed so happy and contented. She'd been too nice, really. Hadn't realized that there were evil people about. She'd never be without that knowledge again, but it was wonderful the way she was recovering. They'd all been very lucky.

Pike continued to count his blessings as he drove away from London down the A23. The super for instance. It'd been a real stroke of luck to be assigned to work for him, even if old Romford was a bit of a pain in the neck. He grinned as he thought of his face yesterday. It was amazing how a bloke could deal with crime for twenty-five years and still be capable of shock at something any vicar could take in his stride. Of course

Romford had been with Stolen Vehicles for years and there wasn't much sex there. Pike remembered that last case he'd been involved with in the Regional Crime Squad and tried to imagine how Romford would have coped with it. He shuddered and put it out of his mind.

He set himself to thinking about this old girl he was going to visit. The super had seemed apologetic about asking him to take on another one. But he quite enjoyed talking to them. He was good at it and he didn't have any ambitions to take on what he wasn't fit for. It didn't sound as if there was a lot in it. She was ninety-five, after all, and she hadn't said much except that Mrs Thomas had been a nasty piece of work. But young Ellis had got all excited and the super seemed to think there might be something in it. And though the coroner had been certain her death was an accident, you never knew. It was a disgrace that that inquest report hadn't come in till yesterday. Shocking inefficiency on someone's part. The super had really let off steam with the inspector responsible. He didn't often do that.

He stopped the car to consult his map, drove on and then turned right and sharp left. That must be it just ahead with the gables. He drove up the short drive and parked in front of the house. He was pleased to see there was a pleasant garden with plenty of seats for the old folks. But as he walked through the open front door he felt less happy with the interior. There was no denying that the place had a pokey look to it. He wrinkled his nose at the smell of old food that hung heavily over the hall and rang the hand-bell on the desk. As he waited he looked at the pictures. Must have come with the house, he concluded. No one in their senses would deliberately choose for a place like this paintings so dark you could hardly make them out.

Hearing footsteps behind him he turned and came face to face with a neat middle-aged woman in a flowered nylon overall. She looked at him enquiringly.

'Detective Sergeant Pike, ma'am, from Scotland Yard.' She seemed impressed. It amused him how often the mention of the Yard seemed to add a glamour to the person of a nondescript sergeant.

'I'm Mrs Oliveira, sergeant. I'm the matron. Will you come in here for a moment?'

She led the way into a small sitting room containing a large television set and about twenty easy chairs.

'Please sit down, sergeant. I just want a word with you before you see Mrs Jameson.'

Pike took the nearest seat and she sat beside him. She lowered her voice. 'I gather you have come to see her in connection with that awful poisoning case.'

'That's right, ma'am. She saw someone from the local force the other day and I've just come to ask her a few follow-up questions.'

'I just wanted to give you a word of advice, sergeant. I don't know if you have much experience of old people?'

'A fair bit, ma'am.'

'Well then you probably know how they get little fancies and like to make themselves important.'

'I suppose we all do. From what I've seen, I'd say that you're not much different when you're old to what you are when you're young. It's just that some characteristics get more exaggerated.'

Mrs Oliveira shot him a look of dislike. Pike was untroubled by it. He didn't care for her either.

'Much as I'd like to, I haven't got time to debate this with you. I just thought you should know that you shouldn't attach too much weight to anything Mrs Jameson says.'

'Do you mean she's gaga, ma'am?'

'We don't use words like that here, sergeant. We prefer to call it "wandering a little".'

Don't tell me, thought Pike. I bet they pass over and don't die.

She continued, 'No. She's got her senses, but she's inclined to be a trouble-maker. I'm only telling you this for your own sake. She'll say anything to stir things up.'

'I'm grateful for the warning, ma'am,' said Pike, in as natural a tone as he could summon up. He got to his feet. 'Now, if you'd just ask her to come in.'

Mrs Oliveira was shocked. 'We don't allow the residents to have visitors in here. Only in their own rooms. This lounge is for the use of all residents at any time. We can't have them upset by seeing strangers in it.'

She rose and began to lead him out of the room. 'Where are they all at present, ma'am?' he asked her floral back.

'Asleep. I always make them take a nap between two o'clock and four o'clock. It's for their own good.'

As Pike followed her through the hallway and down a narrow dark corridor he looked at his watch and saw that it was just three o'clock. He didn't take the point up with her. He knew a natural bureaucrat when he saw one.

She stopped abruptly and flung open a door on the right. 'Mrs Jameson, dear,' she cooed. 'I've brought you a visitor. Now don't keep him long. He's a busy man, I'm sure.'

Pike stepped into the little room after her. The old woman sitting ramrod-straight in the button-backed velvet chair by the window looked up at him and nodded. She turned her head towards Mrs Oliveira and said, 'Dolly, dear. I'm afraid you're getting very forgetful. You know I like you to knock. Now run away and get us a nice cup of tea.'

Pike noted that Mrs Oliveira's hands were clenching and unclenching and her lips were tightly pressed together, as if by a physical effort to restrain the appropriate words from tumbling out. Then without a further word she turned on her heel and left.

'You've got to show them who's boss,' said Mrs Jameson. 'Otherwise they'll take advantage of you. That's the way I've lived and that's the way I'll die. Now sit down here opposite me and listen to what I've got to tell you about the Thomas family.'

Sunday, 27 February

Milton described a small circle with his glass.

'Of course I'm bearing her age in mind, but Sammy said he believed her, and on someone like that I'd trust his judgement absolutely.'

Rachel still looked perplexed. 'All right. Let's accept for the purposes of the argument that she's correct. All it seems to reveal is that Bill has been exceptionally long-suffering throughout his adult life.'

'I just find it all very depressing,' said Amiss gloomily. 'It was bad enough that he was negative about everything, but at least I thought he took a twisted pleasure in it.'

'There's no reason to suppose he doesn't by now,' said Milton. 'After all, Mrs Jameson said his bids for freedom were made in his twenties. Presumably he settled to liking a life entirely composed of work and Mother. He doesn't seem to have changed it much since she died.'

'Unless you count attending the Annual Dinner Dance as a sign of his real desire for the bright lights?' said Amiss.

Rachel drained her gin and tonic. 'I can't believe he'd have put up with her keeping him at home unless he really didn't mind too much. It wasn't as if she was bed-ridden or anything. He could just have told her to get stuffed and suited himself if he wanted a different kind of life.' She got up and went to the bar to order the next round.

'What about his father?' asked Amiss.

'Mrs Jameson only said that he was hen-pecked until he died. Bill was about eighteen then. It was just before he did his National Service, in fact. She did say that Mr Thomas probably deserved it.'

Milton pulled Pike's report from his pocket and searched for the relevant paragraph. 'Yes. Here we are. She said he was a nebulous sort of creature who needed to be kept up to the mark. What she complained of was the way Mrs Thomas behaved towards Bill afterwards.'

'You mean she hadn't been so hard on him before?' asked Ann.

'No. According to Mrs Jameson, Bill had a more or less normal childhood. She remembers him playing in the street like any other kid, even if he was very much trailing along after the local charismatic personalities. It was when he came home after National Service, apparently, that his mother began to stop him socializing.'

Rachel returned bearing a tray of drinks and Amiss filled her in on the information she had missed. As she sat down she asked: 'How did Mrs Jameson know all this anyway?'

'Oh, she was quite thick with Mrs Thomas. She rather admired her forcefulness, though they fell out a few times when Mrs Thomas mentioned that Bill had wanted to do X or Y and she'd told him he couldn't. And then there were a couple of rows in the garden that she overheard. She says that by the time he was in his thirties he was so set in his ways that there was no aggro any more.'

Milton looked at Pike's report again and then shoved it back in his pocket. 'There was one more interesting thing she said. Bill didn't create that garden. It was his mother who planned it and laid it out. He just learned to tend it as a kind of under-gardener. That's rather changed Sammy's view of him.'

He had taken the line up till then that no man capable of such artistry could be a potential destroyer of life. Sammy's got a romantic streak.'

'But damn it,' said Rachel. 'If he'd been capable of murder, surely he'd have seen off his mother.'

'Ah,' said Milton. 'That's the other thing. Nearly two weeks after this investigation started, some imbecile has just informed us that, owing to an oversight, we hadn't been told that Mrs Thomas died from an accident.'

'What kind of accident?'

'She fell down the stairs and broke her neck.'

'Any chance that Bill was responsible?' asked Rachel. 'Though I must say it would seem strange that he shouldn't get homicidal until she was eighty-five.'

'We don't know yet. All we've got is the bald inquest report. Those bloody clowns haven't even managed to send us the record of the evidence yet.'

Ann, who had been listening silently for some time, suddenly intervened in a decisive manner. 'He's always been my favourite candidate. Now I'm prepared to put my money on him. I bet you'll find there's something peculiar about her death, even if the coroner was prepared to accept that it was a *bona fide* accident.'

'You're hung up on the psychopath theory,' observed her husband.

'Maybe I am. And I admit that I am a bit out of touch with how this case has been progressing while I've been away. But I'm convinced that whoever sent those chocolates suffered from a severely warped personality. I think someone should be trying to work out a profile of the murderer, so that you'd know what traits to look for.'

'You're not in Los Angeles now,' said Milton wearily. 'Anyway, as far as I can see we've got several suspects who could be accused of being distinctly odd. I don't think Bill Thomas stands alone as a candidate for the funny farm.'

'I agree with Jim,' said Amiss. 'I think you're getting carried away by the idea of Bill just because he has no motive. Anyway, you said something just now about being prepared to put money on him. How much and at what odds? And will anyone give me 4-1 against Tony Farson?'

Milton's face assumed an expression of distaste. 'I think

that's the most contemptible suggestion I've heard in a long time, Robert.'

Amiss looked uneasy. 'Oh, come on Jim . . .' he began.

'No Robert. I really do. I think it's downright greedy to expect anyone to give you better than 2-1.'

30

I'm getting neurotic, thought Milton, as he fingered the little stack of paper. I shouldn't be going over and over this ground again. Tony Farson, still the favourite, and agreed to be generously priced at 7-4. Graham Illingworth 4-1, largely because Sammy's belief that there was some domestic trouble had carried so much weight with Rachel. Bill Thomas was running strongly in third place at 8-1 because Ann had put her shirt on him. Henry was 100-8 since Amiss had decided to hedge his bets. Tiny was still a rank outsider, with only the Commander showing the faintest interest in him. He seemed to think that the intelligence brought back by Robert and Rachel that Tiny was totally absorbed in his Kenya plans vindicated the theory that he had had an overwhelming desire for freedom but lacked the guts to abandon Fran. Milton struggled yet again to understand why someone should think mass poisoning an easier option than abandoning his wife. He sighed and awarded Tiny a price of 50-1.

When there was a knock at the door he guiltily thrust the slips into his drawer. He was relieved that his visitor was Pooley rather than Romford. Though he regretted that Romford should so obviously be keeping out of his way, their estrangement had its compensations. Until the contretemps over Henry, Romford had seemed to resent the direct contact between Pooley and Milton. Now, apparently having washed his hands of his superintendent, he was doing his routine work and refusing to get involved in what he termed highfalutin speculation. Except in his morals, reflected Milton, Romford was daily becoming more and more like a denizen of PD2.

Pooley was looking rather downcast. 'I've got some stuff for you here, sir, but it's pretty negative on the whole.' He thrust several files in Milton's direction.

'No. Sit down and give me the gist. I can look at the papers later.'

Pooley, clearly discouraged, slumped on to his chair. 'Come on,' said Milton, 'Don't forget that elimination is important too.'

'Oh, I realize that, sir. It's just that I had some real hopes of the National Service checks, and now it all looks like a waste of time.'

'Whatever the result,' said Milton gently, 'I think it was a clever idea. Now get on with it.'

'Well, sir. None of them got into any formal trouble. The only one with whom there was any divergence from the norm was Bill Thomas. Apparently he insisted he was a pacifist but was too unconvincing to be excused conscription. They made a gesture by assigning him to admin work.'

'I suppose it's a point in his favour? No, it isn't really, is it? He might just have wanted to be allowed to stay in Civvy Street.'

'It's impossible to judge, isn't it? I mean the fact that he was unconvincing doesn't mean he wasn't a pacifist. From what you and Sammy said about him, I can't imagine him easily persuading anyone of anything.'

'No. I've never seen him as an alumnus of the "How to win friends and influence people" school that whatshisname used to run.'

Pooley looked blank.

'Sorry, Ellis. You're too young to remember. Continue.'

'There isn't much more to say about it, really. Bill Thomas and Henry Crump spent most of their National Service with the army in Germany. Tony Farson was in the army in Hong Kong for a year. Graham Illingworth was a sort of unskilled fitter in the air force and never went abroad. And Tiny Short had a spell in Singapore. He got to be a sergeant. No one else was promoted except Farson, who made it to corporal.'

'I suppose we were unduly optimistic in expecting anything from official records,' said Milton thoughtfully. 'I'd like to hear something from their colleagues.'

Pooley's eyes lit up. 'Just what I was thinking, sir. Couldn't we get lists of the men in their platoons or whatever, and have them interviewed?'

Milton shifted unhappily. 'It's the same old problem, Ellis. We've been using manpower with abandon, and the top brass are complaining that we're showing no results. I'm even under pressure to call off the tails. Apart from DC Richmond's foray, the most exciting thing anyone's had to report is that Tiny is spending most of his time in the local gym and the rugby club.'

'Just one or two interviews each?' suggested Pooley hopefully.

Milton drummed his fingers on the desk indecisively. 'All right,' he said finally. 'Get the names and addresses as quickly as possible and do the initial chasing up yourself. It's going to be a matter of simple drudgery – going through telephone directories to locate the few chaps whose families haven't moved house or died. It's as good a method of random selection as any. Though I should think your chances of tracking down any of Henry's comrades from over thirty years ago are slim. I'll authorize you to request assistance from the local forces to interview a maximum of two per suspect, if it proves necessary. But if you can do it all on the telephone, so much the better.'

'Thank you, sir. I'll get on to it straight away.' Pooley jumped up and headed for the door.

'Ellis,' said Milton patiently. 'You came in here bearing several files for my perusal, all of which you're now disappearing with.'

Pooley stopped in his tracks and returned to his chair. 'Sorry, sir. I got carried away. I haven't told you yet that we drew a virtual blank on the passports. None of them has one except Crump, and only Illingworth's had one in the last ten years. If anyone except Crump's been abroad in search of poison supplies, he's done it on a false passport. But I suppose you haven't changed your mind about going through the application forms?'

'Look, you know I couldn't do it if I wanted to.'

'It's just that several of them have some experience of abroad. And I still believe that they might be prepared to take more risks in finding a supplier if they were away from their own patch.'

'Ellis. I'll make a bargain with you. You and Sammy between you can check with the wives and neighbours. If you can find evidence that any of our suspects has had the opportunity to be out of the country for a couple of days in the last six months, then I'll reconsider the matter. I can see the sense in your theory. But keep quiet about it. The only person who seems to have had the necessary freedom and a passport is Robert Amiss. And I don't really want to draw him to Romford's attention.'

He stopped abruptly, shocked at his own indiscretion. 'Forget what I just said. It was highly improper. I have the utmost confidence in Inspector Romford. It's just that we don't quite see eye to eye on the question of whether Robert Amiss is a likely murderer.'

Pooley nodded tactfully. 'Of course, sir. Now, there's just one other matter. All the papers on Mrs Thomas's accident have now come in. At least they're conclusive as well as negative. The circumstances were investigated thoroughly. She fell down the stairs in the middle of the afternoon, and Bill had been at work all day. A couple of neighbours had seen her in the morning and she was in lively form. She was found by her next-door neighbour who had front-door keys and used to keep an eye on her. And the police checked the stairs. There was no tripwire or anything like that. She was dead for an hour before Bill got home.'

'And they confirmed his alibi.'

'They did. And what's more, there was a comment on the file that he was utterly distraught.'

Shit, thought Milton. Then he wondered what he was coming to. Did he really want to discover that Bill had pushed his poor old mother down the stairs? No. It was just that he was sick of dead ends. 'All right, Ellis. Is that the lot?'

'Yes, sir.' Pooley deposited the files on the desk and left the room.

Milton reached out compulsively to the drawer and took out the familiar stack. Then he dialled a number and asked for his wife.

'Sorry, Mr Milton. She's in a meeting. Can I give her a message?'

'Yes, please.' He made a rapid mental calculation. Pacifist and mother-mourner. 'Would you tell her I said the odds on her horse have just lengthened to 50-1. And tell her that's an ungenerous price.'

31

'I'm very sorry if I've caused you any distress, ma'am. Goodnight.'

Pooley put down the receiver and crossed another name off his master list. He felt exhausted and dispirited. It had seemed a good omen that the army and air force had responded so quickly to his request. He had been overjoyed when the names and addresses started coming over the telex at the end of yesterday afternoon. And though it had been frustrating that so few of them could be located via the old addresses, at least that promised to keep the numbers to be interviewed at a manageable level. But now, after many hours of solid telephoning, he had nothing to show for his work. His main achievement had been to upset a couple of families whose sons had died prematurely.

He looked at his notes and tried to be positive. Wasn't he looking at this the wrong way? As the super had said, elimination was important too. It must count for something that two blokes remembered Tiny Short extremely well and with great affection. One of them had said he'd been the life and soul socially in Singapore. The guy must have real leadership qualities, thought Pooley. How awful for him to have landed up in such a foul job. He hoped he'd get to Kenya and have a good life. But wasn't it possible that he had been driven mad by PD and had turned his talents in a vicious direction? Hell. This information was not necessarily helpful. On one reading, the thing his old corporal had said about him being on for anything daring was a black mark against him.

The only old comrade of Graham Illingworth had hardly been helpful, and he had no other name to try. It had taken ten minutes before he had placed him at all, and then all he could remember was that he was a dull sort of chap. Tony Farson's old comrade hadn't been much more use, although after a few leading questions he did admit that old Tony had been a bit tight when it came to standing his round. No joy at all with

Henry, and only the two Bill Thomas contacts left. His first pessimistic conclusion had been right. This had proved to be a waste of twenty-four hours.

He looked at his watch and saw that it was now 9:45. He just had time to try the two remaining numbers before the magic hour of 10:00, after which it was regarded as impolite to ring.

He dialled the Darlington number.

'Hello. I'm trying to get hold of Peter Kelly. Does he still live at this number?'

'Who are you?' asked a suspicious female voice.

'Detective Constable Pooley from Scotland Yard. I am making a series of routine enquiries about someone Mr Kelly used to know many years ago and I thought he might be able to help.'

'Well, Detective Constable Pooley. You can do something for me. I've been trying to find Peter Kelly for about five years, since he disappeared out of my life without a forwarding address. If you catch up with him, you might mention that his wife would appreciate a postcard.'

Pooley mumbled his apologies and rang off. He mopped his brow. He was the wrong man for this kind of job. Sammy would have been able to do it better and without getting so embarrassed when things went wrong. 9:55. Well, he wasn't leaving until he had rung his last number. Surely the dramatic conventions required this to be the winner. There must somewhere be some reward for effort. He dialled the Oxford number.

'Yes?' said a rather impatient voice. 'Roland Eastty here.'

Pooley's stomach tightened with mingled excitement and the fear of another anti-climax. At least there couldn't be any danger that there were two Roland Easttys. This one sounded as upper-class as his address. He must have inherited the family home.

'Hello, Mr Eastty.' Pooley went through the preparatory rigmarole. He tried to make it as crisp as possible. This chap sounded as if he would tolerate fools ungladly.

'I see. Bill Thomas indeed. What's he supposed to have done?'

Pooley made a rapid decision. He looked around him and saw no one within earshot. He thought he knew the type he was dealing with. They didn't like pigs in pokes. Apparent

145

frankness was what was called for.

'He is not supposed to have done anything, sir. It is merely that we are investigating a murder case and Mr Thomas is unfortunately though almost certainly coincidentally among those in a position to have . . .'

'Done the evil deed, eh? Well, well. And you want me to tell you if he showed any homicidal tendencies in the army?'

Pooley couldn't decide if it was an advantage that Eastty was this smart. On balance it probably was. He offered a silent prayer that Eastty was more pro the police force than anti snooping into the private lives of citizens. 'Frankly, yes, sir.'

'What kind of murder?'

Pooley outlined the main facts. 'You've probably read about it, sir,' he concluded.

'It does ring a faint distant bell. But *The Times* is a bit lax in its coverage of such titillating events.'

Pooley thanked the gods. If Eastty had said the *Guardian*, he'd have been more worried. He had a flash of memory of his own activities as a left-wing undergraduate and wondered if he could really have changed so fundamentally in so short a time. Just pragmatism, he reassured himself. 'I'd be grateful for anything you can remember about him, sir. It's a matter of trying to build up a pattern of behaviour.'

'I don't remember a lot. In fact I probably wouldn't remember anything at all if it wasn't that one thing he did once stuck in my mind. For most of the time he was a boring little bugger.'

Patronizing swine, thought Pooley. He felt a sudden sense of shame. Then his natural ambition reasserted itself.

'I should be most interested in hearing about it, sir.'

'It was a row about pornographic pictures.'

Pooley gaped at the telephone.

'That's right,' went on Eastty. 'We all went out one night on the piss. And when we came back Bill suddenly got furious about the pin-ups in our quarters. When I say pornographic, you understand, I'm talking about pornography *circa* 1957. Nothing much you wouldn't get in one of those prole papers nowadays.'

'I understand, sir.'

'Yes, well . . . we were all lying on our beds when he suddenly went rushing round tearing the pin-ups off the walls, shouting about it not being right or some such thing. We managed to stop him when he'd torn up about half of them.'

'Why did he object to them so much?'

'Oh God. Don't ask me. I assumed he was some kind of religious zealot. Come to think of it, he was behaving like an adherent of one of those fundamentalist sects in the Deep South. All to do with the purity of womanhood, motherhood and apple pie, you know. As I remember, he was a trifle incoherent. He'd had a few pints and they didn't seem to agree with him. But the gist of it was anyway that he didn't approve. The other chaps were furious. A couple of us had to intervene to save him from being lynched.'

'And this was an untypical outburst, you say?'

'Oh, absolutely. He was normally inoffensive to a fault. He apologized next day and explained it was brought on because he felt protective about his mother who had been recently widowed. And he explained he didn't usually drink. Everyone forgot about it and in due course another lot of lovelies replaced the old ones.'

'I see, sir,' said Pooley, who was trying vainly to arrive at some conclusions.

'I don't suppose I've really helped you, have I? In so far as it points towards anything, that story shows him to be rather more pro than anti women. In fact what he did would be approved of by modern feminists, I dare say.'

'I suppose it would, sir.' Pooley felt really drained now.

'Well, if that's all, I'll say goodnight to you, officer. I hope Bill doesn't turn out to be your man. From what I recall he was a rather pathetic, timid little chap. In fact, now I come to think of it, he had a thing about not killing spiders.'

'And that's absolutely all you remember, sir?'

'The lot, I'm afraid.'

'I'm grateful to you, sir. Thank you very much and goodnight.'

'Goodnight, officer. And good hunting.'

Pooley sat and stared at his list. Another bloody dead-end. Unless? . . . He scribbled a couple of questions on a pad, picked it up and left the office. He would go home, have a bath and try to unwind. Then he'd see if he could come up with any bright ideas over a whisky and soda. A large one.

32

Wednesday, 2 March

'I'm sorry, Milton,' said the Commissioner, 'but you must see I have no choice. I'd leave you in control if you seemed to be about to make a breakthrough, but by your own testimony you are really flailing around. It may be that Detective Chief Superintendent Randall will be able to make quicker progress through bringing a fresh mind to the case.'

'Does this mean I'll be moved off it on Monday?'

'No. Well, that is to say, it's really a matter for Randall. But I expect he'll want you to work under him.'

And he'll ultimately take all the credit himself, thought Milton, who knew Randall of old.

'Very well, sir. Did you want to talk about anything else?'

'No. The AC wants a word, though.'

He nodded a dismissal and returned to his paperwork. Milton trailed disconsolately out of the room and went in to see the AC, who was wearing his unconvincing 'this hurts me more than it hurts you' expression.

'I'm sorry about this, Milton, but you must realize that we can't stand much more of this public criticism about our slowness. We need results.'

Milton reflected that for all that they pretended to despise the popular press, they were strikingly thin-skinned about accusations of inefficiency, even when they were unjustified.

'You see, putting Randall on the job when he gets back will show what a high priority we are giving to it.'

'It's all right, sir. You don't need to explain.' It was bad enough to be humiliated, he thought, without having to put up with all this bullshit.

'In the meantime, of course, carry on as you are. Who knows? You might have got your man before Monday. There's nothing like a spur to get chaps cracking.' The AC gave the sniggery laugh that Milton so much disliked. 'This isn't a reflection on you, you understand. Except in so far as you are perhaps a little too prone to give your fellows an easy ride. It

148

may be that what is needed is a bit more hustle and firmness.'

'If that's all, I'll get back to my office.'

'Oh, there is just one other thing. I've agreed with the three Chief Constables that there's no need to keep those tails on the job.'

'Had you consulted me, sir,' said Milton as evenly as he could, 'I would not have agreed with you.'

'That's as may be, Milton. But there's a lot of bad feeling about the waste of time involved. If any of them intended to skip the country, they'd have tried by now.'

'The reasons for having them tailed were more complicated than that.'

'Oh, yes. I know. I remember what you said. I just don't think there's anything in it. Anyway, we can't afford to alienate our provincial colleagues unless there's a very good reason.'

Like catching a murderer? thought Milton. He knew from experience that there was no point in arguing when the AC had made up his mind.

'Well, that's all, Milton, unless you want to consult me about anything.'

'No thank you, sir.' Milton walked out of the office hating himself. He should at least have put up a symbolic fight. But pointless battle had never been his style. He preferred to reserve his fire for the occasions when it might force the enemy to back off.

When he reached his office, he sat looking again at the newspaper article that had sealed his fate. 'WIVES IN DANGER, YARD DRAWS BLANK,' it began. 'The Chocolate Poisoner May Strike Again,' ran the sub-heading.

A source at Scotland Yard today revealed that the cruel murderer who sent hoax love-gifts to six women on St Valentine's Day may strike again.

The police have so far failed to trace the source of the deadly strychnine that killed beautiful wife, Fran Short, 34, grannie Edna Crump, 54, little Tommy Farson, 7, and husband and father Charles Collins, 32.

ROPE

Heartbroken widower Henry Crump said yesterday, 'No woman is safe from this maniac. I wish I knew what the

149

police are doing. I know they've got a lot on their hands coping with muggers and rioters, but I don't see why they can't find the maniac who killed my Edna. I suppose when they get him some judge will give him life and he'll be out to kill again within a few years. It is time the government brought back the rope.'

NO PROGRESS

When we put this to Chief Superintendent Milton, he said, 'I'm afraid I have no progress to report.'

The unfair selectivity of the rag so maddened Milton that, without reading on, he scrunched it into a ball and hurled it into the wastepaper basket. He picked up the pile of messages on his desk and riffled through them. When he came to one from Pooley asking if he could see him for a moment, he hesitated and then rang through to him. He felt in need of being cheered up.

'It's ingenious, Ellis, but you're really twisting the facts to suit the case. It's far more likely that he was a bit of a prude than that he disliked women.'

'But it's possible, sir.'

'Of course it's possible. Everything's possible. I'm just saying it's highly improbable. Anyway I have to say that you've built a somewhat tenuous link between your basic hypothesis and his deciding to poison fully-clothed respectable women like grannie Edna Crump, 54.'

Pooley looked bewildered for a moment and then recognized the reference. 'I was sorry to read that article, sir. They seem to be gunning for you. It was very unfair.'

'Life's unfair. Now carry on. You're telling me that at least we now have reason to believe Bill Thomas is peculiar about women and that therefore you think we should be turning the spotlight on him. Have you forgotten Farson?'

'Oh, no, sir. I still think he is by far the most likely of all of them. I just think Thomas looks very promising. Apart from anything else, he's had more freedom than any of them during the last year or so and he could have easily gone to Amsterdam or Hamburg or somewhere to get hold of some suitable poison that couldn't be traced to him.'

'With this mythical false passport?'

'Yes, sir.'

Milton's mind ran through the latest state of play on the strychnine hunt. Even Trueman now seemed to have given up hope. There was a lot to be said for the idea that an ordinary Englishman working in London and living near it might find it safer to seek villains abroad.

'Are you and Sammy making any progress in finding out who could and who couldn't have gone abroad recently?'

'We're working on it, sir. But a lot of the neighbours and relatives we're ringing are out. I don't know when we'll be finished.'

'Our bargain stands, Ellis. But I have to warn you again that the chances of getting agreement to a *prima facie* wild-goose chase are slim. And for reasons I won't go into now, they'll be slimmer next week.'

Pooley jumped up. 'I'll get on with it immediately, sir.'

When he had left, Milton looked at his watch. He had fifteen minutes before the co-ordination meeting. He looked through the messages again to determine which were the most urgent. Then he dropped them on to the desk and reached into his drawer. Against his better judgement, he thought he had better shorten the odds on Bill. It was only iron self-control that stayed his hand from vindictively shortening Henry's also.

33

Thursday, 3 March

The telephone rang several times. When Val answered it she sounded breathless.

'Mrs Illingworth? This is Superintendent Milton. May I call to see you this afternoon?'

'Yes, of course. But why?'

'I'd prefer to explain that when I see you. Shall we say half past two?'

'That'll be fine. Goodbye.'

'Goodbye, Mrs Illingworth.'

Milton replaced the receiver. Pike and Pooley, who were sitting in front of his desk, gazed at him expectantly. 'I'll go alone,' he said. 'I don't think she'll tell me the full story – always assuming there's anything to tell – if I have anyone with me. With any luck you two can give me the final answer to the foreign travel question when I return.'

'Come on, Ellis,' said Pike. 'We've still got a lot to do.' Pooley, manfully concealing his disappointment at being left out of a potentially dramatic interrogation, gave Milton a half-smile and followed his colleague out of the door.

Three hours later, Milton listened to the loud sobs emanating from Val and hardened his heart. The AC would have been proud of him, he reckoned. He had shown exemplary firmness, not to say harshness, in wearing her down. If she didn't spill the beans now, she never would.

'Mrs Illingworth, I can stay here all day if necessary. Let me start again and this time please do not insult me by expecting me to believe the feeble denials you have been repeating for the last half hour.'

There was a strangled sound which he elected to ignore. 'According to the evidence I have received from a number of sources, you frequently left the public house at which you worked just after eleven and did not arrive home until at least an hour later. The journey at that time of night should take no more than five minutes. I am asking you what you used to do during the intervening period.'

She sat up straight, stopped crying and said defiantly, 'I don't see what it has to do with you, anyway.'

Jesus Christ, thought Milton, she's just like her bloody husband. Except, if anything, slower off the mark. That line of obstruction has only just occurred to her. Well, I'm not going to put up with it.

'What it has to do with me is easily spelled out, Mrs Illingworth.' He spoke slowly and carefully. 'I'm trying to find out who wanted to murder you. Specifically, at the moment, I am trying to find out if your husband had a reason to want to do so. If he did and he has failed to achieve his objective, he may try again.'

This time he thought she was going to have hysterics. He

found that he was too mad to care. 'Are you going to answer me? Or should I repeat my original question?'

She left the room and returned carrying a box of tissues, with one of which she mopped her eyes and blew her nose.

'I don't know what to think,' she said. He was reminded of a 1930s movie queen.

'With respect, Mrs Illingworth, I am not asking you to think. I am asking you to give me some straightforward information.'

She peered cautiously around the second tissue, which she was now dabbing at her eyes in a slightly coquettish way.

'If I tell you, you won't tell Gray, will you?'

'I will not tell . . .' Milton hesitated. It was more than flesh and blood could stand to be expected to call anyone Gray. 'I will not tell your husband unless I have no option.'

She seemed satisfied. He recognized the signs. She was over the tragedy queen bit and about to cut the crap and start talking.

'I met this man, you see.'

'Yes?' Milton attempted to sound avuncular and cosmopolitan.

'Well, there wasn't anything in it really. We just used to sit in the car for a while after I finished work and talk to each other.'

'And?'

'Well, I told Gray about it.' She seemed embarrassed. 'That is, I told him I was having an affair with someone else.'

'And were you?'

'No. All we ever did was talk. And it only lasted for a few weeks anyway.'

Milton shook his head in an effort to clear it. 'But according to information received, it is only since the murders that you have been coming home straight from work.'

He was pleased to see at least that Val's face was no longer tear-stained. She looked up at him from underneath her lowered eye-lids, adjusted the pose of her shapely body to better effect and asked rather tremulously, 'Are you married, superintendent?'

Milton thought rapidly about what was expected of him. Humphrey Bogart or Paul Newman? He did the best he could by bending towards her, fixing her with his sincere look and saying in a voice redolent with understanding, 'I am indeed, Mrs Illingworth. Now why do you ask?'

'She can't really be as stupid as her behaviour suggests,' he told Pike and Pooley at about six o'clock. It was a relief that Romford had already gone home and he could talk to them without appearing to slight their boss.

They looked at him encouragingly.

'I mean that it became clear that she's quite sharp in some ways. And she can be quite amusing. But I conclude that for the most part her head is stuffed with the ideas that women's magazines used to peddle years ago. Making your man jealous and all that sort of thing.'

Pike was containing his impatience; Pooley barely. Milton took pity on them. 'The substance of what she told me was that while this harmless flirtation was going on, she told "Gray" . . .' – he pursed his lips in distaste – 'that she was having a passionate affair with a wonderful man and was thinking of leaving him – "Gray", that is. The bright idea behind this was to make him take more interest in her. As Robert informed us, she's decidedly jealous of his obsession with little Gail.'

'When did she tell him this, sir?' asked Pooley, breathless with anticipation.

'About two weeks before he went berserk at Twillerton. Take a bow, Sammy.'

Pike smiled rather sadly, as if he had been here before.

'She, of course, knew nothing about his way of letting out his frustrations. She concluded that he couldn't love her or he would have shown signs of rage instead of being cold and distant. Yes, that's the way she talks. Hence, even though the chatty lover moved away from town shortly afterwards, through revenge she kept up the fiction that they were still involved in a frantic liaison. The more Illingworth failed to react, the more she flaunted her non-existent love-life at him.'

Pike was a man who liked to get the details right. 'You mean she hung around for an hour after work each evening?'

'Precisely. She would leave the pub and sit in the car for an hour. The silly bitch obviously understands nothing about Illingworth. One of her ploys was to ask him how he'd feel when she left him, taking Gail with her. If she didn't actually drive him to murder – and she may have done – she certainly did her very best.'

'Does she think he might have done it?' asked Pooley eagerly.

'She was frightened that he might, though she won't say so in so many words. That fear is ultimately why she came clean with me after all that play-acting.'

'It's a good motive, anyway.' Pike seemed distressed but resigned.

'The very best. I bet Graham Illingworth reads every article he comes across on fathers who are denied their children when an unfeeling judge awards them to the sinning mother.'

'How have you left it, sir?'

'I've promised to say nothing about what she's told me, although I told her she should tell him the full story. Their whole problem, if you'll forgive my sounding like a marriage guidance counsellor, is that they are hopeless at communicating. It's clear that she's fond of him but petulant at the lack of attention. On the other hand, I would hazard a guess, he's a poor confused idiot who takes her carry-on as a sign that she doesn't love him. Therefore he concentrates ever more on the child who does.'

Pooley was looking very impressed. Pike looked at Milton seriously. 'I don't want to get involved emotionally in this case, sir. But it would be a terrible tragedy if Illingworth had done this awful thing through a misunderstanding about his wife. Somehow it wouldn't seem so bad if it turns out to be Farson or Crump or someone who had a real motive.'

'I share your feelings,' said Milton with a sigh. 'But I'm afraid it's all too possible. As you pointed out so cogently yourself, he had nothing to live for except his private life. Well, enough of my afternoon. Have you two finished your researches?'

Pike and Pooley looked at each other conspiratorially. Pike generously indicated that Pooley could have the floor. 'I'm afraid it's turned out a bit unexpectedly, sir. As we guessed, apart from the Twillerton weekend, neither Illingworth nor Farson has ever stayed away from home during the past six months. We can't be sure about Crump, since his neighbours wouldn't have known and his wife is dead. Short spent two weeks walking in Scotland during the autumn while his wife went off on a holiday with some other women, and it's highly unlikely that he could ever prove he was there all the time. Bill Thomas is the great disappointment.' Pooley seemed very choked. 'The woman who lives across the road is prepared to swear that he has never since his mother died been away from home – apart from Twillerton, that is.'

'How the hell can she do that?' asked Milton, interested to discover from his reaction that he had had some faith in the theory himself.

'She says she takes her dog out every evening at half past six. She follows a regular route and always gets back almost dead on seven o'clock. That's the time he draws the curtains of his front window. It's a sort of joke between them, being so precise in their habits. She can never remember his missing being there waving at her before he draws them.'

'No one could be that precise.'

'Well, it's part of the joke that if one of them is late, the other gives them the necessary few seconds.'

'You don't think she's just exaggerating?' asked Milton.

Pike came in at that point. 'I'm afraid she's backed up by the next-door neighbour, sir. Apparently she's a keen gardener like Thomas, and every Saturday and Sunday morning he's out there with his radio, rain or shine. She's sure he's never missed.'

There was a long silence. 'Well, that's that,' said Milton. 'I might have been prepared to pursue the Thomas possibility, but I can't easily believe that Henry or Tiny sneaked off to the opium-dens of the continent. You'll have to take it up with someone else. I'd better tell you about what's going to happen on Monday.'

'I'm sorry, Jim,' said Amiss. It was eleven thirty and he was tired, but his fury at the treatment of his friend had woken him up.

Milton was tired too. 'I see their point. I've got as far as I can go now. I don't have a single lead left that hasn't been followed up. Ann's nearly persuaded me to leave the Met anyway. I don't think I want to spend the rest of my life contemplating people at their worst.'

'You can't leave, Jim. You're just feeling depressed. You know you couldn't do anything else.'

'Oh, I don't know. Maybe I could be a social worker.'

The murderer decided to check once again. It was possible that the police were being clever and trying to lull him into a false sense of security. Not that they'd been particularly good at following him. He'd spotted that big fellow in the grey suit days ago. Still, there was no denying that car had gone from up the street. But he'd better make another test so he could be sure.

He put on his overcoat and closed his front door behind him noiselessly. He went to the gate slowly, giving even a dim copper plenty of time to spot him. He walked steadily down the street, turned a corner and suddenly dodged into a lane-way. He stood there for several minutes, waiting for the sound of footsteps. None came. He smiled as he began to retrace his steps homewards. Barring an unexpected obstacle, Friday was on after all.

34

Friday, 4 March

It was four o'clock in the morning and Tiny, dressed in a loud check suit, was doing a roaring trade in the middle of a suburban estate. 'Roll up, roll up,' he shouted. 'You won't get better prices anywhere. 3–1 against Tight-fisted Tony.' Amiss came forward and thrust a bundle of notes at him. He was elbowed aside by Pooley, strangely clad in a Chief Superintendent's uniform topped by a rowing cap. 'What are you offering on Graham Illingworth?' he called. 'Joint favourite, Grotty Graham. 3–1. Price has shortened, but I tell you you won't find better.' 'Hundred quid then,' said Pooley, 'and here's a tenner from Sammy.' 'And fifty from me,' said Rachel. 'Come on, Robert. You know it makes sense.' Amiss was looking cross. He pushed Pooley violently as he passed him and put his bundle on Tony.

Everything stopped for the deafening sound of a jet airliner passing overhead. Ann parachuted out of it. She landed just beside Tiny, opened her attaché case and exposed the tightly packed wads of ten-pound notes.

'£50,000 on Bachelor Bill,' she cried. As Tiny picked up the money, Milton tried to intervene, but he could neither move nor speak until after she had climbed the rope ladder into the hovering helicopter. He rushed frantically to Tiny, crying 'I want a bet, I want a bet!' 'Who on?' 'I don't know.' 'We've got a prize joker here,' observed Tiny. 'Wouldn't you like a nice 20–1 on Horny Henry?' Milton dithered, while Amiss took up the offer. A huge crowd had gathered, cheering and booing. Suddenly the Commander forced his way through, grabbed Tiny by his wide lapels and said, 'I'm putting a thousand quid on you. Any objections?' 'Business is business,' said Tiny. '50–1.' 'Exploiters! Pigs! Oppressors! Violators!' screamed Melissa and her hundreds of Amazons began to belabour the crowd with their placards.

'You're all disgusting,' came the cold voice of Romford, distorted through his loudhailer, as he led his uniformed squad through the mêlée. 'Betting should be outlawed.' 'Get him, men,' he shouted, and half a dozen coppers fell on Amiss, punching and kicking him. As Romford intoned the murder charge, Milton intervened to try to save Amiss. Romford turned on him and said, 'I don't know who you are, but get off my patch or I'll have you arrested for obstruction.'

Milton was glad to wake up, though as he tried to reconstruct the nightmare he found it only marginally worse than the reality. That bit about Robert was only a hangover from the Lorre/Greenstreet past, but the rest wasn't far wrong. Reluctant to wake Ann deliberately for comfort, he emitted a low groan which he hoped would do the job for him. She stirred. He groaned again and she turned and put her arms around him. 'Let me tell you about my dream,' he said plaintively. 'Of course, darling,' she responded sleepily.

Before he even got as far as the arrival of her plane, he had bored them both back to unconsciousness.

Amiss was thrilled by the call from Rachel in the middle of the afternoon. 'It is a bit of good luck, isn't it?' she asked. 'Though it probably scuppers next weekend instead. The Ambassador is certain he'll be recovered by then and he's given orders to try to fix the meeting for tomorrow week.'

'Doesn't matter. Things couldn't be as bad then as they are now. I'll meet you. When are you arriving?'

'No idea. I can't reserve a seat, but they've said I'll get one on stand-by. I'll ring you when I get to Heathrow, probably between six o'clock and nine. 'Bye, darling.'

He sat for a couple of minutes revelling in his good fortune. The weekend, which had promised only a depressed session with Jim and Ann, now looked full of promise. He wondered if it might be the time to raise the question of marriage. Rushing it a bit? Maybe. That's what she would say. He could hear her now arguing that decisions shouldn't be taken at a time of emotional turmoil. Too bloody sensible, that was her trouble. Well, he could raise it cautiously and see what happened. He fell into a fantasy of a candle-lit supper over which she said, 'Oh, yes, please. Let's do it as soon as possible.' It would be the making of him, wouldn't it? He'd become a man full of purpose, forging his way up the civil service ladder determined to succeed for the sake of his family. Stupid fart, he said to himself. It's more likely that she'll be forging her way up the Foreign Office ladder. And I'll be trailing around as her escort as she gets her appointments to Botswana or Mongolia. Why couldn't I have fallen in love with a traditional woman – like Val Illingworth? With a start he realized that unless he left the office soon there wouldn't be any supper at all. He cleared up his desk, put on his overcoat, looked at his briefcase doubtfully. No, he wouldn't be doing any work this weekend. He shoved it into a cupboard, locked the door, pocketed the key and left the room.

'I'm going off a bit early,' he told his staff. 'I've got some urgent shopping to do.'

Four pairs of eyes looked at him with neither resentment nor curiosity. He suppressed a slight feeling of guilt that he was entitled to take such a decision without consulting anyone, whereas the conventions required them to negotiate with him. 'It's been a rough week, hasn't it? If there's someone to cover the phones up to five o'clock, I don't see why three of you shouldn't piss off now as well.'

No one showed any enthusiasm. 'I don't mind staying, if the others want to go,' said Henry.

'Neither do I,' chimed in Tony and Bill.

'Well, I'll go in that case,' said Graham.

Amiss wished them all a good weekend and departed. He found it poignant that, since St Valentine's Day, no one ever said, 'Don't do anything I wouldn't do.'

159

35

It was just six o'clock when Rachel's plane landed. Having with her only hand-luggage, she was through customs and into the arrivals area within fifteen minutes. She peered around in search of a telephone, cursing yet again the inadequacy of the spare glasses she had been stuck with since Tiny had managed to knock her good pair on to the pub floor and trample them the previous weekend.

She could see no free booth, so she decided to go up to the departure floor to make her call. She'd be able to buy a newspaper or book there for the long tube journey. As she came off the escalator at the edge of the concourse, she stood for a moment or two trying to get her bearings. She couldn't read any of the signs and couldn't bring herself to ask anyone for directions. I must be more vain than I imagined, she thought. Castigating herself in a half-hearted way for her unreasonable inhibitions, she walked twenty or thirty yards to the left, stood in the centre of the check-in area and looked around her. She removed her glasses, rubbed them with a tissue and put them on again. On her second uncertain sweep of the environs, she had her reward and walked off at speed towards the clump of telephone booths she had sighted on her right.

The murderer, who had been checking in for his 6:55 flight to Hamburg, had been horrified to see her approaching from the escalator in his direction. He averted his head while the formalities were being concluded, and hoped she would have passed him by before he had to move away to make room for the next person in the queue. The airline clerk handed him his ticket and boarding pass, smiled professionally and said, 'Have a pleasant flight, Mr Jones.' He turned around and saw Rachel only twenty yards away, staring right at him. Terrified, he stood quite still for a moment, and then saw her suddenly stride off towards the public telephones.

He followed her quite mechanically. His heart was thudding

and he felt ill. She must have seen him. Why hadn't she acknowledged that she recognized him, bad as that would have been? It could only be that she realized the significance of his being at a check-in desk. But would she? Of course she would. She'd have known from that conversation they'd had that there was something odd about his being here at all. She'd call Robert and he'd tip off the police. They'd guess the significance all right. Ahead of him she stopped and waited in a four-man queue for a telephone. The murderer stood out of sight and tried to think what to do. One way or the other, he'd be done for. If he took the flight they'd be waiting for him when he got back and they'd look at his passport. If he went straight home now, they'd check the flight lists and find that Andrew Jones had checked in and then disappeared. They weren't stupid. It wouldn't take them long to track down his passport application form. Then they'd know the truth. They mightn't be able to prove much at the start – except that he was a liar – but they'd get there in the end. Could he go to Hamburg and just disappear? Impossible. He didn't have enough money and the German police would pick him up eventually. Nor could he trust his contacts. They'd shop him if the pressure was put on.

He had almost decided to go home, prepare for the police and steel himself to brazen it out, when he saw Rachel move back into his line of vision. She walked over to the bookstall. He leaned forward and checked the queue she'd been in. No, she hadn't made her call yet. She must be getting something to read while she waited around. There came to the murderer the sudden inspiration that he might – he just might – now have the chance to stop her telling anyone. He'd need a lot of luck but it was worth the try. He took from his pocket the Swiss army knife he always carried and, covertly, selected the vicious little marlinspike. The handle of the knife lay crosswise on his palm, the blade extending a couple of inches from between his fingers when he clenched his fist. A hard, punching stab at the vertebrae was the thing to go for. As he began to move towards the bookstall, he felt a momentary regret. Robert was a nice bloke, and he'd be very distressed by this. But that was just too bad. It wasn't his fault that she was at Heathrow. She wasn't supposed to be. A man had to save himself, didn't he? And after all, if he managed to kill her, it would be two birds with one stone.

The French businessman standing running his eye across the paperbacks saw Rachel beside him, similarly engaged. They reached out simultaneously for the same book. Their hands collided in mid-air and they both smiled and apologized. At his insistence, she took the Wodehouse, looked at the blurb and passed it over to him. 'I've read it anyway,' she said, and began to look at the books spread out on the bottom shelf. The Frenchman, who was about to go home after three weeks at a language school and was conscientiously buying recommended English novels, began to read the blurb with intense concentration. He was stymied by an unfamiliar hyphenated word that appeared to be central to an understanding of the plot. He put the book under one arm, bent down to his briefcase and searched within it for his pocket dictionary.

When he emerged from his researches a minute or two later, he was no wiser. He tried vainly to make sense of the concept of a *vâche-crémeuse*. Having failed, he replaced the book and turned to try the shelves on his right. It was then that he saw that the pleasant girl in glasses was no longer sitting on her heels beside him. She had fallen over awkwardly on her face. He knelt beside her, put his arm around her and tried to help her up. Then he realized that she was not just ill. She was either unconscious or dead.

36

At the moment when the ambulance men arrived at the Terminal bookstall, Amiss was sitting in his flat reading, smoking and imbibing a refreshing gin and tonic. He was feeling a sense of well-being, brought on by the satisfaction of knowing that he was wholly in control of practical matters. The casserole was in the oven, the champagne was in the 'fridge and the cork had been pulled from the claret. He had purchased the ingredients of a memorable meal and he was hoping that the way to Rachel's heart might prove to be through her stomach. He would have ample time to set everything up between the time she rang and the time she arrived. He was at peace.

The telephone rang at 7:15. He rushed to it eagerly.

'Robert, it's Helen.'

'Helen. Hello. How nice to hear from you.' Although he was disappointed she was not Rachel, Amiss was very well disposed towards her flatmate.

'It's about Rachel,' said Helen haltingly.

'You don't mean she can't make it?'

'Oh, no. Well, yes.' To Amiss's horror, the normally calm and competent Helen dissolved into sobs of anguish.

'Tell me, for God's sake. Has she had an accident?'

'She's been stabbed, Robert. At Heathrow.'

Amiss found a strange detachment coming over him. In a calm voice he asked, 'Is she dead?'

'I don't know. They rang me from the airport as soon as they found her diary. All they could say was that she was still alive and they'd let me know when there was any news.'

'Where is she?'

'I'm sorry, Robert. But I was so shocked I didn't think to ask. I'll let you know as soon as I hear.'

'Don't bother, Helen. I won't be here. Find someone to be with you and I'll ring you as soon as I have anything to tell you.'

'All right, Robert. I'm sorry. I know how you must be feeling.'

'And I know how you must be feeling. Try to be optimistic. You know what a toughie she is.'

Helen managed a half-laugh and they said goodbye.

Amiss's legs gave way and he fell on to the sofa. He lay for a minute or two torturing himself with unrestrained grief and terror. Then he made a huge effort to regain control of himself. He began to think hard.

Pike answered Milton's telephone. 'Sorry, sir. He's not here. He should be back in about ten minutes. Can I. . .'

Amiss interrupted with the news about Rachel.

'Don't sympathize, Sammy. It's time for action. Two things. Tell Jim it's vital that he gets some local police round to Bill's house immediately, in the hope of getting there before he arrives home. And please find out for me where Rachel's been taken and how she is. I'll be round within fifteen minutes if I can get a taxi. Oh, and Sammy. In case I'm held up, tell Jim to tell the coppers to stick with Bill until told otherwise. Goodbye.'

Milton was deeply shocked, but before he started asking questions he telephoned the Surrey force and issued an urgent request. By the time he had elicited from Pike all the information he had, Amiss had burst in on them.

'What can I say, Robert?' began Milton.

'Nothing, Jim. Have you found out yet where she is, Sammy?'

Pike told him. 'She's having an operation, Robert. We won't know for a while if she's going to be all right. But they've promised to ring here as soon as they've got anything to tell us.'

Amiss sat on the edge of Milton's desk. 'Thank you, Sammy.' He suddenly realized that Pike had called him by his Christian name and found that somehow consoling.

'Right,' he said, hoping he was as much in charge of himself as he sounded, 'I am now not thinking about Rachel. I'm thinking about her attacker. Have you done what I asked about Bill?'

'I have. But purely on a basis of simple trust. Please fill me in.'

'Is Pooley around?'

'Yes. I expect so. He always stays late these days.'

'I think he should be here. We're probably going to need him.'

Pike looked enquiringly at Milton, who nodded. Pike left and returned within a minute with Pooley, who was looking distressed. Milton made the introductions. 'Ellis,' he added, 'you should know that Robert has been fully in touch with the progress we've made up to now.'

Pike and Pooley sat down in their usual chairs. Amiss stayed on his perch, and began to speak, emphasizing the occasional point by kicking Milton's desk viciously.

'I might have saved us all a lot of trouble. . . And indeed, I might have saved Rachel's life . . . or, to try to be optimistic, saved her from serious injury, had I remembered before now that I thought I saw Bill Thomas at Heathrow last December.'

'Don't start the masochistic stuff,' Milton warned. 'Just tell us about this.'

Amiss got a grip on himself. 'One Friday in December I went to Paris – as I often did – to see Rachel. I saw someone I thought was Bill Thomas. I then realized it couldn't be him, because he always said he never travelled, so I dismissed it as a chance resemblance.'

'As one does on these occasions,' interjected Pooley.

'Thank you for that, Ellis. I appreciate it. I suppose one does. I am merely expressing the view that it was something I might have remembered when I heard you were plugging the idea of the foreign strychnine source. As it was, it took the shock of hearing about Rachel and trying to imagine what had happened to bring the memory back.'

'I'm sorry, I don't quite understand,' said Pike. 'Are you saying that Bill Thomas tried to kill her this evening because she saw him at the airport?'

'I see no other explanation.'

'It could have been one of the others, Robert,' pointed out Milton. 'The December episode could really have been a non-event. She might have seen someone else tonight. . . Christ! What am I doing sitting here?'

He jumped up. 'Sammy, you and I are going to see Thomas now. Ellis and Robert, stay here. You'll be able to get news of Rachel as well as act as co-ordinators. Ellis, get a check made on whether any of the suspects has been out tonight. You've got Thomas's phone number. Ring me there when you've got something to tell me. And I want you both to think hard about his character, his possible motives, and anything remotely relevant that might be useful to me when I talk to him.'

As Pike closed the door behind them and they started to stride down the corridor, he said, 'Just one thing, sir. If Miss Simon survives she'll be able to identify her assailant, if this theory is correct.'

'Yes, Sammy. But we don't know yet if she's going to survive.'

37

Milton thanked the local police and explained that he no longer required their services. He and Pike sat in the armchairs of Bill's three-piece suite, and looked at the mild little man on the sofa.

'You were just out for a walk?'

'That's right, superintendent. I went out for a little exercise about half past seven, and when I came back all these policemen were waiting for me. I don't know what's going on. I really don't.'

Milton felt his faith in Amiss's theory begin to crumble. He steeled himself. 'Rachel Simon has been stabbed at Heathrow Airport. You will understand that we have to assume there is a connection between that event and the PD murders.'

'Is that that nice girlfriend of Robert's?'

'Yes.'

'Oh, that's dreadful. Poor Robert. Is she all right?'

Milton looked at him intently. 'Yes,' he said. 'She's going to be fine.'

Bill smiled with apparent delight. 'I'm so pleased,' he said. 'It would have been dreadful if she had been seriously injured.'

'She is however unconscious and therefore cannot yet tell us the identity of her attacker, so we are making enquiries independently.' He wondered what reaction he would have got had he said: 'She is alive and says you were the attacker.' Sometimes he wished he suffered from fewer ethical hang-ups.

'Oh, I quite understand, superintendent. I know you're only doing your job. But, as I say, I just went out for a walk for about half an hour.'

'Can you tell us your movements since you left work?'

'I left the office at five, as usual, and caught my normal train at ten to six from Victoria. I got to the local station about twenty-five past and was home fifteen minutes later. Then I had something to eat and went out at half past seven.'

'Can anyone confirm this? Did you meet anyone on the train, for instance? Or did anyone ring you?'

'No, superintendent. But I did wave at Miss Kipling at seven when I drew my curtains. She was just coming home with her dog.'

Shit, shit, shit, thought Milton. 'She lives opposite, does she?'

'Yes. At number fifteen.'

'Sammy, would you just pop across and have a quick word with her?'

During Pike's absence, Milton attempted to make polite conversation, but his mind was racing. It would be just his bloody luck if it turned out that every bugger had an alibi. But coincidences like that just couldn't happen. Could they?

Pike came in looking solemn. 'Miss Kipling confirms Mr Thomas's statement, sir.'

'Very well. Mr Thomas, I don't need to trouble you any more. But I should be very grateful if you would permit me to make a reverse-charges call to my office.'

'Of course, superintendent. The phone is on that table in the corner. I'll just pop out to the kitchen and leave you to have your conversation in private.'

'That is most considerate of you, sir.'

As Milton went to the phone, he and Pike exchanged expressive looks. While he waited for the operator to put him through, he tapped his foot impatiently. He was desperate for news of Rachel. He spared a fleeting thought for Amiss, who would be deeply disappointed that his idea had proved to be a non-starter.

'Hello, Ellis. Anything from the hospital?'

'Yes, indeed, sir. Just come in. She's going to be fine. He missed all the vital bits, if only by a fraction. All pretty superficial, but she won't be out from under the anaesthetic for a couple of hours.'

'That's marvellous. Hang on.' He put his hand over the mouth-piece and passed the good news on to Pike. 'Ellis. Have any witnesses been found?'

'Afraid not, sir. Everyone who was in the vicinity was absorbed in reading, looking at magazine pictures, that kind of thing.'

'I expected that. It must have been the best spot in the whole departure area. Now, Bill Thomas has an alibi, so I need to know about the others. Have you made contact with them?'

'Just a moment, sir. I'll tell Robert.'

He came back on the line. 'He wants to know what the alibi is.'

Robert is being stubborn, thought Milton impatiently, but he gave Pooley the brief facts. Pooley came back again. 'He's thinking.'

'Good, good, good. Let him think away. Maybe Miss Kipling is Bill's secret lover. Now will you answer my question?'

'Sorry, sir. You can rule out Farson. He's definitely been at home all evening. Graham Illingworth wasn't there. His mother-in-law answered the phone and said that he and his wife have gone away for the weekend. She's looking after Gail.'

Milton allowed himself a moment for self-congratulation. He might well have a future as a marriage guidance counsellor. 'They haven't gone abroad by any chance?'

'No. They've gone to a hotel in Bognor.'

'Sounds like a suitable place for him. And the others?'

'There's no answer from Crump or Short. But we've got a car outside both their houses. Crump isn't with his family and Short isn't at the rugby club. But we'll keep trying.'

'I'd better come back to the office, then. There's no point in dashing off to sit outside deserted houses.'

'Just a moment, sir. Robert wants a word.'

'Jim. There's a question you must ask Bill.'

'Miss Kipling, Robert.'

'Screw Miss Kipling. She might have dreamed it. Ask him to show you his briefcase.'

Milton considered this statement for a moment. 'Of course. You mean he might have a bloodstained knife in it.'

'He might have his pyjamas. His passport. Anything.'

'OK, I take your point. Hold on.'

He went into the kitchen, where Bill was washing a shirt. 'Excuse me, Mr Thomas.' He felt distinctly embarrassed. 'Just one small thing. Could I have a look at the contents of your briefcase?'

If Bill was disconcerted, he showed no signs of it. He began carefully to wring out his shirt and said, 'I'm afraid you can't, superintendent. I lost it on the way home tonight.'

'I see. On the train?'

'Yes indeed. I hope British Rail will be able to find it for me. It has a few personal effects in it that I'd be sorry to lose. Of

168

course, it may have been stolen. There are some dishonest people around these days, you know.'

'I see. I'll get someone to chase it up for you.'

'You are very kind, superintendent.' As Milton left the room, Bill placed his shirt on a hanger and hung it carefully on a hook over the sink.

Milton wondered if he should get a search warrant. No. Better to wait until British Rail confirmed or denied their possession of that damn briefcase. Anyhow, he'd have difficulty in getting a warrant. Unless someone came up with some dirt on Miss Kipling, Bill was in the clear. And on requestioning, she had been adamant about the curtain-drawing episode.

He sat, as he had been sitting for the past hour, staring into space in Bill's sitting room. When no further conversation seemed possible and Milton had indicated that he and Pike would be staying with him for an indefinite period, Bill had politely asked permission to read his gardening catalogues. He sat under the light of his reading lamp, apparently engrossed. Milton was tempted to ask him searching questions about his relationship with his mother and the pin-up episode, but he thought that for the moment he'd better hold them in reserve. He couldn't quarrel with Amiss's thesis that Bill shouldn't be left to his own devices lest he dispose of something incriminating around the house. But the whole evening was becoming ridiculous. It was already 10:15. He couldn't stay socializing with Bill all night. Sooner or later he would have to come to a decision. If either Henry or Tiny couldn't prove an alibi, he'd quit on Bill. If both could, he'd follow through.

Bill's voice interrupted his unhappy thoughts. 'Excuse me, gentlemen, but would either of you care for a cup of cocoa? I usually have one at about this time. Or, if you would prefer, I could make you tea or coffee.'

Both Milton and Pike declined. Bill got up and walked towards the door. The telephone rang. 'You might like to answer it, superintendent. I can't imagine that anyone would ring for me at this hour.'

It was Pooley again. Milton nodded affirmatively at Bill, who left the room, closing the door quietly behind him. 'I think I've got it, sir. Can't think why it didn't occur to me earlier. I've been concentrating too much on why Miss Kipling might have lied.'

'Well, get on with it, for heaven's sake.'

'Electrically operated curtains, with a time switch.'

Milton put the phone down and went over to take a look behind the sofa that had its back to the curtains. It took him less than a minute to prove Pooley right.

38

'Miss Kipling?' said Milton after he had talked to Pooley for another couple of minutes and passed on the gist to Pike.

'I'll see her now, sir. Then I'll probably need to try an experiment with the curtain for her benefit.'

'Carry on. I'll give Thomas no advance warning.'

Bill came in carrying his cocoa mug just after Pike had left. 'Was there any news of my briefcase?'

'Yes. The train has been thoroughly searched and there is no sign of it.'

'What a pity. I hope the BCC won't mind giving me another one. Now, superintendent, I don't want to be inhospitable, but are you likely to be staying much longer? I'm a bit of a stick-in-the-mud, you know. I like my beauty sleep.'

'I'm sorry to disrupt your evening. We will be off as soon as our business is concluded. There are a couple more things I'd like to ask you, but, if you don't mind, I'll wait until my colleague returns. He's just gone across the street.'

Bill evinced no curiosity, and began to drink his cocoa. When Pike came in, he smiled at him welcomingly. Pike walked over and stood beside him. 'Would you mind getting up for a moment, sir?'

'If that is what you want, sergeant.' It was clear that Bill was happy to humour his visitors.

Pike pulled the sofa a few feet forward, walked behind it, and switched the controls to manual. Standing well away from the window, he pressed the button. The curtains opened smoothly. He pressed the button again to draw them. He repeated the sequence a couple of times, and then, leaving the curtains closed, he pushed the sofa back and said, 'Perhaps you would care to sit here again now, sir? I'll be back shortly.'

My God, he's an inscrutable little sod, thought Milton, vainly looking for any reaction in the face opposite. Bill took another sip from his mug. They waited silently.

Pike returned within five minutes. He smiled broadly at Milton. 'She assured me that she had seen me doing what I said I intended to do – that is, waving at her before drawing the curtains.'

Milton adopted his most formal tone. 'Thank you, Pike. That is most helpful. Mr Thomas, do you think you could lend us a torch?'

Bill hesitated.

'I would hate to have to bother Miss Kipling again. It would really be very convenient if you could find one for us.'

Bill got up without a word, left and returned with a torch which he handed over.

'Thank you,' said Milton, passing it to Pike. 'Now, if you'll just bear with us for another couple of minutes, Mr Thomas. My colleague would like to have another look at your lovely garden.'

Bill looked as if he were about to speak. Then he shrugged and sat down again. His nerve is good, thought Milton apprehensively. They sat together and waited.

When Pike returned he carried a clock radio in his arms. He shook his head at Bill. 'Really, Mr Thomas. I'm surprised at you leaving this out in the garden at night. Even if you did have it covered against the rain, I'm sure it can't be good for it.'

It was 11:30 and the tension was getting to Amiss and Pooley. The former was lying well back in Milton's chair, with his feet on the desk. His habit of changing his position every two minutes was taxing his companion's nerves. Pooley himself was pacing up and down, as he had been for the previous twenty minutes. That was beginning to make Amiss want to scream.

When the telephone rang, Pooley's 'Yes' was almost a squeak.

'It's Sammy. He's admitted it.'

Pooley turned round to Amiss and held out his hand. As Amiss shook it he felt the tears well up – some tears for Rachel,

171

but most for Charlie. Pooley waved him to the extension on Pike's desk.

'I know the super would want me to congratulate you both.'

'Thanks, Sammy. But please get on with it.'

Pike ran quickly over the explosion of the alibi. 'And then we were able to wreck his weekend alibis as well. Just like you'd said, he'd got his radio in the garden, timed to go off at ten in the morning. As long as he was back early on Sunday the lady next door would swear he'd never been away.'

'Did he admit it at once?' asked Pooley.

'Not him. That's not his style. It was only when the super told him we'd track down all missing passengers and then look into the passport question that he saw he was done for. He was booked on a flight to Hamburg, on a false passport in the name of Jones.'

'Why did he do it?' broke in Amiss.

'Well, he's still telling the super about it all in the kitchen. He says it was out of the kindness of his heart. Claims that he knew from the office how unhappy all these blokes' marriages were and he wanted them to be free like him. And then, when he met the wives he thought they seemed so discontented that they'd be better off out of it anyway. He said it was really mercy killing. He got the strychnine in Hamburg a few months ago.'

'Good God,' said Pooley. 'He must be mad.'

'Of course he's mad. You'd almost be sorry for him. He seemed bewildered that the super didn't think his motive a good one.'

Amiss spoke through clenched teeth. 'I don't quite see that trying to kill Rachel was a form of euthanasia.'

'He does say he's ashamed of that. He just panicked when he saw her looking at him.'

'Has he produced the briefcase?'

'No. He says it's in a left-luggage locker at Victoria. The weapon's in there all right. He was afraid that the police might get to him before he had time to dispose of that and the passport.'

'Is that it, then?'

'Except that he says it's all his mother's fault. Says she led his dad a dog's life and nagged him rotten. Admits that probably turned him funny.'

Amiss had been gnawing at a fingernail as an aid to

concentration. 'Sammy. There are two things all this doesn't explain. Tearing up the nudie pictures and visiting Hamburg again.'

'He says he tore up the pictures because he didn't approve of pornography. He didn't explain very well why he should be going to Hamburg again. Said he just wanted to get away for a night or two, and that was a place he knew his way round.'

'Since National Service days?' asked Pooley. He was feeling rather smug.

'That's right.'

'I'm not entirely convinced that it all hangs together,' said Amiss. 'But he's presumably going to spill it at greater length in the future. What happens now?'

'I've just rung for a squad car. We'll be taking him down to the local station to charge him. I'd better be off. I'll go and pack some essentials for him. Goodbye.'

The three receivers went down virtually simultaneously.

'Ellis. What do you think?'

'I don't want to think any more. We've got him. We can think again tomorrow.'

'What you need — and indeed what I need — is to drink up the contents of the bottle I've got at home. I'll just ring the hospital again and make sure Rachel's still sleeping peacefully. Then we'll go out and find a taxi.'

Pooley had a brief moment of hesitation as he thought about the squash game he had booked for 9:00 the following morning. 'Sod it,' he said cheerfully. 'You're on.'

39

Pike found a small suitcase in the spare bedroom and carried it through to Bill's. In a practised way he searched for pyjamas, socks, a shirt, a razor and assorted toiletries. He wondered why he was feeling little other than compassion for the murderer of four people and the attacker of a girl he liked. He couldn't help it, he said to himself. He's mad. He's not bad. What an awful life he had. Tyrannized by that mother and never allowed any social life. It was horrible that stuff he'd come out with about how he'd always wanted a wife and children but his mother wouldn't let him go out with anyone. She was the one who ought to be in court. Poor old Bill was just weak by nature and frustration had driven him insane. Pike hoped he'd be sent to a psychiatric hospital. It would be wicked to send him to prison. The inmates would make his life hell and he wasn't strong enough for that.

'I was dreadfully sorry about Tommy Farson.' Bill stirred his second mug of cocoa and shook his head regretfully at the workings of fate. 'You see, I'd thought it all out. I knew he and his sister would be at the circus. It wasn't fair that it was cancelled.'

'What about Gail Illingworth?'

'Oh, I knew she'd be safe. I heard her mother say at the dinner-dance that she never ate chocolates.'

Milton ran a hand through his hair. He was finding this very difficult. Bill sounded so sane as he explained the crazy logic behind his actions. 'You knew a lot about your colleagues and their families?'

'Oh, yes. I knew a lot. I listened, you see. I think they usen't to listen to each other much. Everyone tried to get in with his own troubles. You know how it is.'

Milton knew all too well.

'But I used to listen all the time. They'd ring home quite often, and they were always sounding cross. You had to be sorry for them.'

'But what made you decide to act as a sort of god?'

'They were my friends, you see. I didn't have any others. I only wanted to do them a good turn.'

'But you weren't doing them a good turn by exposing them all to suspicion, were you?'

'I thought it would all blow over. That you'd have so many people to suspect, you'd just have to give up. I mean, it *was* a bit of bad luck that PD1 had that meeting early on Friday morning and were all ruled out, wasn't it?' Bill spoke in a voice of sweet reason.

Milton hoped the squad car would be along very soon. He didn't think he could stand much more of this. He had just found himself on the verge of sympathizing with Bill about the unfairness of it all. 'Tell me, Mr Thomas, why did you. . .?'

He stopped as Pike came through the kitchen door. 'I want to show you something, sir. Something in Mr Thomas's bedroom. Perhaps he will come up with us.'

Milton shot a puzzled look at him and then at Bill. He saw that Bill had gone white. Then with an obvious effort Bill said, 'Of course, sergeant. Anything you like.'

The three of them gathered in the bedroom. 'I think you'd better sit down here, both of you. You'll be able to see the television set best from this position.'

Milton speculated on whether the events of the evening had made Pike lose his marbles. But he sat down obediently and awaited an explanation.

'When I saw this television, I thought nothing of it. Then I remembered something from one of Robert's letters. He said specifically that Mr Thomas didn't like television and wouldn't have one. Said it kept him out of office conversations.'

Bill was sitting rigidly on the end of the bed. Milton looked helplessly at Pike. 'And?'

'And I began to wonder why he should have a television if he didn't watch the programmes. Then I saw he had a video machine in this cupboard underneath.'

Pike opened it with a flourish. There was a shelf under the video on which about half a dozen tapes were stacked. He took out a couple. 'As you can see, sir, they are apparently blank.'

'What's on them?'

'I think you'd better look at a sample. I've got one set up.'

I suppose they must be pornographic, thought Milton. He wasn't particularly surprised. It probably fitted in with Bill's frustrations.

Pike pressed a button and a film came up on the screen. A small brunette who bore a passing resemblance to Ann was chained tightly to a long bench. She was being whipped brutally by a hooded man.

Milton winced and averted his eyes. 'All right, Sammy. It's revolting. But we're more concerned with murder than with Mr Thomas's unpleasant taste in video nasties.'

Pike's voice was shaking slightly. 'It's more than that, sir. Do you remember that case I was on before I came to you? That vice ring I told you about?'

Milton felt sick. He looked at Bill, who had got his colour back and wore an air of resignation. He turned to Pike. 'All right,' he said. 'I'll watch it.'

'You only need to look at one particular bit.' Pike pushed a button and the film speeded up. As the torture became more varied and intensified, Milton realized that his face was contorted into a grimace of loathing. You're a wet copper, he told himself. Come on, you can take it. You've seen enough dead bodies.

Pike pushed a button, and the film returned to normal speed. The hooded man had decided that it was now time to kill his screaming victim. He took up a sword. Milton knew what was coming. In snuff movies the actress didn't just die realistically. She really died. With his head in his hands he continued to watch the screen. The sword came down and the head was severed from the bleeding body.

As Pike switched off they heard the doorbell ring.

'I'll get it,' said Pike. He was half-way down the stairs when he heard the sound of choking. He ran back to the bedroom and forced Milton's hands away from Bill Thomas's throat.

Epilogue

Amiss was in a benign mood as he waited for his career manager to arrive from the meeting that had unexpectedly overrun. He felt refreshed after the three-week holiday with Rachel in Italy. Even though technically she was convalescing and he was on gardening leave – that civil servants' perk that brightened the lives of those found temporarily unplaceable – it was a holiday in the truest sense of the word. It was not just that they had both shaken off the shock of recent events. They had had time to think at length about priorities and make plans about the future.

He fell into a daydream of how life would be when she was transferred to London in a few months. She was right, of course. They must live together before thinking about marriage. But he was sure it was going to work out triumphantly successful. As long as he now got a reasonable job to compensate him for all his sufferings in BCC, he wouldn't have any justifiable grievances. It was not after all the DOC's fault that the past year had not gone according to plan.

He speculated on how life was going on in PD without him. Horace at least would be a happy man: he was poised to step into Shipton's shoes when he took early retirement in May. And maybe under an enthusiastic boss the integrated department might get some pride in itself. He mentally ticked off the signs of hope. Henry, since he had moved in with his daughter, was beginning to boast boringly about the cleverness of his grandson. Graham, in the days before Amiss left, had agreed immediately to at least two requests that would have hitherto met with a 'Can't be done'. And Tony, at the farewell party, had not been the very last to buy a round. That party had been a heart-warming occasion, by PD standards. He still couldn't get over his amazement that Melissa had come specially back from the Midlands to say goodbye. He had feared she would crow over being proved right about male violence but she had been strangely muted about Bill. She seemed to understand that he was hardly typical of his sex.

He looked at the office clock and saw that the bloody personnel fellow was now twenty minutes late. His mind slid back to Bill. Poor bastard. He surely couldn't be held responsible for his actions. What was that Jim had said? That the reason he'd lost all control had been the sight of Bill's happy face after the climax of the snuff movie. Maybe his mother had been partly to blame. She had done the best she could in keeping him under her thumb once she had realized he hated women, but she shouldn't have counted on being immortal.

He found he could still not think without a shiver of what would have happened had Rachel's weekend meeting not been cancelled. Bill had flipped to such an extent that he didn't seem sure himself whether he was off to Hamburg for more videos or more strychnine. A pacifist! God, it was astounding how that had blurred the picture. That envy of the Yorkshire Ripper that had come out in conversations with Jim. How had he put it about Sutcliffe? 'That bloke had the courage of his convictions. I was always a coward.' His knifing of Rachel could so easily have given him a taste for physical contact had he not bungled it.

Amiss shivered. That was one aspect of the case he could not bear to think about. He found the episode worse in retrospect than she did. But then, she'd been unconscious during the hours when he'd been terrified.

Half past four. He speculated idly about what job would be on offer. It would be hard to smile agreeably if it turned out not to have much intellectual challenge. The only time he'd really used his brains during the past year had been on the night Rachel was stabbed. Could she be right in believing he should leave the service unless he got a marvellous offer? No, no. One had to accept the ups and downs. It wasn't a bad life and anyway, he couldn't think of anything else he wanted to do.

He felt a pang of envy for Jim. He had known so clearly that the police force was his *métier* at the time when he feared he would have to resign. It was decent of Bill to refuse to lodge a complaint against him. How could a chap capable of killing people just to feed his sexual fantasies be so considerate?

Twenty to five. If this didn't work out he could always join the police, couldn't he? No, he couldn't. If he found the BCC bureaucracy too much for him, he'd never stand the constraints Ellis had to put up with. Funny that a bloke that bright should be over the moon about receiving an official commendation. And Sammy had seemed to think that making him an inspector was a piece of overwhelming generosity, even though apparently he'd been stuck as a sergeant for years. And Jim had been firmly promised his promotion this time. He deserved it if anyone did. He didn't often come up with the wild inspirational ideas himself, but he knew how to get them from other people. He was a superb boss. Amiss envied his staff.

That had been an interesting conversation he'd had with Ann the other day about the essence of good management. He hoped she'd write a successful book about it. It was a brave decision to give up that fat salary and live off Jim for a year or two. That must be a sign of great confidence in the strength of their relationship. He smiled as he thought of the way Rachel had told him he could live off her if he decided to throw up his job with the civil service. She had moments of great romanticism. Although he was certain they had a wonderful future before them as a couple, he was not going to risk the strain that financial dependence would create. It could take him months to find another job, the way the unemployment figures were going. There was a lot to be said for security.

His career manager entered the room at 4:50. 'Sorry about keeping you,' he said, as he hung his overcoat and umbrella on the stand. 'I got tied up. One of those things.'

He sat down behind his desk and looked fruitlessly for Amiss's file. 'I'm awfully sorry. Can't seem to find the papers. Can you hold on just a moment?'

He began to ferret in a filing cabinet and finally, with a snort of triumph, withdrew his find. Sitting down again, he skimmed through the papers on the top. After a couple of minutes he looked up. 'Quite a time you've had.'

'You can say that again.'

'You must have learned a lot?'

'In what way?'

'About business organization, decision-making in the 1980s and all that sort of thing.'

Amiss didn't believe this. He spoke slowly. 'I have learned a great deal about human nature during the past year. I can't say that I've picked up much else.'

An expression of embarrassment flitted across the face of the man opposite. 'Oh, yes. Of course. Sorry about all that. It must have been rather beastly.'

'It was . . . decidedly beastly.'

'Well now. You'll want to know what we've come up with? By the way, you've had a good gardening leave, I trust?'

Amiss thought of trying to get through this man's defences by explaining brightly that he had spent it with his lover, who had been stabbed by his psychopathic ex-colleague. He decided against.

'Yes, thank you.'

'Good. Just the job. Now, as I was saying, you'll have learned a lot. I think we've got the very thing for you.'

Amiss leaned forward anxiously.

'It's very important that these secondments shouldn't be wasted, you will appreciate. Our aim is to put what you've learned to good use.'

A feeling of unease began to creep over Amiss. 'You have read my report on my secondment, haven't you? I mean, you do realize, don't you, that for practical purposes it was a complete waste of time? Unless you're thinking of seconding me to the Home Office to devise policies for improving the running of institutions for the criminally insane.'

His career manager was embarrassed once again. He said, in a somewhat haughty tone, 'I think you're rather harping on the negative aspects. I like to look on the positive side. This is what I've selected for you.'

He pushed over a piece of paper. Before Amiss could read it he added, 'I must warn you that if you turn this down you are unlikely to be offered another Principal post during this calendar year. You're a bit out of touch with what's been going on in the Department, after all. You can't expect a central policy job or anything like that.'

Amiss skimmed the job description. The first thing he took in was that he would be working in Stockton-on-Tees. The second was that the job was the running of a small team organizing centralized purchasing for the Department. The third was that this section had recently been somewhat reduced in strength owing to a policy of decentralization. The fourth was that, despite this, it was a challenging job with considerable scope for streamlining of procedures.

He raised his head and stared across at the man opposite.

'This *is* a joke, isn't it?'

'I find that a very strange remark in the circumstances. I have put a considerable amount of personal effort into finding a suitable slot for you.'

Amiss forgot that in the civil service people with no talent for the job were frequently pushed into personnel work. He forgot also that there was such a thing as the right to appeal. He could see only Stockton, purchasing procedures, demoralization and the faces of his ex-staff. He got slowly to his feet.

'Well?' His career manager sounded impatient. Presumably he was fearful of missing his train.

Amiss politely pushed his chair forward until the edge was touching the desk. He walked over to the corner of the room, removed his overcoat from its peg and put it on. Then he turned again towards the desk.

'My dear chap,' he said. He made his voice sound pleasant. 'Would you like to know what I think should be done with this job?'

'What?'

'I think you should stuff it up your Whitehall arse.'

He walked out of the room, feeling like a free man.